PANDEMIA

A NOVEL OF THE BIRD FLU AND THE END OF THE WORLD

Books by Johnathan Rand:

American Chillers:
#1: The Michigan Mega-Monsters
#2: Ogres of Ohio
#3: Florida Fog Phantoms
#4: New York Ninjas
#5: Terrible Tractors of Texas
#6: Invisible Iguanas of Illinois
#7: Wisconsin Werewolves
#8: Minnesota Mall Mannequins
#9: Iron Insects Invade Indiana
#10: Missouri Madhouse
#11: Poisonous Pythons Paralyze Pennsylvania
#12: Dangerous Dolls of Delaware
#13: Virtual Vampires of Vermont
#14: Creepy Condors of California
#15: Nebraska Nightcrawlers
#16: Alien Androids Assault Arizona
#17: South Carolina Sea Creatures
#18: Washington Wax Museum
#19: North Dakota Night Dragons

Freddie Fernortner, Fearless First Grader:
#1: The Fantastic Flying Bicycle
#2: The Super-Scary Night-Thingy
#3: A Haunting We Will Go
#4: Freddie's Dog Walking Service
#5: The Big Box Fort

Audio CD: Creepy Campfire Chillers

Michigan Chillers:
#1: Mayhem on Mackinac Island
#2: Terror Stalks Traverse City
#3: Poltergeists of Petoskey
#4: Aliens Attack Alpena
#5: Gargoyles of Gaylord
#6: Strange Spirits of St. Ignace
#7: Kreepy Klowns of Kalamazoo
#8: Dinosaurs Destroy Detroit
#9: Sinister Spiders of Saginaw
#10: Mackinaw City Mummies
#11: Great Lakes Ghost Ship
#12: AuSable Alligators
#13: Gruesome Ghouls of Grand Rapids

The Adventure Club:
#1: Ghost in the Graveyard
#2: Ghost in the Grand
#3: The Haunted Schoolhouse

Books by Christopher Knight:

St. Helena
Ferocity
The Laurentian Channel
Bestseller
Season of the Witch

This book contains the complete
unabridged text of the original work.

An AudioCraft Publishing, Inc. book
published by arrangement with the authors.

For information, address:

AudioCraft Publishing, Inc.
PO Box 281
Topinabee Island, MI 49791

ISBN: 1-893699-87-0

AudioCraft Books are published by
AudioCraft Publishing, Inc., PO Box 281, Topinabee Island, MI 49791

Printed in the United States of America

First Printing - May, 2006

Special thanks to Lynn DeGrande and Terah Peek

PANDEMIA

"Nobody's doing anything. We've been warning the world for years. A flu pandemic is coming. It happened in the early part of this century, and it's going to happen again. People just don't understand: if we don't do something now, we just might see the end of civilization as we know it. Mark my words: bird flu is coming, and it's going to be a worldwide killer."

—Dr. Tomas N. Laakonsenn, Helsinki World Health Watch International Director, quoted from the World Health Watch Weekly Review

Chase: "So, in your opinion, if H5N1, the bird flu, mutates and can jump from human to human, what will happen?"

Dr. Michaels: "Most everyone will die."

Chase: (pause) "You . . . you can't be serious."

Dr. Michaels: "I am serious. More than ninety-nine percent of the world population could be wiped out in a matter of weeks. Maybe even faster. Of course, our governments aren't telling us this. Instead, they kill millions of birds in an effort to stop the disease from spreading."

Chase: "So, what do we do to prevent this pandemic from happening?"

Dr. Michaels: "We don't. It's already too late. The governments, the health organizations of the world . . . we've waited too long. If this thing gets going, there's no stopping it. Mark my words: bird flu is knocking at our front door. It will *not* go away."

—Dr. G.K. Michaels, interviewed by host Allen Chase, courtesy WKYK Channel 34-TV, Los Angeles

PART ONE: WILDFIRE

1

My name is Sierra McConnel, and I live on Castlebury Drive in Saline, Michigan.

Well . . . that's where I *used* to live, anyway.

On my 16th birthday, I invited thirteen friends over for a party. Seven showed up . . . the other six had the flu.

Two days later, the sick ones had died.

A week after that, nearly everyone in the city had the flu. Within weeks, almost everyone in the world was dead.

No matter what, one thing was certain: once you were infected, you were going to die.

It was as simple as that.

2

The official name for the infection was H5N1. However, it was more commonly known as the bird flu, because that's where it began: with birds. First in Asia, where it killed millions of birds over the past few years. Hundreds of millions more were killed in an effort to prevent the disease from spreading and jumping to humans. No one knew it yet, but it was too late. Too many birds had migrated, carrying the disease to far corners of the earth. I saw it on the news a lot. Every few days, there were reports of birds in another country, infected with the deadly strain of H5N1. Doctors and health officials said that millions more birds needed to be killed to prevent the spread.

It didn't work.

It started slowly at first. In the beginning, only a few hundred people died over several years, and they were mostly in Asia. The Centers for Disease Control tried to warn the world, saying it was only a matter of time before the flu mutated and became a human disease, a super-flu that would be a worldwide pandemic, but not many people paid attention. I remember seeing a few things about it on the news, but I thought the same thing everyone else did:

It won't happen to me. Not to us, here, in Michigan, in the United States. They'll stop it, they'll find some sort of vaccine or something.

It was just that sort of thinking that probably helped spread the disease even faster.

3

Symptoms were this: A tired, achy feeling, followed by a cough and a fever, just like a normal flu. Vomiting began within hours. By the next day, you couldn't get out of bed. Your body temperature would rise and you would sweat and hallucinate.

Then, the worst.

The bleeding would start. First from the eyes or ears, or both. Then the nose. There would be blood in your vomit. When this happened you knew the end was coming, and fast. Once you began puking blood, you were going to die within hours.

And those last hours . . . wow. Victims writhed in pain, delirious, screaming, pleading, praying. Some people simply killed themselves to end the suffering. I saw a woman on the street leap in front of a car. She bounced up and over the hood and hit the pavement like a bloody rag doll. The car never stopped. On the street where we live, we saw a man bleeding from his ears, eyes, and nose. He shot himself in the head with a pistol. By then, I had become numb to such displays of vulgarity. Sure it was awful and terrible.

But the worst was yet to come.

4

"D'ja here about Mr. Theraldson?" Tracie asked. "He's dead. Died last night."

It was Tuesday, May 1st, the day after my birthday, and what would be the last day of school for a week. We all knew the bird flu was already a huge problem, but it was still one of those things you don't think will happen to you. There had been an announcement that morning that school was being closed for a week, until the flu was under control.

I was in Government class, and it wasn't very full. This was, of course, before anyone knew what was *really* going on. Lots of people were sick by then. Tracie Spencer, my best friend, was sitting next to me. Tracie is very dark complected, with jet-black hair and eyes just as dark. She's thin, and her face is tight and narrow. And, although she's my age—sixteen—she looks like she could pass for eighteen or nineteen. I could easily see her as one of those models in a swimsuit magazine, but she has no interest. She's a bit shy and quiet, and has no idea how pretty she really is.

There were only a handful of students in school that day. Most others were home, sick with the flu. Some of them were already dead, but I didn't know it yet. At that time, no one knew how serious the bird flu was. On television, they kept telling us that everything was under control, that a vaccine was on its way, that it was only a matter of days. They told us not to panic, that we'd all be okay.

Yeah, right.

5

Someone was screaming in the hall.

Tracie had just told me that Mr. Theraldson, the physical education teacher, had died last night. I was about to say something, but the shrieking in the hall diverted my attention.

The classroom door was closed, and Mrs. Fleming was talking. I don't remember what she was saying.

What I do remember is the wailing that began way down the hall. A boy. Even with the door closed, we could hear the commotion clearly. There was more screaming and shouting. Someone banged against a locker, then slammed into the classroom door and fell, leaving a thick streak of blood on the door window. Mrs. Fleming went to the door, but she didn't open it. Someone else slammed into the door, and she leapt back. There was more shouting and screaming. Fighting. Somewhere in the hall, someone was crying.

And I'll never forget the look on Mrs. Fleming's face. She locked the classroom door and turned to us. She looked devastated, tired. Like she had played the game, given it her all, and lost. Mrs. Fleming is only twenty-eight, but there were now lines etched into her forehead, and dark, heavy droops beneath her eyes. She looked like she'd aged twenty years in less than a week.

"Class," she said very calmly, "it's time for you to leave."

It was kind of weird. Although she didn't say it, we just knew she meant for us to leave . . . *permanently*. And we knew in some odd, psychic way, we should leave by climbing out the window. Pandemonium had erupted in the hallway, and the window seemed the only viable option.

No one said a word as we got up from our desks. Joey Speers walked to the window, pushed it open, and crawled out. Tracie was next. One by one, my classmates stood, walked to the window, and climbed outside. There was more shouting, more screaming in the hall. Mrs. Fleming sat at her desk, put her face in her hands. Sobbed.

I stood up, picked up my purse, but I left my textbooks. Somehow, I knew I wouldn't be needing them again.

Ever.

6

"Sierra! Hey! Sierra! *Sierra!*"

My brother was yelling at me from the parking lot. It was just past noon, and there were no buses lined up yet. I had climbed out the window into a beautiful May day, with a gemstone-blue sky and a blazing, lemony sun. The trees were calm and serene, perfectly still, their leaves unruffled.

Yet, despite the perfect weather, turmoil was breaking out across the campus. All around me, students were running and shouting. Some were crying. Cars were squealing out of the school parking lot. Matt McKinley ran into me so hard I almost fell. He dropped his backpack, but he didn't stop to pick it up. I don't even think he knew he dropped it.

"Sierra!" Eddie shouted again. He waved his arms frantically, and his black leather jacket shined like a beetle shell in the midday sun. "Get over here! *Now!*"

I'd never heard that tone in his voice before. It was a mixture of anger, warning, alarm, and pleading. We've had our fights, and he's gotten pretty mad at me, but this was a different thing altogether. Eddie needed me. He was warning me, calling me, saving me.

From what, I wasn't sure.

I waved to him and started running. My purse slapped my waist, and I gripped it in my hand to keep it from flopping around. Everywhere, students were scurrying like scared mice.

In the parking lot, Eddie got into his car. It was an old Pontiac Grand Prix he'd bought last summer. A fixer-upper, for sure. There was rust around the wheel wells. The right front corner was dented . . . battle scars from a party at Dunnigan's Hill, when someone tried to leave the scene a little too fast and hit Eddie's car. He was mad. He never found out who did it.

As I approached the car, Eddie leaned over and pushed the passenger door open.

"Get in!" he ordered. "We've got to get out of here!"

I tossed my purse on the seat, tumbled into the car, and pulled the door closed. "Eddie," I breathed. "What's going on? What's happening?"

"What's going on?!?!" he exclaimed. Tires squealed, and I was thrown back into the seat before I could even get my seatbelt on. "What do you think is going on, Sierra?!?! Everybody's sick!"

"Yeah, but everybody is freaking out," I said. *"Watch out!"*

A blue Ford pickup swerved in front of us as Eddie tore out of the parking lot. Jimmy Swayne, I think, but I couldn't be sure. Eddie swerved and cursed as the truck whizzed by. Then he hit the accelerator, and the Grand Prix tore onto the highway. Tires squealed again, and the engine roared as Eddie frantically shifted.

"Haven't you heard the news?" Eddie said. "Haven't you seen what's going on? It's not just here, Sierra. It's *everywhere.* Everybody is dying. This isn't just the flu. This is the end of the world."

7

"I heard Mr. Theraldson is dead," I said.

We'd been driving through the city, heading home. Cars were speeding by. A few had veered off the road, crashing into trees in yards, or coming to rest at a house or building. We could see smoke rising from various corners of town. It hadn't been this way in the morning.

"So is Mr. Visnour," Eddie said. Mr. Visnour was the school principal. He'd been home sick for the past couple days. "Like I said," Eddie continued, turning onto Castlebury Drive, "everybody's dying. Sick and dying. Or dead already. I was listening to the news during lunch. The president has called out the National Guard and the army. This is big-time serious, Sierra. This is an epidemic. The bird flu made the jump from birds to humans. Not only that, they say the virus mutated and now is passing from human to human. People are sick and dying. Not just here, but all over the world. This is what they've been talking about. They said it was going to happen. They've been talking about a bird flu pandemic for years. They warned us. They told us this was going to happen. And it has."

That scared me. It scared me a *lot.*

3

A month before that day in May, I was helping Mom with the dinner dishes. It was Friday. Dad was watching television in the living room, and Eddie was getting ready to go out with Carrie, his loser-girlfriend. Carrie had a chest that stuck out so far it had another zip code. A five digit address, and a double-digit IQ. Carrie didn't have a lot upstairs, but she packed a lot on the main floor, which made her popular with the jocks—Eddie included. After a month, however, Eddie got bored with the Carrie Carnival, and he was already plotting his breakup act.

The news was on. Mom was quiet, pondering her day at work, no doubt. She was a nurse at University of Michigan Hospital in nearby Ann Arbor. When she wasn't there, the hospital worked on *her*. She was always thinking about work, always bringing problems home with her. She tried to separate her work life and her home life, but I could tell it was hard for her. I imagine it's hard for anyone who cares a lot about their job and other people.

I was washing the dishes, and Mom was drying them and putting them away. I could hear the TV in the living room.

". . . health officials say that if H5N1 jumps to humans and mutates, a worldwide pandemic would likely wipe out a billion people. If that were to happen, and a vaccine wasn't found quickly, the H5N1 strain could conceivably end human life on this planet as we know it."

It was a scary thought. I couldn't even imagine a million people sick and dying, let alone billions. Besides—

" . . . working hard to develop a vaccine that will immunize—"

—they would come up with a cure fast enough. It might kill a bunch of people over—

"—likely to begin in Asia, but officials fear that with today's mobile society, the flu could rapidly spread over the globe within hours. Officials say that a worldwide pandemic is long overdue, and that—"

—we'd be safe here. Saline isn't a big city at all. We'd be safe here.

"—might be virtually impossible to contain once it breaks out. Still, officials are working—"

Safe. They wouldn't let something like that happen.

Not *here.*

9

Weeks later, when people first began to get sick, nobody made a big deal about it. It was, after all, the flu. I've had it a couple of times, and so has Eddie. Mom and Dad, too, for that matter.

But not *this* kind of flu.

The news confirmed that thousands of people in Asia were already dead or dying. The H5N1 virus had finally mutated, leaping from bird to human. It had become a highly contagious disease, easily jumping from person to person, spreading around the world overnight, as officials had feared. The news reports made it sound horrific . . . but that was their job. Every disaster, every tragedy was magnified on the television news, making it sound worse than it was. When hurricane Katrina hit the southern gulf coast, the TV news had predicted over a hundred thousand people were killed. They reported murders and rapes in the shelters where people had been moved to. None of this, of course, turned out to be true. It was just the nature of television news to make the tragedy even larger and more devastating than it was, to strike an emotional cord with viewers. It was, as my dad said, all about ratings.

"The news isn't news anymore, Sierra," he'd told me once. "It's entertainment. It's ratings and money, especially television. Don't believe anything you hear, and half of what you see."

Last year, there had even been a made-for-television movie about the bird flu. Sort of a 'what if' type thing. I watched it, but it seemed over-dramatized. It was just an exaggerated movie created to scare people. You know . . . a bunch of hype. Like Dad said: television was entertainment. It was all about ratings and money.

That's the way everyone treated the early reports about H5N1. We watched and gasped and thought how terrible it was. But I couldn't help but think what was being reported was much worse than the situation really was. I think everyone was certain it couldn't be *that bad,* that the television reports were overstated for the purpose of entertaining viewers. A ratings game.

10

There was a body on the street. *Our* street.

It was lying on its stomach, and its face was turned to the side. At first, I couldn't tell if it was a man or a woman. Eddie slowed and had to steer the car around it.

"Cripes," he said as he looked out the side window. "It's Mrs. Morton. She's dead."

"Are you sure?" I asked, turning to look out the back window. The car had passed, and I could see Mrs. Morton's face. Her eyes were wide and bloody. Blood had dribbled down her face and pooled on the black pavement. Her arms were out, puffy and white. Eddie didn't have to answer. Mrs. Morton had punched out.

I winced and turned back around. Millions of questions began buzzing in my mind. Fear inflated inside me like a balloon.

What if I'm already infected? I wondered. *What if Eddie*

is? Mom? Dad? Are we all going to die? Is everybody going to die?

Our home came into view, and Eddie tapped the garage door remote clipped to his visor. The big door began to roll up. The garage was empty.

Eddie whirled the car into our drive. He parked in the garage, in Dad's spot. Dad was in Pittsburgh, and wouldn't be home for another couple of days. Mom, of course, was still at work. She wouldn't be home until five-thirty.

"Let's click on the news," Eddie said as we both got out of the car. The garage door began chugging down, and we skirted through the breezeway into the house. Eddie went right for the television, and I went to the phone. The message light was blinking red, and I pressed it.

Hi guys—

Mom.

—gonna be late tonight. Lots of nurses sick. Lasagna from last night is in the fridge. Sierra, take the clothes out of the washer and put them in the dryer, would you, sweetie? I'll be home when I can. Love you both. See you tonight.

Beep.

Howdy, folks—

Dad. He always began his messages that way.

Coming home early. Everybody's sick, and no one is coming to the meetings. I'll be home in the morning. Love ya. Over and out.

Beep. Bip-bip-bip.

End of messages.

The news was on in the living room.

"Sierra." Eddie's voice sounded oddly stale. Apprehensive, serious. "Holy shit, Sierra," he said. "You gotta see this."

11

We stood in front of the television, watching wordlessly. Breathless.

A Fox News commentator was talking about the outbreak. He was off-camera, and the live images on the screen showed people at a hospital. There were hundreds of them, and they were all shouting and screaming. Some of them were bleeding. They looked panicked and scared. Angry. Desperate. Apparently, they were locked out. While we watched, a large mob succeeded in smashing the emergency doors. Glass splintered. People pushed their way inside.

"*—think they will find a cure somewhere in the hospital,*" the news reporter was saying. "*These people mistakenly believe they will find a vaccine somewhere in the hospital, although officials tell us there still is no known cure for the avian flu pandemic which has now spread to virtually every country in the world. They're calling this* *situation a 'pandemia', the result of mass hysteria brought on by the bird flu pandemic."*

The scene on TV changed, showing a small town in some third world country. Dust was rising into the air. Bodies were stacked six feet high along a dilapidated city street, while dozens of people hurried past, holding cloths to their mouths.

"Officials say nearly thirty million people have died in the past twelve hours—"

"Oh my God," Eddie breathed. I reached down and took his hand in mine. I don't think he noticed.

"—even more contagious than originally thought. With me is Dr. Michelle Altman from the Centers for Disease Control in Atlanta. Dr. Altman . . . what is the likelihood of a vaccine being developed in time to stop this epidemic?"

Dr. Altman was an attractive woman, probably Mom's age. She had dark brown hair and tired, dark eyes. Her cheeks were sunken, though, and she looked exhausted, like she hadn't gotten much sleep.

"We've been working on this around the clock for the past year," she replied. *"As everyone knows, the bird flu has been around for several years, and we've known that a pandemic was not only possible, but probable. We have a vaccine in its early stages, but these things take time. We're working on this as fast as we possibly can. The main thing now is for people not to panic, and to stay away from those who are already infected."*

"At least they've got a vaccine in the works," Eddie said.

But this was before we realized that Dr. Altman's comments had been scripted. It was a lie. We found out later there was no vaccine, and she knew it. The government knew it, too. They lied to try to stop what they knew would be inevitable. They figured if they lied and said there was a vaccine, people wouldn't panic. Dr. Altman was just a mouthpiece for the government, repeating what she had been told to say.

I know it sounds terrible, lying to millions of people like that. But, in the end, I don't think it really mattered. Bird flu was a killer . . . and it wasn't going to be stopped.

12

I nuked the lasagna in the fridge, but I wasn't all that hungry. Eddie and I ate in the living room on the floor, seated cross-legged in front of the television. Eddie skipped from channel to channel, and the only thing we saw was coverage of the pandemic. It was weird. Even stations like HBO and QVC were covering the flu outbreak. Public officials were holding press conferences, urging people to be calm, telling them what to do. Some preacher with a very bad hairdo was urging everyone to pray. One of the channels had a picture of the H5N1 virus, magnified thousands of times. It looked like blobs of colored jelly.

"This is insane," Eddie said as he flipped to another channel. Rioting had broken out in many major cities including Detroit, Los Angeles, Dallas, Houston, Phoenix, Miami, Boston, Toledo, Atlanta, and others. New York was the worst. A live skyline shot showed hundreds of buildings burning. It was beyond unbelievable. Close up shots showed people smashing storefront windows and looting. People were fighting. While we watched, a man was held up at gunpoint and his car was stolen. The whole thing seemed surreal, like we weren't watching a news report at all. It was like we were watching a movie.

"Why are people doing this?" I wondered aloud. It made no sense. People were sick and dying, and many that were healthy were using the opportunity to loot and destroy.

Eddie shrugged. "Human nature, I guess," he said.

"It's not human nature at all," I replied. "There's nothing human about it."

"Things'll calm down overnight, I bet," Eddie said. "You heard the president. He's using the cops and the military to crack down on everybody."

"I'm going to call Mom," I said, getting to my feet. "Hand me your plate."

I walked into the kitchen and placed the dishes in the sink. Evidently, Mom had been thinking the same thing I was. As I reached for the phone, it rang suddenly, surprising me. The caller ID displayed *Univ of Michigan* on the LED screen.

"Hi, Mom," I said as I put the phone to my ear.

"Hi, Honey," Mom said. There was a sluggish weight in her voice. She sounded tired. "Where's Eddie?"

"He's right here. We're watching the news. When are you coming home?"

"Not for a while, I'm afraid. We're—"

"Are you all right?" I interrupted. "We saw on the news where people were breaking into hospitals and—"

"I'm fine, everything is fine here," Mom said. "Just

busy. So many sick people. Half the staff is sick. We're telling people who are sick to go home and—"

(die)

"—try to be comfortable. There's just nothing we can do for them. You're okay?"

"Hmmm?" I said. I had been momentarily distracted by shouting on the television. Cops were shooting at looters in some city.

"You're okay?" Mom repeated. "You feel all right?"

"Me? Sure. I'm fine. Eddie is, too."

"Good. Stay inside. Don't go anywhere, and don't let anyone come into the house. No friends. Don't have anyone over. If someone comes to the door, don't answer it."

"Mom," I said, mentally rolling my eyes.

Mom's voice sharpened. "Sierra . . . listen to me. I don't know what's going to happen. *Nobody* does. This flu has spread too fast, and nobody knows how to stop it. Stay in the house, and don't come into contact with anyone else."

"But what about *you?"* I asked.

"I'll be fine," Mom said. "I've got a mask. Everyone is being careful."

"But once people catch the flu, they die, don't they?" I asked.

There was a pause.

"No, there's no cure or vaccine," Mom breathed.

"That's not what I asked."

"That's all I can say. Your father called. He's on his way home."

"I know," I said. "He left a message."

I promised Mom we'd stay indoors, that we wouldn't let anyone in and we wouldn't go anywhere.

I hung up, not knowing I had just spoken to my mother for the last time.

13

Eddie and I sat in silence, watching the television in disbelief. I remember seeing images of the World Trade Center coming down, and how I had been horrified into a stupor, unable to speak, unable to tear away from the sickening video of the giant buildings reduced to rubble.

Now we were watching much the same thing, only it wasn't a building collapsing . . . it was civilization. We were watching the human race being felled before our eyes, courtesy of the bird flu and our local cable provider.

Dad called half an hour after I'd hung up with Mom. He said he was stuck in traffic west of Toledo, but he thought things were going to start moving, and he'd be home in a couple of hours. He sounded sick, and there was a tense sound to his voice that I don't hear very often. Dad is pretty easy-going and mellow. He doesn't get upset very often, and he doesn't show it when he does.

"Are you okay?" I asked. He'd had a coughing fit.

"Yeah, I'm fine," he said. "Frog in my throat. I'm fine."

Dad never made it home.

14

I called Kevin Martinchek at seven o'clock. We'd been dating on and off for about six months. I wouldn't call our relationship serious, but Kevin was a year older than me, and a lot of fun. Cute and smart. He just didn't know what he wanted. One day he'd tell me he wanted to be with me and only me, and a day later he would tell me we should keep dating, but see other people. Which was fine. I just wanted him to stop flip-flopping.

"Are you watching the news?" I asked him.

"Who's not?" he replied. "God, Sierra . . . this is awful. Did you see New York?"

"We're watching it on TV right now. Are you okay?"

"Fine," he replied. "The gas station is closed, though, so I don't have to go to work." Kevin worked evenings at the Marathon station a few blocks from his house. In the summer, he also worked at a landscaping business. One thing was for sure: nobody could ever call Kevin lazy.

"That's probably a good thing," I said. "I mean . . . with everything going on."

"Mom's sick."

My heart felt like a brick. I didn't say anything.

"She's okay, though," he continued. "She locked herself in her bedroom yesterday. She'll . . . she'll be all right."

We both knew better, but there was no point discussing it.

"How are you feeling?" I asked.

"I'm okay, so far," he said. "I'm not sick, and I feel fine. How are *you* doing?"

"Me? Fine. Eddie's here. We're fine. We just can't believe what's happening. People are sick and dying, and others have gone crazy."

"It's going to get worse, Sierra," Kevin said. "It's going to get a *lot* worse."

"No," I said. "Things will get better. They won't let it get worse."

"Who's 'they'?" Kevin laughed. "The police? The government? Hospitals?"

"They have a vaccine on the way," I said. "I saw it on TV."

"There's no vaccine, Sierra," Kevin said. "It's all a lie."

"No, I saw it," I insisted. "There was some doctor—"

"Babe, it's not true," Kevin said. "Everybody knows it. They're just trying to tell us something—anything—to keep everybody calm and stop the looting and the violence."

Suddenly, there was an enormous crash outside. It sounded like a thousand pounds of metal fell from the sky. Even Kevin heard it through the phone.

"What was that?" he asked.

"I don't know," I said. "I've got to go. Call you later." I hung up.

Eddie was at the window. "Oh my God," he said.

15

A dark blue minivan had slammed into a parked car on the other side of the street. Steam was hissing out from beneath the hood. While we watched, a woman scrambled out. She walked slowly, stumbling, dazed. Then she tripped over the curb and fell into the grass.

"She's hurt," Eddie said, and he started toward the door. I grabbed his arm and stopped him.

"No, she's not," I said quietly, still looking out the window. "She's not hurt, Eddie. She's *sick.*"

The woman rolled over on the grass and got to her knees. She tried to stand, but was too weak. Then she vomited. A geyser of dark brown liquid sprayed into the grass as her body convulsed. She continued heaving, spewing a seemingly endless amount of puke. When she stopped, she sat on the curb, facing us. She was crying, and a stain of muddy liquid trickled down her chin and onto her shirt.

And she was *bleeding.*

At first, I thought is was just vomit, but then I noticed it was red. Blood was dripping from her nose, trickling at first, then turning into a stream. The woman didn't seem to notice. She was dazed, and had a forlorn, faraway look in her eyes.

Eddie and I watched through the living room window. We both knew there was nothing we could do. It was painful, watching the woman in the state she was in, knowing we couldn't help her. If she was sick and we came into contact with her, we would likely become infected with the disease ourselves.

Which was another thing.

Suppose we're already infected? I wondered. *Suppose Eddie or I picked up the virus from someone at school?* Then, it would be only a matter of time before we, too, began to feel sick. It would be only a matter of time before we—

A movement caught my attention. It was a man, perhaps in his early twenties. He was running up the street, his feet pounding the cement. At first, I thought he was running to help the woman, but he flew past her and leapt into the van.

"What's he—" Eddie started to ask, but in the next instant, it was clear what was happening. The man suddenly sprang from the vehicle and ran off . . . carrying the woman's purse. The woman, still sitting on the curb, watched passively, like it wasn't her purse. Like it wasn't happening, like she didn't care. She couldn't have done anything if she tried.

"They're wrong," I told Eddie.

He looked at me. Studied my face. "Who?" he asked.

"Wrong about what?"

I shook my head. "Everyone is wrong. It's not going to get better. Like Kevin said: it's only going to get worse. A *lot* worse."

16

Night came.

It came with yellow flickering—fires—in the distance. I watched the clouds above, their bellies glowing yellow, red, and orange, reflecting the burning structures across town. It came with the sound of sirens, of breaking glass, and squealing tires. Of people shouting in the distance. Screams. Gun shots.

But there was another sound, too.

No, it wasn't a sound that was as much *heard* as it was *felt.* It was the sound of something dying, of giving way. The sound of loss, of despair. It was a whisper in my ear that said something was really, *really* wrong.

And things would never be the same again.

17

The woman on the curb had died, we were certain. Earlier, we had watched her slump forward and fall, laying spread-eagle in the street. Her body convulsed violently, and she let out with a shower of bloody puke. Her body twitched once, twice. A brown-red stain of vomit pooled around her. Then she stopped moving.

Eddie kept flipping through the television channels. The networks were jumping to locations all over the world, but it was impossible to tell what city or country we were seeing. Fires, disaster, looting . . . I couldn't believe what people were doing. The bird flu epidemic had turned the world upside down, but in major cities in every country, people seemed less concerned about getting sick, and more concerned about hauling off televisions and stereos they looted from homes and businesses.

"Turn to one of the local channels," I said.

Outside, a police car flew by, its lights flashing and siren blaring. It swerved to miss the dead woman on the street, but the car never slowed.

Eddie pecked at the remote, and the images flashed on the screen. The local NBC station was interviewing the mayor of Ann Arbor.

"*. . . most importantly,*" the mayor was saying, "*we need everyone to remain indoors. Stay in your house. Lock your doors and windows. We expect troops to begin arriving soon. Until then, the police are doing all they can do.*"

"That's a good idea," I said, walking to the front door. I locked it. Then, I went around to each window in the living room. Eddie got up and went into his bedroom, locking his window and closing the blind. Then he went to Mom and Dad's room and did the same. There was a sliding glass door that opened to a patio in our backyard, and I made sure it was locked.

"I've got all the windows," Eddie said as he walked back into the living room. He picked up the remote and surfed through the channels until there was another doctor being interviewed.

"*. . . appears to be a highly-communicable disease, easily transmitted from one person to another. The only thing we can stress is for people to stay completely away from any and all infected persons.*"

A news reporter posed a question. "*Are people catching this flu from eating contaminated birds?*"

The doctor shook his head. "*No,*" he replied. "*That's not possible. This is a different strain altogether, one that appears to be exclusive to humans.*"

The reporter asked another question. "*Can the disease be spread by someone who is infected, yet doesn't show signs of being sick?"* he asked.

The doctor nodded. *"Yes. We think that's one of the reasons the mutated H5N1 has spread so quickly. Generally, we believe it takes only twelve to twenty-four hours for symptoms to show. During that time, the infected person wouldn't necessarily have any way of knowing they are infected."*

That scared me.

"Both of us could be infected," I said to Eddie. "We could be infected and not even know it."

"We'll know tomorrow," he said glumly.

13

The phone was ringing.

The loud chirping jolted me awake, and I snapped up from the couch. I'd fallen asleep. Eddie had conked-out in the recliner, and the television was off. The house was dark.

The phone was on the coffee table, and I snatched it up. The caller ID displayed Dad's cell phone number.

"Hi, Daddy," I said sleepily.

"Hi, Sierra," Dad said. He sounded distant, distracted. "Mom home?"

"No, not yet," I said. Suddenly, everything began coming back to me. The flu pandemic, the rioting, the looting. The dead woman who was probably still laying in the street in front of our house.

Eddie awoke, got up, stretched, and walked into the kitchen.

"Where are you?" I asked Dad.

"I'm still outside of Toledo," he answered. "All traffic has stopped."

"Are you all right?"

"Yeah, yeah, I'm fine," Dad replied, but I could tell by his voice that everything wasn't fine. It wasn't fine at all.

"What's wrong?" I asked, clearing my throat. I heard a noise in the hall and saw Eddie's shadow. He walked into the kitchen and opened the fridge. White light splayed.

"I just don't know if I'm going to make it back by morning," Dad said. "With this traffic and all. How about you and Ed? You guys . . . all right?"

I knew what he meant. He wanted to know if we were sick.

"We're fine," I said. "There's . . . there's a dead woman on the street. Dad . . . what's going to happen?"

"Everything will be fine," Dad said. "Just . . . just stay indoors. Don't open the door for anyone, don't come into contact with anyone. Mom should be home soon. Let her know I called."

"I will," I said. "I love you lots."

"Love you, too," Dad said.

I clicked off the phone. "That was Dad," I said, standing up.

Eddie was in the kitchen, swigging milk from the gallon jug. "Where is he?" he asked.

"Still in Ohio. He says the traffic isn't moving."

"Turn on the television," Eddie said as he replaced the milk and closed the fridge.

I clicked on the lamp on the coffee table . . . and that's when the living room window suddenly exploded, showering the room with glass.

19

The blast was so sudden that I didn't have time to move. Shards of glass fell like rain, and a massive hole the size of a beach ball defiled the curtain. It was over in an instant, but the shocking effect, the suddenness of the impact, remained. I was stunned. I didn't even realize I was bleeding.

Then the shouting began. Outside, in our yard.

"Sierra!" Eddie yelled. *"Get back! Get over here!"*

I ran into the kitchen, and Eddie grabbed my arm. Blood streaked from my elbow to my wrist, and I gasped.

"Does it hurt?" Eddie asked. He yanked the dishtowel that was looped over the oven handle and draped it over my arm.

"I didn't even know I was cut," I said, looking down at the blood, which had run down to my finger and was dripping on the kitchen floor.

The shouting in the yard continued, and there was a

gunshot. That's when I realized that the window had been shattered by a shotgun blast.

"Into my bedroom!" Eddie shouted, and we raced down the hall to his room. A small nightlight cast a thin, sugary light, barely illuminating posters of rock bands and race car drivers on the walls and ceiling. A few model airplanes dangled from fishing lines. Eddie had built them years ago, when he was still in elementary school, but he never took them down. A dresser drawer was open. There was a disheveled pile of clothing on his unmade bed. Eddie wasn't really into folding and putting away his clothes.

My arm was throbbing, and the dishtowel was quickly staining with blood. I pulled it away, revealing an inch-long slice. Not very deep, though, and I didn't think it would require stitches. Good thing, since there was no way I was leaving the house to go anywhere. Blood continued to ooze from the wound, and I replaced the towel and pressed it hard, thinking how glad I was I hadn't been any closer to the window.

"Man, they just shot a guy!" Eddie gasped as he pulled the drape back and peeked out the window. I walked to his side and looked over his shoulder into the yard.

A streetlight lit up the area. The dead woman was still laying in the road, but her van was gone. Instead, there was a dark-colored Corvette, parked partially over the curb. The driver's door was open, and, a few feet away, a man was laying on his back in the street in a pool of dark liquid. Under the streetlight, the blood looked like a shiny oil slick. Another man, carrying a shotgun, was shuffling through his pockets.

"Can't we do something?" I asked.

Eddie shook his head. "He might come after us," he said. "I think he shot out our living room window by accident."

"I don't think he shot that guy by accident," I said.

While we watched, the man with the shotgun stuffed the dead man's wallet into his pocket. Then he bounded over to the Corvette, threw the gun into the passenger seat, and leapt behind the wheel. The car roared to life and rocketed off the curb. It vanished in a cacophony of squealing tires.

"What time is it?" I asked.

Eddie walked to his bed. A T-shirt covered his clock radio, and he plucked it off and tossed it on the floor. The green numbers glowed.

12:44.

It was after midnight, and Mom still wasn't home.

20

"I'm going to call the hospital," I said, and I walked out of Eddie's bedroom.

"What about your cut?" Eddie asked.

It was weird, but I'd actually forgotten about the cut. Even though I was still holding the towel to my arm, I wasn't actually aware I was doing it. I guess when there is so much going on, when your heart is pumping and your adrenaline is raging, it's easy to overlook other things.

I lifted the dishtowel and exposed the wound. The bleeding had slowed to a trickle.

"You call Mom," I said. "I'll go take care of this." I walked down the hall and into the bathroom. Flipped the light switch, and squinted. I looked at myself in the mirror. My eyes were puffy, my light brown hair messy. I ran my fingers through it, decided it didn't matter what I looked like, anyway, and turned the water on. I ran my injured arm beneath the warm stream, then washed it with soap. The cut stung, but not bad. The dribble of blood was slowing.

"Did you get hold of Mom?" I called out.

"I'm on hold," Eddie replied from the living room. I could hear the tinkling of glass as he picked up pieces of the shattered window and dropped them into the plastic garbage can he'd dragged from the kitchen.

I patted my arm dry with a clean towel, then bandaged the cut with some gauze and tape.

Could have been a lot worse, I thought. *Glass could have cut me deeper. Or my face.*

I heard the television come on and I left the bathroom, walked down the hall, and stopped at the living room. Eddie was picking glass out of the couch, and I knelt down to help him.

"What's going on?" I asked, nodding to the TV.

Eddie shook his head. He had the phone tucked between his shoulder and his ear, obviously still on hold. "Just turned it on," he said. "Looks like more of the same. Worse."

The screen showed more images of rioting. It was a city in Kenya. Hundreds of small, hut-like homes were on fire. People were running everywhere. The graphic at the bottom read *PANDEMIA STRIKES WORLD.*

"Enough of this," Eddie said, pulling the phone away and clicking it off. He placed it on the coffee table . . . and it rang.

21

Mom. It's got to be Mom.

Eddie snapped up the phone and waited for the caller ID to register. Then he tossed it to me without answering.

"It's Tracie," he said.

I caught the phone, turned it on, and pressed it to my ear.

"Trace?"

"Hi, Sierra," Tracie said. She sounded like she'd been crying.

"What's wrong?" I asked.

She laughed, half sobbing. "What's *wrong?* Geez . . . what *isn't* wrong?"

"I mean . . . with you. Are you all right?"

"As well as can be," she said. "I'm not sick, so that's a good thing."

"Eddie and I are okay, too," I said. "So far."

"My Dad is sick. He's not coming home from work, because he doesn't want to infect me or Mom. But Mom went to the grocery store earlier today. She hasn't come home."

"Did you try her cell?"

"It just goes to her voice mail. I'm really scared, Sierra. I mean . . . I'm watching the television, and this is . . . this is just unbelievable! When is all of this going to end?"

"I don't know," I said. "Dad's stuck in Toledo. He said traffic has stopped."

"Where's your mom?"

"She's still at work at the hospital. She says it's pretty crazy there. But that was a while ago. We haven't talked to her in a couple of hours."

"It's crazy everywhere. I don't like being here alone."

"Where's your sister?" I asked.

"With her boyfriend," Tracie replied. "She moved into his apartment in Minnesota last week. She was supposed to come back yesterday and pick up her car, but she never showed up. I've been calling there, but there's no answer."

There was silence on the line for a moment, and I watched the images on television. A man in a dark green uniform was being interviewed, but Eddie had muted the volume and I couldn't hear what was being said.

"I'm sorry for calling so late," Tracie said. "It's just that . . . well, I'm here alone, and—"

"Don't worry about it," I interrupted. "I'm glad you're okay. Try and get some sleep. I'll call you in the morning."

"Okay," Tracie replied. "Be careful."

I hung up.

Be careful.

That sounded weird.

Be careful.

22

The night air drifting through the broken living room window was chilly and damp.

"We've got to do something about that," I said, pointing at the window. "It's going to get cold tonight."

Eddie went into the garage and returned with a large, flattened cardboard box. It was a couple of years old, from when we got a new fridge. Dad used it on the floor in the garage, because his car sometimes leaked oil, and he said he didn't want it all over the cement. The box had a big, black stain on it.

"Let's use some duct tape and seal the cardboard around the window," Eddie said. "It'll help keep the cold air out."

Working with the cardboard was tedious, but at least it was big enough to cover the whole window. Eddie held it in place while I taped the edges to the walls.

"If the paint peels when we take this tape off, Dad is going to be pissed," I said.

"At this point, I don't think Dad is going to care much about some peeled paint," Eddie replied.

23

Morning came.

After we'd put the box over the window, I went to bed. I took the phone with me in case Mom called, but it never rang.

And Mom still wasn't home.

I climbed out of bed, slipped into my sweat pants and a baggy T-shirt, and walked down the hall. Peered into Eddie's bedroom. He was still sleeping. Then, I went into the kitchen and poured a glass of water.

Next stop: television. A window to the world. I turned it on, but kept the volume low so I wouldn't wake up Eddie. Once again, the only thing on was news reports. Riots, looting, fires. Pandemonium and chaos. Madness. Many channels were no longer on the air. No one was playing any commercials. CNN had some guy on who claimed to be a survivalist, and he was warning that this was only the beginning. He said from here on out, we wouldn't be able to count on law enforcement, the government, no one. He said we were all going to be on our own, and the only ones who would survive were the ones who had been prepared, the ones who had stockpiled food . . . and weapons. The ones who had been ready.

Its only getting worse, I thought. I hated to admit it, but the more I watched and listened, the more I realized the man was probably right. The only people who would survive were going to be the ones who were prepared, the ones who had been planning for a catastrophic, world event like we were seeing.

The interview continued, but the TV now showed images of a supermarket. People were rushing out with their arms full of food, pushing shopping carts as fast as they could. Some people carried guns. Others were fighting one another over items.

I returned to the kitchen and poured a bowl of Froot Loops. I nibbled the cereal dry. Eddie loved milk; I could take it or leave it. Then I took up a position in front of the TV again, sitting cross-legged, dipping into my bowl of cereal.

"Sierra?" Eddie called out from his bedroom. Alarm was in his voice.

I stood. "Yeah?" I replied just as he emerged from his bedroom. He had just slipped into his jeans and was pulling a T-shirt over his head. He saw me.

"Get dressed," he said.

"What's wrong?"

"Just . . . just get dressed. Get something else on besides sweats. Put on some pants."

"What's wrong?" I repeated.

"Something's going on," he said, tucking his shirt into his pants. "I heard some noise outside. It looks like there's a group of guys going house to house. Looters. I . . . I saw them pull Mr. Carlson out of his house and stab him. He's dead."

"What?!?!" I exclaimed.

"Get dressed. We've got to hide. Or get out of here, one of the two. Hurry up."

I ran to my room and changed as quickly as I could. Then I reached into my dresser and pulled out a wad of money I'd been saving. Just over one hundred dollars. I didn't know if I could ever use it again, but it was easy enough to stuff into my pocket. There was also a lot of jewelry in the drawer—some of it expensive—but I left it. Then I put on my tennis shoes.

Eddie came to my door. He was carrying the handgun Dad kept in the dresser drawer on his side of the bed. It was a nine millimeter semiautomatic. I didn't know much about it, and I'd never shot it. But Dad and Eddie would take it to the range once in a while for target practice.

"They're across the street!" Eddie said. "They'll be here any—"

There was an enormous pound on the front door, and wood began to splinter.

They were here.

24

"Downstairs!" Eddie hissed. I was still seated at the edge of my bed, and I leapt up. He grabbed my hand and we sprinted down the hall and reached the basement door—just as the front door shattered.

"Hurry!" Eddie hissed, almost pushing me down the stairs. We descended two steps at a time into the dark basement. From the living room, I heard voices . . . angry sounding, vicious voices, and wild, frenzied laughter . . . and once again, the craziness of the whole situation rattled through my head.

What good is it going to do to steal people's things if you're going to get the flu and die? The more they come into contact with people, the sooner they're going to be infected. Didn't they know that?

Yeah, they probably did. But, like we saw on television when hurricane Katrina hit the gulf states: during a crisis, people act differently. When faced with pressures they hadn't planned on, when the stuff really hits the fan, they can't cope. A reactionary mode kicks in, and they do what they know how to do. Some people, faced with catastrophe, just don't *think*. They become different. They show what they're *really* made of.

Some become animals—like the ones who had kicked in our front door.

25

Our basement steps are made of wood. There's a single, bare bulb on the wall, but Eddie didn't turn it on. Instead, we plunged down into the darkness, intent on finding a place to hide. Besides: we both knew the basement inside and out. As kids, it had been our play area. We made forts out of old boxes, played hide-and-seek and board games like *Chutes and Ladders* and *Operation.*

And, thankfully, there wasn't much of value in the basement. It was cluttered with a lot of useless junk. There was a broken treadmill, an old couch. A large wooden crate still held all kinds of toys from when we were little. The washer and dryer were on the far wall, next to the hot water heater.

"Behind the couch!" Eddie hissed. *"Let's pull it out a little and hide behind it!"*

Upstairs, things were breaking. There were loud

voices. Laughter. Crazy, insane laughter. A window shattered.

We pulled the couch out from the wall—only a few inches—and wriggled behind it on our hands and knees. When we were growing up, it had been one of our favorite hiding places.

I hoped it still worked.

We had just snuggled behind the couch when I heard the basement door crash against the wall, thrown open. Footsteps on the stairs. Then, the light came on. The footsteps continued until they reached the bottom of the basement steps.

I was terrified, and I hoped that, whoever it was, would decide there was nothing in the basement worth stealing. I hoped they wouldn't find us. I hoped they would just go away. Sure, Eddie had Dad's gun . . . but he'd be no match for a bunch of looters. They probably had their own guns, anyway.

Footsteps. This time, they were going back up the stairs.

"Nothin' down here," someone yelled. "Just a bunch of crap."

Relief washed over me.

Upstairs, the looting continued. I could hear lots of things breaking and smashing. And, although this may sound weird, I was *glad*. Let them take anything. Let them take it all. I just wanted them to leave. Get whatever they want, then go.

I heard the garage door open, followed by Eddie's car starting. Tires squealed. Someone shouted something.

After a while, the noises faded. Ten minutes later,

there were no sounds at all, except for outside. We could hear more shouting and yelling, but it was distant. Then we heard a gun shot. And a scream.

It was then I realized we couldn't go back. There was no way the world was ever going to be the same.

Not anymore.

26

After a few more minutes, Eddie climbed out from behind the couch and stood. I followed.

"I think they're gone," I said.

Eddie shook his head. "They just moved on to the next house," he said. "There might be more. We're just going to have to keep an eye out. Let's go upstairs."

"They stole your car," I said, almost apologetically.

He shrugged it off. "We're still alive," was all he said.

We walked up the steps quietly. Eddie led the way, holding out Dad's handgun in front of him, just in case.

Upstairs, the house was in shambles. Wrecked. The television was gone, along with the DVD player. My radio in my bedroom was gone. Lots of things had been stolen.

But I couldn't figure out why there had been so much *damage.* There was a picture that used to hang on the wall in the hall. It was a picture of me, Eddie, Mom, Dad, and Lucy, our chocolate lab who died last year. The picture hadn't been stolen . . . it had been smashed to pieces. It was just senseless vandalism. Stupid. Other things were wrecked, too. Someone had taken a knife to our leather couch and sliced it up. Dad's recliner was upside down, and the arm was broken. The coffee table was broken into three or four pieces. Even the cardboard Eddie and I had used to cover the window had been slashed with a knife.

Eddie walked to the breezeway and pressed the remote button that controlled the garage door. There was a mechanical jarring sound, a chain-and-spoke sound, as the garage door lowered.

A feeling of desperation welled up inside of me, and I started to cry. Mom wasn't home, Dad wasn't home, and animals had destroyed our house.

Eddie hugged me, which is something he hadn't done in a long time.

"Hey, hey," he said. "It's going to be all right. We're going to be fine. Mom and Dad will be home soon. They'll know what to do."

He pulled away, but his hands gripped my shoulders. Eddie is a few inches taller than me. Strong.

"Meantime, we have to be prepared. We have to be ready to hide. And to fight, if we have to. Get your backpack, Sierra. Fill it with some clothes, and only the things you *absolutely* have to have."

"Where are we going to go?" I asked.

"Nowhere," Eddie said. "But we have to be ready. If, for some reason, we have to leave the house, we'll need to have whatever it'll take to survive."

"What about food?" I asked.

"I'm not all that worried about food," Eddie said.

"Why?" I asked.

Eddie dropped his hands from my shoulder, and they hung at his sides. "Because, Sierra, if half the world dies from this flu, there's gonna be a lot of food to go around."

27

My backpack is small, and I wasn't going to be able to put a lot in it. I managed to fit a change of clothing and a few toiletries, which, by some miracle, hadn't been stolen or trashed. I guess looters don't give a hoot about toothpaste. As I'd suspected, all of my jewelry was gone. I didn't care. At that point, I was thankful I was still alive. And thankful, at least for the time being, that I wasn't sick, and neither was Eddie.

I carried my pack into the living room. Outside, I could still hear occasional shouting and distant screaming. Gunshots were becoming more and more common.

And another thing I noticed:

No more sirens.

There weren't any sirens to be heard, anywhere. Which, of course, could only mean one thing: the police had given up. The firemen, the rescue workers. All had given up.

If the National Guard had been sent to restore order, they had taken a detour, because they sure weren't anywhere near Saline.

But I had Eddie. Sure, I couldn't stand him sometimes. Sometimes, we didn't get along. But Eddie was smart. He was smart, and he was fearless. If I had to face a situation like this, without Mom and Dad, I was glad I had Eddie.

The phone rang, startling me. Actually, I was surprised it still worked. The unit had been tossed to the floor, and it took me a minute to find the receiver, which was under the upended recliner. I looked at the caller ID.

Tracie.

I pressed the 'talk' button and placed the receiver to my ear. "Tracie!" I shouted into the mouthpiece.

"This is nuts!" she said. "This is crazy, Sierra!"

"Are you all right?" I asked.

"I'm fine," she replied. "I'm not sick. But there are people all around, and they're—"

"I know, I know," I said. "They came and looted our house. A mob of animals. Eddie and I hid, and they didn't find us. We're fine. We're not sick."

"I'm coming over!" Tracie said.

"What?!?!" I exclaimed.

"Sierra, I can't handle this! I'm alone! Do you hear me?!?! I'm *alone,* Sierra! The whole world is going to hell, and I'm *alone!*"

"How are you going to get here?" I asked.

"I'm going to drive!" she said. "I'm taking my sister's car! And if anyone tries to stop me, I'll mow them over! Just promise me you'll be there for me. Promise me!"

Eddie emerged from his bedroom, and I mouthed the word *Tracie* to him. He nodded.

"Yeah," I said into the phone. "We'll be here. Be careful."

Tracie hung up.

Eddie went back into his bedroom.

Then—

A shadow fell over the front doorway.

A *human* shadow.

23

I had an instant of total fear, an accelerated moment of complete horror. Then, as fast as the emotion had hit me, it slipped away when I saw who was at the door.

Kevin.

He rushed inside and we hugged. "I'm so glad it's you," I said. He held me tightly, and it felt good.

"I'm glad you're all right," he said. "I was really worried."

"Why are you here?" I asked, pulling back. He was wearing his varsity jacket with a tank top beneath it. "What about your—"

"Mom's dead," Kevin said. There were the beginnings of tears in his blue eyes. "This morning. She's been locked in the bedroom. Early this morning, she said she was going to die. It was horrible." A tear slid down his cheek. I had never seen Kevin cry. "She was in agony all night. I could hear her moaning and groaning, throwing up. I tried to kick in the door, but she screamed at me. She told me to stay away, that I'd catch the flu if I got near her. It was horrible, Sierra. There wasn't anything I could do."

Outside, we heard a shout from across the street and a gunshot, just as Eddie came out of his room with his backpack. Dad's handgun was tucked in the right front pocket of his jeans. Upon hearing the blast from across the street, he drew the gun and let it hang, barrel pointed toward the ground.

"Hey, Kev," he said in greeting, looking him over. Eddie and Kevin aren't what you'd call 'friends', but it's not because they don't like each other. They've just never spent any time together. Actually, they have a lot of the same qualities. Both are thin but solid. Kevin is a little bit taller, Eddie has shoulders that are a little bit bigger and broader than Kevin's. But Kevin's sandy-blonde hair is longer, flaring over his shoulders and several inches down his back. He's seventeen, but, like Tracie, he looks older.

"You guys are all right?" Kevin asked.

"If you mean we don't have the bird flu, we're fine," Eddie replied. "Everything else has gone to hell."

And it had. We no longer had a television or radio, but we knew what was going on. Our window to the world was now our front doorway. The door had been shattered by the looters, and it lay on the floor.

But beyond it, a new world was emerging. In the distance, fingers of smoke rose, merging to create a dirty brown film in the sky. Closer, there was a house burning—the Freeman's, I think. It was on the next block, and I could see tongues of yellow leaping in the air. Thick smoke swirled and licked at the sky. Sporadic gunfire could be heard, some of it close, some of it a long way off. There were shouts, screams, yells. Tires squealing. Glass breaking.

It was a new world, all right.

There was a sudden, loud squeal of tires and an even louder crashing sound. A car had hit something. Then the engine roared, getting louder as it approached.

Eddie bounded to the door and peered out cautiously. Kevin and I followed.

The car was flying down the street, its engine racing.

"That's Tracie!" I exclaimed. "She made it!"

Not quite.

At that moment, a kid came running out from the side of a house. I say 'kid' as in someone my age. Maybe younger. He was wearing black boots, dirty blue jeans. No shirt. There was a cut that extended from his shoulder to his elbow. Dried blood caked on his arm.

And he was carrying a shotgun.

He ran to the curb, shouldered the weapon, and aimed it at the oncoming car.

"No!" I shrieked . . . just as the sharp blast of the shotgun filled the air like cannon fire.

29

The moment the gun barked, there was a simultaneous explosion as the right front tire of the car Tracie was driving blew out. The car lurched sideways and hit the curb, out of control until it slammed into a parked car that had burned last night.

I could see Tracie behind the wheel, her face twisted in shock and fear. Her eyes were wide, white with black dots. I could hear her muffled screams.

The kid with the shotgun approached the car, the weapon still drawn to his shoulder. He fired again.

Tracie sprang just in time. She scrambled across the passenger seat, threw open the door, and leapt out . . . just as the windshield exploded. She started running toward us.

The kid with the gun swung the weapon.

Eddie stepped onto the porch, brandishing Dad's pistol with both hands. There was a thundering explosion—I'd never heard the gun go off before—that made my ears ring.

Most importantly, though, the kid dropped the shotgun. It discharged again as it clattered to the pavement. He stood frozen for a moment, a dark red splotch on his belly growing by the second. Then, he clutched the wound and fell to his knees. Blood gushed from the gaping hole, and he fell forward onto the pavement. I winced as his face slammed into the rock-hard surface, but I'm sure the kid couldn't have felt it. He was already dead.

Tracie had never looked back, and now she ran up to us. I reached out and took her into my arms.

"Sierra! Oh, God, Sierra!" She was sobbing, hysterical, her face streaked with tears. Her mascara had run, giving her a tired, goth look.

"You're all right now," I said, holding her thin body tightly. "You're all right. It's going to be okay."

Her head was buried in my shoulder. "It's never going to be okay! Never, ever! We're all going to die!"

"No, no we're not," I insisted. "We're going to be okay. Really." I'm not sure I believed my own words, but I didn't know what else to say.

I could still smell gunpowder in the air. Eddie stood on the porch, the nine millimeter hanging limp at his side. He stared at the dead kid in the street. I knew he was a good shot with the pistol . . . but he'd never shot anyone before.

He turned. His face was pale, but color was gradually returning. There was no doubt he was shook up about what he had done.

"Let's get back inside," he said. "We have to start thinking about what we're going to do to stay alive."

30

The phone rang.

We were in the living room. Eddie and Kevin had turned the recliner back over, and Eddie was sitting in it. The phone rested on the broken arm. Tracie, Kevin, and I were on the torn-up couch. When the phone rang, it surprised all of us. Tracie jumped. Eddie looked at the caller ID.

"It's Mom," he said, pressing the *talk* button and placing it to his ear. "Hey," he spoke into the receiver.

His brow furrowed in surprise. "Yes?" he said. He looked confused. "Okay. Uh-huh." His composure was fading, and the dread was contagious. I knew the news was not good.

"Yeah," Eddie said, barely a whisper. His eyes had grown watery. Glazed and distant. I buried my face in my hands, already knowing what had happened.

"Yeah, it's all right. Thanks. Did . . . did

she . . . hello? *Hello . . . ?"*

He pulled the phone from his ear, pressed the talk button, then placed it to his ear again. "Lines are down," he said as he slowly placed the phone on the recliner's broken arm.

I spoke, but I already knew what Eddie was going to say. "What's the—"

"Mom's dead," he interrupted, his voice trembling. "She . . . she was sick. I guess she was sick when she talked to us, but she didn't say anything. She died this morning. She told one of the doctors to call here and tell us. She told him to tell us she loved us."

We were all crying now. Tracie was in my arms, and Kevin had his arms wrapped around both of us. Eddie sobbed quietly in the recliner.

Time passed.

31

"We've got to get some news and find out what's going on," Kevin said. "Maybe they've got a vaccine or something. Maybe there's an emergency shelter we can go to."

We were in the kitchen, sitting around what was left of the dining room table. Amazingly, the chairs had been spared. The table was another story. It had been broken into several pieces, its legs stripped away. For no reason.

Eddie said the phone died while he was talking to the doctor at the hospital. Not just our phone, but the lines. We tried a couple of times throughout the day, but it was no use. The phones were out.

And the computer was trashed. It hadn't been stolen, but the monitor was shattered and the box looked like it had been stomped on.

"The only thing I've got is my radio," Eddie said, "and the batteries are dead."

"Cars have radios," I said, looking out the kitchen window. "There are cars all over the place."

"There are also people with guns and knives all over the place," Tracie said.

"But there's four of us," Kevin chimed in. "We'd be safer if we stick together."

Eddie looked outside. It was now late evening, and it was nearly dark. All day long, we heard the sounds of chaos: shooting, yelling, screaming. Car engines racing, vehicles crashing in thunderclaps of metal, steel, and shattering glass. There were several loud explosions, like bombs going off. Twice, when gangs of people got close to the house, the four of us had scrambled into the basement. There wasn't anyplace for all four of us to hide, but Eddie stood at the foot of the basement stairs, waiting with Dad's pistol. Thankfully, no one else came into our home.

And there were more deaths. Outside, we could see people who were sick, walking along, dazed. Some of them were moaning, pleading for help. Sometimes they simply fell to the ground and died on the spot. Other times, another person came along, knocking them to the ground. They would take their watch, ring, necklace . . . whatever the person had. I couldn't help but wonder: *Don't they know that, by touching an infected person, they are probably going to get sick and die? Don't they know it doesn't matter how much they rob and steal, it's not going to matter, anyway? What good is a diamond ring if there's nobody around to buy it? What good is money if you can't spend it?* I still had my money in my pocket but it didn't look like cash was ever going to have any real value. Not anymore.

"I'm getting hungry," Eddie said. None of us had eaten all day. We talked about what we would do for food, but there were just too many things we didn't know. Had all the supermarkets and grocery stores been looted? Probably. Houses? Who knows. Thankfully, our food hadn't been stolen. There was *some* food missing, but it was mostly cookies and snacks the looters grabbed.

Then again, like Eddie had said earlier: with so many people dying, there would probably be enough food to go around. We just had to find it without getting ourselves killed.

"I can put together something," I said, getting to my feet. "We still have a few boxes of macaroni and cheese."

"My favorite," Tracie said, and it was the first time I'd seen her smile all day. Granted, it was only a weak grin, but there was a flicker of optimism in her eyes.

I opened three boxes of macaroni and cheese. While I boiled the noodles, Kevin and Eddie talked about where they might find a radio.

"There's got to be one in someone's house," Kevin said. "The looters couldn't have taken them all."

"Maybe," Eddie agreed. "The problem is finding one without running into other people. There are people with guns who are killing others without even thinking about it. And we also have to make sure we don't get near anyone who's been infected with the bird flu. I mean . . . take a look outside. Are the dead people—the ones who died from the flu—are they still contagious?"

While I was fixing the meal, I glanced out the window. From where I stood, I could see several bodies. One, a man, had been beaten earlier in the day, and robbed. Others had died from the flu. All in all, there were probably a dozen people on our street, in yards, and along the sidewalk, dead.

"Well, we've got to get a radio," Tracie said. "Or a television. Or something."

"I say we wait for it to get dark," Eddie said, "then I'll go house to house to see what I can find."

"What if there are other people who have the same idea?" Tracie asked.

The macaroni noodles had finished boiling, and they were soft and tender. I added the milk, butter, and mix into the pot, and began to stir. I've always loved the smell of macaroni and cheese. It smelled like home.

"Maybe," Eddie said. "But I can't believe that *everyone* is out to kill people. We're surviving, and *we* aren't going to hurt anyone."

"Yeah, but they might not know that," Kevin said. "But you're right. We need to find a radio or something. At this point, we know the bird flu has spread around the world. We need to find out if there's a vaccine, or a shelter, or something."

I was able to find three plates that hadn't been smashed by the looters, and I scooped out lumps of macaroni and cheese onto them. Then I handed the plates to Eddie, Kevin, and Tracie. We still had utensils, thank God. I was able to find a small plastic bowl to use for myself, and I scooped a mound of the yellow mush into it. Then I sat down in my chair.

Conversation ceased as we ate. I don't think any of us had realized how hungry we were.

"There's more in the pan," I said, motioning with my spoon.

"I'm all for that," Eddie said, getting to his feet.

"Anybody else?"

"I'm fine," Tracie said.

"I'll take some," Kevin replied.

I shook my head. "I might have to drive," I cautioned, and Eddie snickered. Dumb joke, I know. But I was trying to find a little humor. Somewhere.

Eddie retrieved the pan and scraped some of the macaroni onto Kevin's plate. "Anyone else?" he said, looking at Tracie and me. We shook our heads, and he plopped the rest of the macaroni and cheese onto his plate. Then he returned the plate to the stove and sat down to eat.

"That's what we'll do then," Eddie said, shifting the topic back to our search for a radio. "We wait for it to get dark, and then I'll go house to house and try and find a radio. I'll take the flashlight from the basement. Who knows? I might get lucky and find a television."

"If the cable is out, that won't do us much good," Tracie said.

"No, but there might be some stations still broadcasting over the airwaves," Eddie said. "The local affiliates."

"I'll go with you," Kevin offered.

Eddie shook his head. "You stay here. I'll leave Dad's nine millimeter with you, and I'll take a knife. You stay and watch Tracie and Sierra."

"We can take care of ourselves," Tracie said with more than a hint of annoyance.

"Yeah, maybe so," Eddie said. "But we're not taking any chances. Besides . . . I'll be fine. If it's just me, I can sneak around without being seen. Most of the houses have been looted, anyway. I don't think I'm going to find very much, but we won't know until we try."

We could still hear the sounds of a world coming apart at the seams: distant gunshots, yelling, tires squealing. But, for the most part, it seemed farther away. Castlebury Drive was out of town a little, and we figured most of the damage had already been done.

Suddenly, there was a tremendous explosion that shook the entire house. I felt it in my chest, as it seemed to take my breath away. It rattled what was left of the glass in the windows.

And then the power went out.

32

The four of us sprang from our chairs and crowded the front door, anxiously looking around. We stayed back a little, wary of being seen—but it was so dark outside by now, that it wouldn't have mattered. There were no streetlights on. Not a single light glowed in any surrounding houses. It was an odd sensation to look outside at night and not see any lights whatsoever.

However, to the north (left of where we were) light was growing. A house was on fire. Yellow tongues were quickly becoming larger and longer. Truck headlights winked on, and there was excited shouting.

"What in the hell—" Eddie started to say. Right then, however, a small bundle of flame arched up into the sky. It had been thrown from someone in the truck. The glowing ball smashed onto the porch of a darkened home. Suddenly a pool of flame spread, fanning out over the porch, climbing the walls, snaking up to the roof.

I'd seen this kind of device on the news. It was a small bottle or jar filled with gas or kerosene, called a Molotov cocktail. A rag was stuffed into the end, lit, and thrown. The result was a highly-flammable, homemade bomb.

A cheer went up from the vehicle on the street . . . and the truck started to move.

"They're torching houses!" Kevin exclaimed.

"Oh my God!" Tracie gasped.

Another wad of flame flew into the air, spiraling beneath the black sky, landing on the roof of the next house. Yet another flaming ball went sailing in the opposite direction, hitting the outside wall of yet another house.

"We gotta get outta here!" Eddie said. "They're setting fire to every house on the block!"

We backed away from the door.

"Everybody stay here!" Eddie said. "I know right where the flashlight is downstairs! Get your packs together! We'll leave out the back!"

I could hear Eddie cautiously making his way down the hall. Then I heard his feet thundering down the basement steps.

Outside, the whooping and hollering grew stronger. I could hear the roars of the fires, too, as they built into raging infernos.

It can't be like this, I thought. *It can't be like this everywhere. There has to be people left with decency and common sense. Somewhere.*

We had a discussion in my class, shortly after hurricane Katrina wiped out New Orleans. We talked about the senseless looting and violence, and how some people were actually shooting at the very people that were coming to help them. It was as if they'd all gone mad. One of my classmates said it was because they were all caught up in the craziness, and, since everyone around them was acting that way, it would only be normal for everyone to do the same.

"Should they be held accountable for their actions?" my teacher asked the class. Many of the students said 'no', that it was because of the situation they were in. They said the rioters probably wouldn't behave like that if they weren't in such a deplorable situation without food or water or shelter. It was the government's fault for not coming to help sooner, some said, and it was only natural people would behave that way.

My teacher saw me shaking my head in disgust. "Sierra," she said, "what do *you* think?"

I paused and drew a breath. "I think—"

Everyone was looking at me. I don't say much in class in the first place, so this was something new for the students. *Hey . . . let's all watch the shy girl speak and make an idiot out of herself.*

"I think . . . if you don't do what's right in a situation like that, how can you possibly be trusted to do what's right in *any* situation?"

"They know the right thing to do," a student said. I think it was Ashley Garrett. "They just *can't.*"

"They know what to do," I shot back. "They just *don't.*"

"So, Sierra, you're saying the rioters should be held accountable?" my teacher asked.

I looked around. "I think they should be *shot,*" I

replied flatly.

My teacher's expression soured. Clearly, I'd struck a note. "See me after class, Sierra," she said. There was no further discussion about rioters and personal responsibility.

33

The truck was inching along the street. With every firebomb thrown, there was an uproar of whooping and hollering from the mob, followed by a dull shattering of glass and the whoosh of spreading flames. The fires lit up the neighborhood, and I could see the glowing reflections on the houses across the street.

"Hurry, Eddie!" I shouted down the hall.

"I've got it!" Eddie shouted back, his voice hollow and dull in the basement.

Suddenly, there was a whoosh, a flash, and a crash . . . and our entire living room was engulfed in flames.

34

A loud cheer rose from the mob in the truck. The firebomb had come through the open front doorway and shattered against the wall, spewing flammable liquid all over. Flames licked at the walls like dragon tongues, and a blast of heat suddenly super-heated my exposed skin.

"Eddie!" I shrieked. *"Hurry!"*

Tracie, Kevin, and I snapped up our packs and ran into the kitchen, leaping away from the growing fire. I grabbed Eddie's pack, as there was no way he would be able to save it from the rapidly spreading flames. Already, the toxic smoke was causing me to choke, and my eyes were stinging. The fire was burning the carpeting in the hall. Dirty, thick smoke clouded the room, but Eddie suddenly burst through, coughing and sputtering. He carried a long, black flashlight that was as big around as a baseball bat, and about half as long.

"Out the back! Out the back!" Eddie shouted, and we pushed through the strewn mess in the kitchen and bounded through what was left of the sliding glass doors. They had been shattered by the looters earlier, and my feet crunched on the tiny shards that covered the cement patio in our back yard.

"Let's cross through the yards to the other block!" I exclaimed. "There's nothing burning over there!"

"Not yet," Kevin said glumly.

The four of us started running, single file, snaking across the shadowy lawn. The back yard was dimly lit by burning homes behind us, so we had no difficulty seeing where we were going. We scrambled over the chain link fence that separated the yards. The area here was darker as we made our way farther and farther from our street and the burning houses.

I managed a glance over my shoulder. A dozen homes were torched, their red and yellow fires twisting up angrily into the night sky, spewing dirty smoke and orange embers.

We ran through the darkened back yard. Eddie clicked on his flashlight, and we followed him past a small flower garden and a shed, slowing between two houses. Here, the roar of the fires seemed distant. However, we could still hear the faint revelry of the rioters as they continued burning house after house after house. I noticed the sounds weren't just from behind us, either; they were all around. In every direction, we saw the fluttering glow of fires pressing against the night sky.

We stopped, and Eddie turned off the flashlight. "It's too dark around here," he said. "I don't want anyone to see our light and come after us."

"What if it's someone that will help us?" Tracie asked.

"How many people have you seen today that wanted to help us?" Eddie replied flatly. "We're on our own, Trace. At this point, it's us against the world."

35

The four of us leaned against the side of a garage, concealed in the shadows. Our home and garage had burned completely to the ground, and the only thing left was a large pile of smoldering orange coals.

I thought about everything the house had meant to me. I had always felt safe there. It was more than just a place to sleep and keep my stuff. It was *home.* I had pictures of my friends in my bedroom that were now gone. I had over a hundred books, books that I *loved.*

Gone.

My clothes, my dresser. My doll collection I'd had since I was little.

Gone.

All of my letters and cards I'd saved.

Gone.

Mom and Dad . . . .

Knock it off, Sierra, I told myself. *There's no time to be sad. Not now. Now's the time to think. Use your brain. That's what Mom and Dad would want. Think. Survive. Be sad later.*

I had started to cry, but I wiped the tears on my sleeve.

Think.

A car roared by on the street. Its headlights provided some dim illumination, but the light faded quickly as the vehicle passed.

"All right," Eddie said. "I'm going to go into this house and see if I can find a radio." He handed the pistol to Kevin. "You guys stay here. I'll be right back."

"Be careful," I said quietly.

"I'll be fine," Eddie said, and he slunk silently away.

The three of us remained in the shadows, huddled against the garage. More gunfire erupted. Several more large explosions could be heard, and we heard the sound of footsteps running down the street. It sounded like a lone runner, but it was so dark, we couldn't tell. It may have been someone running from something, to something, who knows. But I was glad when the footsteps faded.

Eddie returned after only a few minutes. "No radio," he said. "The house is trashed. And there's a dead guy in the bedroom. I don't know if he died of the flu, or if he was killed by somebody . . . but I didn't get too close."

"Let's try another house," I said.

"There are a couple of cars on the street," Tracie said. "They'll have radios."

"But we don't know if they have keys in them," Eddie said. "Probably not. And we might attract too much attention."

"We could—"

Kevin started to speak, but he was interrupted by Eddie.

"Shhhh!" Eddie said. "Hear that?"

We listened. Faintly, far in the distance, we could hear a dull, rhythmic thumping sound. A sound that couldn't be mistaken for anything else.

A helicopter.

It was a helicopter . . . and it was getting closer and closer by the second.

36

The thrumming was rapidly growing louder, but we couldn't see the chopper yet. We stepped back from the garage and scanned the night sky.

Suddenly, the aircraft was literally upon us. It had been flying low, at high-speed. The aircraft swooped right over us, its red lights streaming beneath the darkness. It was so loud I had to cup my hands over my ears. Then, as quickly as it had arrived, it was gone, and the thundering of blades began to fade.

"See!?!?" Tracie said. "They're coming to help! They know we're in trouble!"

"Yeah," Kevin said, "but it's only one helicopter. It's going to take more than one chopper to do anything."

"I'm going into the next house," Eddie said. "You guys stay here."

"No way," I said. "We'll follow you through the back

yard, over to the house. If you get into trouble and need help, we'll be closer."

"Fine," Eddie said. "Let's go."

We slunk around the garage and behind the dark house. Several gunshots went off in the distance. One was closer, and sounded like it was only a block or two away. I was glad Eddie had thought to get Dad's nine millimeter. It had already come in handy once—saving Tracie's life—and would probably come in handy again. It wasn't much protection against roving gangs . . . but at least it was *something.*

We approached the next house slowly, creeping across the damp lawn. It was getting colder, and I began to wonder where we would spend the night. Certainly not outdoors, as it was early May, and it still got too chilly at night. No, our best option would be to find an unoccupied home out of the weather.

"Stay here," Eddie told us, and, once again, he vanished into the darkness.

"This is insane," Tracie said. "This can't be happening."

"In the morning, things will be better," Kevin said. "People will come to their senses. The government will get control. They've got tanks and planes and guns. They'll do what it takes."

I wanted to think Kevin was right. I thought hard about what the next day might bring, and I really hoped things would calm down. After all, they couldn't just let everyone fend for themselves like animals, could they?

Could they?

37

A shadow approached, startling the three of us. It was only Eddie, but he'd been gone nearly fifteen minutes.

"We hit the jackpot!" Eddie said excitedly.

"What do you mean?" Kevin asked.

"The house is trashed, and nobody's home. I went into the basement. There are two rooms down there, along with a fridge and lots of bottled water. I also found an AM/FM radio with batteries. Apparently, the looters never bothered to look there. We can stay the night in the basement, and maybe find out what's going on from any radio broadcasts!"

"Did you listen?" I asked.

"Not long," Eddie replied. "Only long enough to make sure it worked. They were talking about what was going on, though."

"I wouldn't think they'd be playing Nickelback,"

Kevin said.

Hope surged. Sure, things were pretty bad, but Eddie had found a radio. We found a place to stay, out of the cold. Away from the roving mobs. The refrigerator probably had some food. Even without power, anything inside it would probably remain cold for a half-day, at least. And bottled water! For whatever reason, the faucets wouldn't work, so we didn't have any running water.

And a radio. We'd finally be able to find out what was going on. I was sure there would be some shelter we could go to, somewhere organized where there was food and water. Somewhere where we could stay away from the rioters.

That's when a bright light hit us. I turned and squinted, and, twenty feet away, saw the dark silhouette of a gun barrel pointed directly at us.

38

"Don't move. You do, and you're dead. Alla'ya."

It was a man's voice. Older. Behind the single bright light, he was impossible to see.

We said nothing.

"You guys got any food?" the man asked.

"No," Eddie replied. "That's what we were looking for."

"You sick?" He moved the light over each of our faces.

We shook our heads.

"You're gonna be. Everybody's gonna get sick."

"We've stayed away from everyone," Kevin said. "The four of us . . . we're fine."

"You sure you don't have any food? In them packs?"

"See for yourself," I said, and I held the bag out.

"I ain't gettin' any closer," the man said.

Eddie spoke up. "Look, we don't have any food," he said. "We're just trying to get by, just like you. And we don't want to get sick, either."

"Everybody's gonna get sick," the man repeated, still aiming the rifle at us. "This is that killer flu they been talkin' about for so long. We're all screwed."

Suddenly, another voice came from farther away, on the other side of the street.

"Andy! What's going on? You find anything?"

"Just these guys," the man with the gun replied. "They ain't got nothin', though."

"Well, then, come on! Let's get movin' and get outta here!"

The man lowered the gun, but he kept the light trained on us. "Good luck," he said. "Y'all better watch yourselves. This ain't gonna get any better."

He turned and walked away. We could hear them whispering—two men, it seemed—as they hustled off into the darkness.

"If those were the nice guys," Tracie said nervously, "what are we going to do when the really *bad* ones come along?"

39

Fifteen minutes later.

We'd crept silently through the house, stepping over furniture that had been smashed, over broken glass and plates. I felt funny, going through someone's house like that. I wondered if the owners would come back, and what they would think if they found us here. Perhaps they would think we were the vandals that destroyed most of their home. Maybe they would think of us as nothing more than the rioters that were wreaking havoc around the city.

Then again, maybe the owners were dead. Maybe they weren't coming back. That seemed more likely.

Either way, we'd at least found a place where we could spend the night. Eddie had been right: most of the house had been trashed by looters, but they hadn't discovered the basement. There were two rooms and two double beds, and a whole closet full of blankets. At least we weren't going to freeze.

Now, we were seated on the floor around a candle Tracie had found. It was a scented candle—pumpkin spice—and it filled the room with a sweet, pungent aroma. The air wasn't that cold, but I had draped a blanket over my shoulders, anyway. Kevin sat to my right, Tracie to my left, and Eddie sat directly across from me. It reminded me of a time, long ago, when Eddie and I would sit outside at night, just the two of us, and tell scary stories to each other. Our faces glowed warmly in the candlelight, and it felt good. It felt good then, and it did now, too.

Eddie held the radio in his hands. The dial glowed green, and he flipped through the frequencies, looking for a station. It took him a moment to find one, which was strange. On any other day, you could dial through a couple dozen stations. Now, there wasn't much to be heard but static and noise.

Suddenly, voices flared. English. Life. News.

". . . no shelters are available at this time," the woman was saying. She sounded very tired and downtrodden. *"Everyone is advised to remain in their homes with their doors locked. Do not open the doors for anyone. If you are ill, please do not come in contact with another human. I repeat . . . do not come in contact with another human. Local, state, and federal officials are doing everything they can to ameliorate the situation and bring the pandemic under control."*

"What's 'ameliorate' mean?" Tracie asked.

"It means they're covering their asses," Eddie quipped.

". . . while it is unknown how long it will be before things are brought under control, it will probably be several days before the pandemic can be contained and order restored."

"This is garbage!" Eddie shouted. "She's not telling us anything! She's just reading a script! We don't need a script! We need to know what to do!"

"Eddie! Shh!" I said.

"*. . . meanwhile, it is recommended that people prepare to be without power for at least a week, if not longer.*"

Eddie angrily turned the dial and found another radio station. As we listened, we learned all we needed to know. Maybe too much, as a matter of fact. We learned the truth.

That was the worst part. It's been said that the truth will set you free.

Wrong.

The truth was going to set the world on fire.

40

The studios of the radio station are dark, all except for the faint glow of the on-air main broadcasting room. There, a single light burns amid several computer screens and blinking lights. There are two men in the studio: the announcer and another man. He is bleeding from a gash on his forehead, but he is not seriously injured. Both men are wearing headphones, each are leaning close to large, bottle-like microphones. The radio station has been powered by generators for several hours; they won't last much longer. Still, the announcer and his guest chatter on, determined to offer as much relative information as possible to their listeners, wherever they may be.

The announcer speaks. "If you're just joining us, we have with us, in the studio, Dr. Jerry Denmore. Dr. Denmore is—*was*—Director of Infectious Disease Response at U of M, a think-tank that has been working for several years, specifically, to prepare for the possible outbreak of a bird flu pandemic, like we're seeing now. Jerry, for those who have just joined us . . . if someone thinks they're sick, if they've got symptoms of the flu, what should they do?"

Dr. Denmore is smoking a cigarette. He'd quit over thirty years ago, but this morning, he'd started again, smoking one after another after another. He pauses, blows a plume of smoke. Looks at the announcer.

"Seriously?" he asks. His voice is deep and strong, but resigned.

"Yes," the announcer replies. "If someone thinks they have the flu, what should they do?"

"Jump off a building," Dr. Denmore says, very matter-of-factly. "But make it a tall one. You'll want to go quick. I imagine you can shoot yourself, too. That would work. Or, an overdose of pills, if you have them laying around."

The announcer seems stunned. "You're saying that if you get sick, there's no hope?" he asks.

"Of course there's hope," Dr. Denmore says with a chuckle. He exhales smoke through his nose. "Hope that you die quickly."

41

We were stunned.

To hear the doctor speaking so gravely, so matter-of-factly about death, was horrible. We'd hoped to find information about what to do, about where to go. We'd hoped to hear someone saying the worst of it was over, that things were getting under control. Instead, they were telling us things were getting worse and worse . . . and didn't show any signs of getting better.

"Turn it off," I said flatly.

"No," Eddie said. "I'll see if I can find something else." He reached down and turned the dial until another station came on.

Music.

Johnny Cash.

42

The announcer sits alone in the studio, sipping an iced tea, listening to the song. The building is empty: everyone went home the day before. None have returned. When the power went out, he fired up the generator. It was only the third time the radio station had to use it to resume broadcasting. Once in 1995 after an ice storm knocked out power, and again two years ago when a blizzard did the same. The generator is powerful, but it will only supply enough electricity for two days at the very most. In an effort to make it last as long as possible, the announcer has shut off all other power in the building. The only things still running are what's absolutely mandatory to remain on the air.

Johnny Cash is singing about being everywhere, man, and the song begins to fade. The man waits until there is dead air, then he opens up the microphone and speaks.

"There's the Man in Black, the one and only, the late,

great Johnny Cash," the announcer says. He speaks coolly, calmly. Effortlessly, not a care in the world, as if he is oblivious to the events that are rapidly overcoming every continent on the planet.

"Folks, I just don't have much more information for you," he continues. "Satellite service is out, phones are down, our internet went out earlier. The only thing I can tell you is you're not alone in your situation. This is going on all over the country, all over the world. Last report I heard before we lost contact, more than half the world's population is dead. That was ten hours ago." He takes a long sip of iced tea, and continues.

"When's it going to end? That's anybody's guess. I've been here since yesterday. My wife called when she was very sick, and that's the last I've heard from her. I know rioting has broken out in every city across the country, but our station, here, is pretty remote, so I haven't had any trouble. Nothing here for anyone to loot, though. I'm down to a single sandwich, a candy bar, and a couple bottles of water."

The announcer coughs, and there is a long pause.

"I, uh . . . I guess it's got hold of me, too," he says. "I just started feeling it coming on a few hours ago. I thought I might have a chance, being here at the station. But apparently some of my colleagues were infected and didn't know it."

The man coughs again, then clears his throat and sips his tea.

"My advice, if you're listening to this and you're not sick, is to hide out for a while. Hunker down. Stay away from everyone, especially the infects. There's no cure. Once you get it, you're as good as dead. Now, I'm not going to be like some radio stations and tell you the best way to kill yourself. I'm sure you've heard them, and I admit, folks . . . this isn't looking good for anybody. But if you start feeling ill . . . the shakes, body aches, fever . . . well, that's the beginning of the end. Get away from people and stay away, or else you'll infect them, too. Most likely, if you're with a group of people and one is getting sick, all of you are going to be infected. So, stay away from everyone. Now, here's Jim Croce, with 'Time in a Bottle'."

The song begins to play, and the announcer shuts off his microphone. Then, as if they were candy, he takes a handful of pills from the table and washes them down with his tea. Then he takes another handful . . . .

43

Jim Croce faded into silence, and we sat on the floor, our faces glowing from the pumpkin spice candle burning before us.

"Where did he go?" Tracie asked after the man didn't speak after nearly a minute of dead air.

"No idea," Eddie said. "Maybe he went to the bathroom."

We waited, but the man still didn't return. The station was dark.

Outside, in the distance, we heard several more gunshots.

"All right," Eddie said, "we've got to sleep. Kevin . . . you and I will sleep in shifts. One of us will have to be awake to keep an eye out. I'll take first watch."

"Where are you going to watch from?" I asked.

"Upstairs. I'll just stay out of sight, and make sure no

one tries to get inside." He looked at his watch. "It's just past ten. You guys sleep. Kev, I'll wake you up at three."

Eddie stood. He picked up the nine millimeter from where he'd placed it on the bed. "I'll leave you guys with the flashlight," he said.

"Be careful," I said as he walked toward the stairs.

"Yeah, right," Eddie said.

44

Morning arrived. I was jolted from a deep sleep by shouting and gunfire. It was distant, but loud enough to wake me up.

I was a bit disoriented, but everything came back quickly, in flashes.

Flu.

Looting.

Death.

Tracie, Kevin, Eddie.

I was still dressed, sleeping on the bed with a blanket pulled up to my chin. Eddie was next to me, and Tracie was on the other side of him.

Great, I thought. *I went to bed with my boyfriend and woke up with my brother.*

Eddie stirred, and Tracie moaned softly, still sleeping. I swung my legs over the side of the bed, stretching and shaking my head to push away the morning fuzzies.

Kevin came down the stairs, and I stood and met him at the bottom of the steps. We hugged and kissed briefly. I drew back.

"Nothing to worry about out there," he whispered. *"A couple cars went by. Someone was shooting at someone."*

"How are you doing?" I whispered, searching his eyes.

"Me? I'm fine, considering. Tired, but not bad. Getting hungry."

"There's a lot of food in the fridge," I said. *"It's probably still cold, but not for too much longer. Not without power. Want me to make a sandwich for you?"*

"No, I'll wait until everyone's up. I would like some more water, though. Sure wish I could take a shower, too."

The thought of a nice, cold drink of water sounded good, but the thought of hot water, of sweet-smelling soap all over my body was *heavenly.* I hadn't showered or bathed for two days, and I felt clammy and sticky. But, with no electricity and no running water, the prospect of bathing didn't even loom on the horizon.

Eddie awoke, propping himself up on his elbows. He yawned, saw that Tracie was still asleep next to him, and carefully pulled the blanket away. Then he rolled to the side of the bed and stood. Tracie slept on.

Kevin hiked his thumb in the air. *"Everything's cool,"* he whispered.

Eddie strode to where we were standing.

"Nothing going on this morning that wasn't going on yesterday," Kevin continued. "Sure are a lot of dead bodies out there."

I cringed. Sure, we'd seen our share of death in the past few days. But I still couldn't get used to the fact that bodies were scattered all over the neighborhood, like road-kill animals. It just seemed so . . . so *inhumane.* So uncivilized.

"That's another problem we've got," Eddie said. "Not only do we have the bird flu to worry about, but with all those bodies laying out there, bloating and baking all day—"

"Eddie!" I said, grimacing.

"—they're going to create diseases of their own," Eddie finished.

"There's nothing we can do about them," Kevin said.

"Right," Eddie agreed. "But we've got to stay away from them. Matter of fact, we've got to get out of here. Far away from people. The more removed we are, the better chance we'll have of surviving. We have to stay away from people, because we don't know if they're infected. And we have to stay away from the rioters. We could get shot—" he looked at me "—or worse."

"Then let's find a map," Kevin said. "Let's find someplace."

"But where?" I asked. "Where are we going to go where we won't run into people?"

"Anyplace away from the city," Eddie said. "We need to get out of here. Maybe not right away, but soon. We need to find someplace more remote. We have no idea what we might find. Maybe the flu hasn't caught on in less populated areas. Maybe it hasn't spread like it has in cities."

Tracie woke. She rolled to the side and swung her legs off the bed. Her dark hair spiked in every direction, and her clothes were wrinkled and disheveled.

I grinned. "Hey, Trace," I said.

She smiled thinly. "What's so funny?"

"You, bed-head," I said.

"You guys don't look much better," she replied. She yawned. "So, what's the great and wonderful news today?"

"The great news is we're all still alive," Kevin said. "It doesn't get much better than that."

"And there is no wonderful news," Eddie added.

Tracie stood and walked to the fridge, retrieving a bottle of water.

"Grab one for me, would ya?" Kevin said.

"Anyone else?" Tracie asked.

"I'm fine," I replied.

"No, thanks," Eddie said.

I walked to the bed and sat. Kevin followed and sat next to me. Tracie handed Kevin a bottle of water, and Eddie remained by the steps, his hands on his hips.

"All right," he said. "Let's figure out what we're going to do from here."

45

Eddie had been able to find an atlas upstairs. In the fridge we found heaven in a fourteen-inch square box: an entire cold pizza. By the looks (and taste) of it, it couldn't have been more than a day or two old. And, even though the fridge had been off since the previous night, it was still cold. There were a few moderately-chilled Pepsis, and even half of a chocolate cake. I know it sounds like a gnarly breakfast, but for us, it was amazing.

It was things like that—little things—that helped me keep a positive attitude. I mean . . . I think I've always looked on the bright side, no matter what. No matter how bad things got, I always tried to look for the good in it. When I was faced with a problem, I always looked for a solution, instead of sitting around whining about it.

But I'd never been up against a situation like this. Who could have even imagined it? My mom used to say something about whatever doesn't kill you will only make you stronger. If that's the case, the four of us were going to either be the strongest people on the planet . . . or we were going to die: that's all there was to it.

46

We sat on the floor, cross-legged, eating the cold pizza and drinking Pepsi. Eddie had the atlas unfolded in front of us, displaying the state of Michigan. The radio was on. We'd found a station that was doing what it could to provide information about bird flu. All the guy was doing was reading from a book, skimming over the parts that weren't important. As far as a place to go or what to do, the radio announcer didn't have a clue. He said that he was defying regulations, as the Federal Communications Commission had ordered all stations to begin airing the same message being broadcast from Washington. He said that it was all lies, that there was no vaccine, and no one was even close. So, he decided to take it upon himself to try to do what he could to help anyone who was listening. Besides, he said, he hadn't heard anything from anyone in Washington since the day before.

"So, what's happened, everyone," he was saying, "is that the H5N1 strain made what's called an 'antigenic shift'. That's where there's a sudden and dramatic change, a major change, with influenza A viruses. There are four antiviral medications: amantadine, rimantadine, oseltamivir, and zanamivir that have been approved by the FDA for use for the treatment or prevention of influenza. Sadly, however, the H5N1 strain has developed an immunity to these drugs. What this means, unfortunately, is that we're no closer to a vaccine today than we were five years ago. They're calling this a pandemia. The aftermath of a global, catastrophic pandemic."

We listened while we ate, and Eddie studied the map.

"We're right here," Eddie said, placing his finger on the map, creating a small pizza-grease smudge. "What we can do is follow Castlebury Drive down to highway 12. We can follow 12 west. There's not much out there, as far as houses go."

We listened to Eddie while we ate. "Or," he said, "we could head straight north. We'd have to go through the river, but we could make it up to Saline Waterworks Road. It all depends on which direction we want to head."

"Or," I said, "we could just stay here."

"We could," Eddie agreed. "But we have to have a plan. We don't know what's going to happen from here on out. When gangs of nuts start going around burning houses at night, we have to think about what we're going to do."

"Maybe the worst is over," Tracie said. "Maybe things are going to smooth out."

"Maybe," Kevin said. "But Eddie's right. We have to have a plan. A plan for anything and everything."

We listened to the radio.

"What appears to have happened is something the experts never imagined or planned for," the announcer was saying. "The Centers for Disease Control never imagined that bird flu could become as contagious as it has in so short a time. When they realized what the world was up against, it was already too late. And that's where we are, people. If you're hearing this, and you're healthy, count your blessings. Use some common sense. I haven't been able to get any reports for a day now, but the last I heard, there's been a total breakdown of order worldwide. The president himself died of the flu within the first few days of the pandemic. Yep, that's the truth. Everything else you heard from him . . . that had been taped. The Centers for Disease Control in Atlanta, Georgia, was attacked by people who thought they might find a vaccine inside. The entire facility was burned to the ground."

We listened, amazed and bewildered.

"The National Guard and the Army troops that were promised never arrived. Or, if they did, they quickly became infected themselves. It's bad, people. This is really bad."

"But we saw a helicopter last night," Eddie said. "It flew right over us."

"I don't think one helicopter is going to do much, now," Kevin said.

"I'd give anything for a little good news," I said.

"Here's good news," Tracie said. "There's one more piece of pizza left. There's hope for the world, after all."

She smiled, and it meant everything to me. There was hope. We might not know what to do, or what we were in for. We had no idea what we would do tomorrow—or if we'd even be around tomorrow—but we were alive. We were alive, and we weren't sick.

That really *was* good news.

47

We finished eating, then we sat around, going over the map. Every once in a while, we'd hear a car or truck roar past outside. Even from where we were in the basement, we could still hear distant gunfire erupting around the city.

We had the radio on, and every few minutes Eddie would change the station. Mostly, however, the news was pretty much all the same: we were all on our own. No one knew if or when order would be restored.

"If there are gangs roaming around, burning and looting," I said, "there's got to be groups of people who have banded together to stop them."

"Maybe there is," Eddie said. "But remember: any person we come into contact with puts us at risk of getting the flu. There's no way to know who's contagious and who's not."

One radio station reported that the entire University

of Michigan campus had been burned, including the hospital. I thought of Mom, and I wondered where she'd been when she died. It hurt . . . it really, *really* hurt to think about it. I hoped she hadn't suffered like the woman on the street, like so many people around the world. I hope she—

"I say we just stay here for a while," Tracie said, interrupting my thought. "We can get ready to leave, if we need to. But think about it. We're pretty safe here. We're not in the city limits, where it seems most of the rioting is still going on. The houses around have been ransacked, but there's probably some food we can find. Canned goods, things like that. If we just hunker down here and stay low, we could probably get by for a few days, if we need to. Maybe even a few weeks."

"Tracie is right," I said. "It would be good to be ready to flee if we have to, but we're safe here. At least for now. I say we stay put. There's enough food here in this house for a couple of days, at least. We can venture out at night and find more food. Maybe, by then, things will have calmed down."

"I don't know about the calming down," Kevin said. "But I agree with Tracie. Let's stay here. Any other options that we have are too dangerous."

Eddie shrugged. "Fine with me," he said. "But we still need to make a plan to get out of here. One firebomb, and *poof* . . . we're out of business. We saw how quick that happened last night."

One good thing: we weren't trapped in the basement. We were free to move about the house, as long as we kept an eye out the window. We all took turns being lookout, just in case anybody was going house to house, searching for food.

Unfortunately, we were a little careless.

Just before noon, when we were all upstairs in the living room, there came a loud pound on the front door.

43

The sudden noise made us jump. Eddie had kept the pistol close at hand all day, and he snapped it up from the floor. Then he placed a finger to his lips, urging us to be quiet. As he stood, a man on the other side of the door spoke.

"I know you're in there," the man said. "I heard you talking."

Eddie approached the door. "What do you want?" he asked loudly.

"Information," the man said. "I want to know what's going on."

"Get back from the door," Eddie commanded.

There was a shuffling sound. Eddie took a few steps to the left and looked out the window.

"It's just a lone guy," Eddie said as he shot a glance toward us. Then he went to the front door and opened it. Kevin stood and walked to Eddie's side. Tracie and I did the same.

The man was probably in his fifties. His gray hair was thin and messy. His clothing was in tatters, and there was a bandage on his left elbow. And he was carrying a rifle in his right hand. The gun hung loose, its barrel pointed to the ground. Clearly, this man wasn't going to be a threat.

"We don't have a lot of information," Eddie said.

"Is anybody coming to help us?" the man asked.

Eddie shook his head. "Not that we've heard. We have a radio, but they don't have much news. The news they do have isn't very good."

"My daughter and me," the man said, shaking his head. "Things aren't good. We're a couple of blocks over. Wife died of the flu last week, while she was in Detroit visiting her sister. Me an' my daughter, we're just trying to stay safe and out of sight."

"Same here," Eddie said.

"You guys got any water?" the man asked.

"Yeah," Eddie replied. "Do you need some?"

"We're getting a little low," the man replied. "Could you spare just a little?"

Eddie looked at me and nodded. Tracie and I hustled down to the basement and returned with a six-pack of bottled water. I handed it to Eddie.

"I'm going to leave it here, on the porch," Eddie said. "You know . . . just in case."

The man shook his head. "I know what you mean," he replied. "Can't take any chances with anyone. This flu. Sheesh. It's a damned killer."

"Good luck," Eddie said, and he stepped outside and placed the bottles of water on the porch. Then he stepped back into the house.

"Thank you," the man said. "You guys take care of yourselves."

We waved, and Eddie closed the door. We could hear the man step onto the porch. Through the window, we watched him walk quickly away, a rifle in one hand, the bottled water in the other.

"Looks like we're not the only ones," Tracie said.

"There's probably a lot of people doing what we're doing," I said. "If we could all get together, we might be safer."

"Problem is," Eddie said, "we don't have any idea who's sick and who's not. I mean . . . that guy seemed fine. But what if he has been contaminated? What did that guy on the radio call it?"

"An infect," Tracie said. "He called people who carried the virus an infect."

"Yeah," Eddie said. "He might be an infect. He might get sick in an hour. We don't know. We just have to make sure we stay away from everyone."

"Sooner or later, this has got to end," Kevin said. "The world can't continue to live like this."

"Yeah," I said. "Sooner or later."

49

Days passed.

The wound on my arm healed fine, and, besides keeping it clean and changing the gauze bandage a few times, I never really thought too much about it. In the scheme of things, it wasn't that big of a deal.

We'd managed to make 'our' home comfortable. We had plenty of drinking water and a fair amount of food. Granted, room-temperature, canned vegetables weren't the best, but we didn't complain. We could have built a fire in the back yard and warmed up our meals, but we thought it would be too risky. We didn't want anyone to see the flames and know we were in the house.

We weren't, of course, able to take a shower, but every night, we would sneak into the darkened back yard, one at a time. There, we would take off our clothes. Using water sparingly, we would soak a washcloth with water and wet our skin as best we could. Then we washed with a bar of soap, and wiped it away with the washcloth. I learned how to wash my hair with a single cup of water. Granted, it wasn't the best way to take a shower, but every day I looked forward to our nightly 'cleanings'.

Going to the bathroom, was, of course, another issue altogether. Eddie found a place behind a shed in the back yard. The back of the shed was overgrown with shrubs, and he pulled a few of them out, making a small area that offered a little privacy. Since we never knew when nature was going to call, we would use the outdoor facilities two at a time: Tracie and I, and Eddie and Kevin. One would keep an eye out with the pistol. It wasn't the most pleasant conditions, but, considering our circumstances, we didn't complain.

Gradually, more and more radio stations went off the air. We listened constantly, hoping to hear good news, hoping to hear the government was back in control, that they'd come up with a vaccine. I wanted to hear that the worst was over, that things were getting better, that electricity was being restored. Nothing we heard, however, led us to believe the situation was getting better. In fact, the more we listened, the more we realized that no one was coming to our rescue. There was no longer a government, law enforcement, or military. It was, as one announcer put it, 'every man for himself'. He said every major city had been burned to rubble and the survivors were now fanning out into the suburbs, trying to find food and water. After a few weeks, there were no more radio stations on the air. The world, it seemed, had gone silent.

Dead bodies littered the street. They became grotesque, rotting cadavers, bloating to three times their normal size. Some of them looked like giant, freakish circus balloons that could just as easily have drifted into the air and floated away. Clouds of flies swarmed over them. But there was nothing we could do. We couldn't risk getting close to them, for fear of picking up the flu or some other disease.

So, they remained right where they were, slowly rotting in the sun, at the mercy of the elements. It was unfair, it was gross, it wasn't right. But there was nothing we could do.

Sometimes, we saw people or cars go by. Almost everyone was in a hurry. They looked ragged and tired. Some were beginning to get sick, others were in the final stages. Everyone had guns. Once, a truck went by filled with eight or nine men and women in the back. They all carried guns, like they were patrolling. We were careful to stay out of sight.

And Eddie and Kevin had managed to find another gun. All day long, we were careful to look for signs of activity in other homes around us. We saw nothing, leading us to believe most of the homeowners were dead, or had left. For us, it became convenient. Most of the looting that had taken place in the first few days of the pandemic had been scattered attempts at theft and vandalism. People weren't thinking about stealing things they would need to survive, and we were able to find many necessary items from the houses around our block. Eddie sometimes ventured outside during the daylight, bringing back arm loads of boxed cereal, canned food, pop, whatever he could salvage. Two homes over, he found a 12-gauge pump shotgun beneath a bed, along with six boxes of shells.

He'd also made other, more gruesome discoveries.

"There are dead people in almost every home," he told us one afternoon. He'd just returned from one of his excursions, carrying fresh towels, toilet paper, and some extra-large T-shirts. That was another problem: we had no way to wash our clothing, so we wound up wearing whatever could be scrounged up. Most of our clothing didn't fit, but at least it was clean.

"There's a whole family in a house down the block, dead," he said. He raised his hand and made a waving motion beneath his nose. "I could smell them from outside. It was pretty rank."

"Eww," Tracie said, and I grimaced.

"Did you see them?" Kevin asked.

"I kept my shirt over my mouth and went up to the window. There were five bodies on the floor. They were all bloated and caked with—"

"That's enough," Tracie said, wincing and covering her ears with her hands. "I don't need to know any more."

The fires gradually went away. We'd seen less and less smoke in the distance, and not nearly as much gunfire. Still, we had no clue what was going on around the city. It was driving us crazy. Was there a place we could go and be safe? Were we living like hidden hermits for no reason?

One day, we saw two cars sailing down the street. Both cars were packed with occupants . . . shooting at one another.

"Just when you thought it was safe to go back into the streets," Kevin cracked.

Days went by without incident. We were getting restless, though, and our tempers were growing shorter. I got into an argument with Eddie about something stupid. He got mad at Tracie for something or another. The close proximity of living together in such conditions was really wearing on all of us, and we knew some changes would have to be made.

And then the dogs came.

50

One night, a wonderful, glorious thing happened: a rain storm. It was now the end of May, and the temperatures had been hot—in the eighties—all week. That's a bit warmer than normal for that time of year in Michigan, but not uncommon.

We could hear thunder rumbling as it grew dark. Rain began to fall around midnight, and it was really dumping. I shot up out of bed, waking Kevin as I did.

"Wake up! Wake up!" I said, nearly shouting. "It's raining! It's pouring!"

Tracie and Eddie woke. Eddie had been sleeping on an air mattress he'd found at another house. He and Tracie took turns sleeping in the bed.

Kevin and I were fine, sleeping together on the other bed. We'd grown closer, but our relationship hadn't bloomed into anything deeper. We both slept with our clothes on, usually sweats and a T-shirt.

"What's the big deal?!?!" Eddie said groggily.

I didn't even take the time to answer. The basement was pitch dark, but I could see the very faint shadow of the stairwell. I got out of bed.

"What?" Kevin said. "What's wrong? What are you doing?"

"I'm going to take a shower," I replied dreamily.

I cautiously walked up the basement stairs, unaware that Kevin, Tracie, and Eddie had arisen and were following behind. Upstairs, I went into the kitchen and retrieved the bar of soap from the counter. Then I walked over to the back door, slipped out of my sweats, and walked outside.

The feeling was incredible. The rain was very warm, and I was soaked in seconds. Tracie, Eddie, and Kevin didn't waste any time, either, and soon, all four of us were parading around in the dark, naked, letting the rain wash all over us. I lathered up with the bar of soap, then gave it to Tracie. She giggled with delight as she, too, washed herself with the soap. I went back into the house, lit a candle, and found the shampoo. Then I went back outside.

Eddie, Kevin, and Tracie were just three dark figures, standing several feet apart from one another. After being cooped up so long without *really* feeling clean, we all felt brand-new. We couldn't care less whether we were nude or not, or even if we saw one another without clothing. We couldn't, but it wouldn't have mattered. We were too caught up in the moment, of the pure ecstacy of a simple rain shower, of the warm water on our skin.

I washed my hair, rinsed it, then washed it again. I didn't want the rain to end, ever.

"This is awesome!" Tracie exclaimed as I handed her the bottle of shampoo in the darkness.

"Better!" I said. "This is the best!"

I rinsed my hair, and then just stood in the wet grass, allowing the rain to soak my skin. The warm water dripped from my fingers, my chin, my nose. I felt better than I had since this whole nightmare began.

"I'll go grab some towels," Kevin said, and his dark silhouette went into the house. I followed him and waited by the front door. He emerged from the bathroom with a towel around his waist, and I realized the glow from the single candle now gave off enough light to see one another. He had a towel on, but I was completely naked.

I didn't care.

He handed me a towel and glanced at my body before turning away. Nothing was said.

Eddie came to the door, and Kevin handed him a towel.

"Trace?" I called out quietly. "You coming in?"

"Just a sec," she called back from the yard. "I'm enjoying this too much."

Then, there was another sound. A low, deep rumble.

Growling.

And then Tracie screamed.

51

Without knowing what they were getting into, Eddie and Kevin bolted into the dark back yard. Tracie was still screaming, and now there was a loud snarling and growling that was unmistakable: a dog. I couldn't see it, but I knew Tracie—and perhaps Kevin and Eddie—were in a lot of trouble.

I could hear Eddie and Kevin yelling and shouting.

The shotgun, I thought. *Get the shotgun.*

I dropped the towel and picked up the single candle. Then, I raced down the hall, down the stairs, and over to the far wall where we'd been keeping the shotgun. I snapped it up and took the steps two at a time, candle in one hand, 12 gauge in the other.

"I've got the shotgun!" I shouted as I returned to the front door.

"Don't shoot!" Eddie shouted. "Kevin! Get the gun

from Sierra!"

Kevin suddenly appeared, and he snatched the shotgun from my hand. I held the candle up in hopes of seeing *something,* but, of course, it was impossible.

"Hit him with the butt of the gun!" Eddie screeched.

Tracie was still screaming. "Get him away! Get him away! Oh, God! Get him off me!"

There was a dull thud and the dog let out a sharp, painful yelp.

"Now!" Eddie shouted. "Shoot him!"

"I can't see him!" Kevin shouted back.

"There! There!" Eddie screamed. "Right there!"

There was a thundering blast, an explosion of white light, and then, like a bolt of lightning, it was gone. But the afterimage burned in my mind: Tracie, on the wet grass, nude, her leg beneath her knee bleeding. Eddie, next to her, getting to his feet. Kevin, the towel around his waist, shouldering the shotgun. I didn't see what he had shot.

But he'd hit the dog, I was sure, as there was a loud, painful screech . . . and then: nothing. Just the rain on the roof, and Tracie sobbing.

I ran into the yard and found Tracie and knelt beside her in the wet grass. "Can you walk?" I asked. "You've got to get inside."

"It hurts *so* bad," she cried.

I helped her to her feet. Eddie and I helped her limp to the front door, where I gave her a towel and then wrapped one around myself.

"Over to the couch," I said, and we helped her across the living room.

"Grab me another towel, Kevin," I said, and Kevin

skirted off, returning with a hand towel from the bathroom.

The bite wasn't too bad. There was one gash that could probably have used stitches, but would have to do without. We really had no way to stitch the wound, and, if we tried, we would probably cause Tracie a lot more pain than she was already in.

I did my best to wash the wound with soap. There was some rubbing alcohol in the bathroom vanity, and it made me cringe just looking at it. It would disinfect the wound, but it was going to sting . . . *bad.*

"You are *not* going to like me," I said, showing the bottle of rubbing alcohol to Tracie.

"Oh, God, that's gonna burn," Tracie said.

"I've got to do it," I said.

"I know," she replied.

"Ready?" I asked.

"No," she replied, shaking her head. "But do it. Do it and get it over with."

"Hold her leg," I said to Eddie. He placed one hand on her thigh and one on her ankle. I placed a towel beneath her leg, and poured the clear liquid over the wound.

Tracie came unglued, but, somehow, managed to hold it together. The alcohol on exposed flesh was incredibly painful, and she cried out, doubled her fists, and pounded on the floor.

"It's done, it's done, it's done," I said, setting the bottle down. She'd started crying again, and I leaned forward and cradled her head against my chest. "That's it," I said. "Shhh. It's done."

Eddie got up and returned a few minutes later, wearing his sweats and carrying a wad of gauze. He handed it to me, and I bandaged Tracie's leg.

"Try and walk," I said, helping her to her feet. Kevin appeared, wearing his sweats and a T-shirt with a cartoon of Homer Simpson on it.

"Ouch-ouch-ouch-ouch," Tracie hissed as she walked. The towel almost fell off of her and I grabbed it quickly, pulling it tightly and securing it over her breasts.

"It's not that bad," Tracie said. "It throbs a lot, though."

"We'll go back downstairs," Eddie said. "You can lay in bed and we can prop your leg up with some pillows. It won't throb so much."

I helped Tracie downstairs, helped her into bed. When she was comfortable, I went back upstairs to retrieve my sweat pants and T-shirt. Eddie and Kevin had extinguished the candle, and the house was dark.

I fumbled my way to the back door, feeling around on the floor for my sweats. When I found them, I stood up.

"Where are you guys?" I asked quietly.

"Over here," Eddie said. "Shhh."

I dressed quickly in the darkness, then made my way through the living room and found Kevin and Eddie. They were standing by the living room window.

Outside, I could hear sounds.

Dogs.

Lots of dogs.

Growling. Snarling. Yapping.

Kevin slipped his arm around me. Nothing was said.

"Let's call it a night," Eddie said. "We'll deal with this in the morning."

52

Morning came—cold, gray, and foggy. Eddie and Kevin were gone. I sat up, stretched. I'd completely forgotten about the dog attack until I saw Tracie in the next bed over, her injured leg propped up with towels and pillows. She was sleeping soundly, however, so I moved quietly, not wanting to disturb her. I tiptoed across the floor and up the stairs.

Eddie and Kevin were in the living room, staring out the window. I walked up to Kevin and we hugged briefly, and he kissed my forehead.

My gaze shifted to the window, and what lay beyond. The rain had stopped, and a mountain of fog had settled in, obscuring the yard, the cars parked on the street, and the houses on the other side.

A dark shadow loped quickly down the street. Small. Certainly not human.

"Dogs," Kevin explained. "We've been watching

them all morning."

"How many?" I asked.

Eddie shook his head. "Hard to say. But we've seen a bunch of them. Probably pets that have gone wild."

I hadn't thought about that, but it made sense. With so many people dead, the animals had no other choice but to fend for themselves.

I shuddered at the thought. Our dog, Lucy, was such a gentle, sweet dog. She wouldn't hurt anyone, never bit anyone. It broke my heart to think that dogs like her, faced with the possibility of starving, would be forced to hunt for their food. Fight for it, in fact. *Kill* for it.

I left Kevin's side and walked into the kitchen. In the back yard was a gruesome sight: the dog Kevin had shot was in bloody tatters, most obviously eaten by other dogs. Its carcass had been chewed and gnawed. Pink, bulbous portions of its entrails had been strewn around the yard like rotting pork. Its fur, what was left of it, was glossy and rain-soaked.

I felt sick, and I turned and went back into the living room before I puked.

"What do we do about them?" I asked.

"Nothing, for now," Kevin said. "They seem to be roving, traveling in a pack. There might be twenty, there might be fifty. But it looks like they've learned to hunt together, like wolves. If we go outside now, we're likely to be attacked by who knows how many."

"Great," I said. "And I have to pee."

"You're going to have to hold it for a while," Eddie said.

I turned to go downstairs to check on Tracie and

find something to eat. I stopped when I saw her at the top of the stairs. She was favoring her wounded leg, using an arm to lean against the wall for support.

"Guys," she said weakly. I started walking toward her, but she pressed a hand in front of her, motioning for me to halt. "Stop, Sierra," she said weakly.

"What's wrong?" I asked.

"Oh, God, guys. I'm so sorry." Her words were choked, and she was crying. Her face was bleach white, and her eyes had dark, puffy circles underneath.

"Trace . . . what's wrong?"

"I'm sick," she said, shaking her head. "I'm really, really sick."

53

"How is she?" Kevin asked.

"She has a fever, and she's really achy," I said. "But she's sleeping now."

Ignoring Tracie's warning for me to stay away, I had walked up to her and held her in my arms. She tried to push me away, but I wouldn't let her. Finally, she just melted into me, sobbing.

"I'm sick, oh, God, I'm sick!" she cried. "I'm so sorry! I'm so, so sorry, Sierra!"

"No, no," I said. "You're going to be okay." I was crying, too.

"No," she said, sobbing. "How did I get it? How did I get it?"

Eddie and Kevin came.

"Let's get her back to bed," Eddie said.

"You don't understand!" Tracie said. "I've got it! I've

got the flu! And you will, too, if you don't stay away!"

"I'll get her downstairs," I told Kevin and Eddie. "She's burning up. I'll get her back to bed."

I held Tracie as she limped downstairs.

"What can we do?" Eddie called out.

"Nothing, yet," I replied. "I'll be back up in a minute."

"I am so sorry, Sierra," Tracie whimpered.

"Knock it off," I said. "We've been through too much together. You're going to pull through this."

I helped her to the bed, helped her get out of her sweats. Then I helped her lay back, propping a pillow beneath her head and placing the mound of towels and pillows to elevate her wounded leg. I pulled the sheet over her.

"How's that?" I asked. "Are you still hot? Cold?"

Tracie didn't reply.

"Can I get you anything?" I asked. "Water?"

"Promise me something, Sierra," she said quietly.

"What?"

"Promise me . . . promise me you won't let me . . . let me die . . . like *that.* Don't let me die like everyone else. I don't care how you do it. Just . . . just don't let me die that way."

"Trace, you're not going to—"

She grabbed my wrist. Hard. "Promise me, Sierra! Please, please! Promise me you won't let me die that way."

I looked into her eyes. She was terrified. Horrified, in fact.

"I promise," I said quietly. "Rest, now."

I left Tracie and walked back upstairs. Eddie and

Kevin were seated in the kitchen. They looked worried.

"How is she?" Eddie asked.

"Not good," I said.

"You think it's the flu?" Kevin asked.

"How?" I asked. "She hasn't come in contact with anyone."

"The dog," Eddie said. "She was bitten by that dog."

"That's what I'm saying," I said. "It could be anything. It could be some illness brought on by the bite. An infection. It doesn't mean she's got bird flu."

"We'll know soon enough, I guess," Eddie said somberly.

And I was scared. I was scared for Tracie, I was scared for me. For Eddie and Kevin. If Tracie had the bird flu, then, chances were, we were all going to get it. Maybe we were already infected.

54

Tracie's fever got worse as the day wore on. At times, she was delirious, talking to people that weren't there. It was difficult listening to her, especially when she was talking to her mom as if she was in the room with her. For a while, she argued with a guy she'd dated a year ago, all the while speaking to him as if he was right there with her, talking to her.

By evening, her fever was still raging. The sheets and bed linens were soaked with her sweat. She drifted in and out of sleep, however, and she wasn't holding conversations with people who weren't there. With Kevin's help, we moved her to the other bed. Then I stripped off the sweat-soaked sheets from the other bed and threw them into the garage.

All day, and into the evening, the dogs darted in and out of the fog, which refused to lift. With the passing of the storm the previous night, a cold front had settled in, and the daytime temperatures barely hit sixty degrees. We heard the howling of dogs, near and far. Occasionally, we'd hear the scratching of paws on the front or back porch. I turned once to see a ratty black Labrador, thin and emaciated, staring back at me. He wore a dirty red collar with a silver tag, and it killed me to know that, only a few weeks ago, this dog was probably somebody's pal, somebody's friend who played with a ball and swam in the lake. Now, the dog looked rabid. If I would have set foot outside, there was no doubt in my mind the animal would have attacked.

That was another thing. Tracie was very sick. If it wasn't the bird flu, it could be any number of other illnesses . . . including rabies. We had no way to treat anything like that. No drugs, nothing. Rabies would kill her. It would be just as bad as if she'd contracted bird flu. The only thing we could do was to try and keep Tracie comfortable.

And hope.

55

I had a hard time sleeping that night. I was worried about Tracie . . . but I also really began to think about our situation. Everything seemed so *hopeless.* I kept thinking about all of the things that had happened, all of the things going on around us in the city, the state, the country. Around the world.

How could this happen? How come nobody did anything? I remembered hearing about the bird flu in the news before the pandemic hit. I read about it in the paper. Over the past few years, I'd heard how the disease had spread throughout the world through migrating birds. I read that scientists had said it was only a matter of time before the bird flu made the jump from birds to humans. The world was warned. It had been warned for years, but nobody did anything. Now, of course, it was far too late.

The more I thought about our circumstances, the more I realized how grave our situation was. We'd gone from living in a technologically advanced, superior society, to a third-world country . . . or worse. Not long ago, I could buy a loaf of bread twenty four hours a day, any day of the week. If I wanted food, I got something out of the fridge, or I went to a fast food place, where I had a meal in a matter of minutes. If I had to go to the bathroom, I only had to walk twenty feet in my own home. Or stop somewhere at a public restroom. Everything was so *easy.*

Now, everything had changed. We had to really think about things before we did them. No more could we simply walk down the street and visit a friend. Gone were the days of calling up someone and talking to them over the phone. No more e-mails. No instant messaging or cellular phones. Convenience—the by-product of necessity and ingenuity, that very staple of American prosperity—was no longer in the picture.

And now there was the Tracie factor. She was sick. As she lay sleeping in bed, I listened to her breathe. She hadn't moved in hours.

I got up and gently felt her forehead. She was still running a fever, but . . .

Was she cooler than she was a couple of hours ago?

I couldn't be sure. Perhaps it was just my imagination.

But I'd made up my mind about something else, too. If Tracie *did* have bird flu, if she got worse and worse . . . I would live up to the promise I made. I wouldn't let her suffer like we'd seen so many suffer already. I wasn't going to watch her wretch and vomit blood, agonizing for hours.

I owed her that much.

As for me, I didn't care anymore. If I got sick, if

Eddie and Kevin got sick, well, maybe it was for the better. Maybe there really was no way out of this. Maybe it was only a matter of time. Maybe it really was the end of the world. The end of human life on the planet. Maybe there really was no escape.

Most of the night went like that. I was only thinking negative thoughts, bad thoughts, and I let it get the best of me. I cried quietly a couple of times, until I finally fell asleep.

But when I awoke, our world had changed again.

56

I was dimly aware of a figure standing over me. How long it had been there, I don't know. But as I slowly awakened, I flinched, startled by the form at the edge of my bed.

Tracie.

She was smiling. She was smiling, and she was wearing an oversized white T-shirt that nearly came to her knees. Black letters on the shirt read: *76% of all statistics are made up on the spot.* She looked tired, drained . . . but she looked—

"I'm feeling better," she said quietly. "I'm really weak, and my leg hurts, but my fever's gone."

I propped myself up on my elbows. "You're . . . you're better?" I asked in disbelief.

"Not a lot," she said. "I'm still achy and weak. But my fever's gone, I think. I just drank some water and ate some Triscuits. They were stale . . . I wouldn't recommend them for breakfast."

I almost cried. I'd spent most of the night worrying, fearing the worst, thinking Tracie was going to get sicker and sicker and sicker and I would have to—

She touched my hand. "Thanks for taking care of me," she said.

"But you need to go back to bed," I said. "If you're getting better, you need to rest."

"I will," she said. "But I had to get up and get some water. I was *so* thirsty."

"Where's Eddie and Kevin?" I asked.

Tracie shrugged. "I don't know," she said. "They weren't here when I got up. I went outside, behind the shed to pee—"

"By yourself!?!?"

"I had to go *really* bad, Sierra," she said. "And besides—I took the pistol with me." She nodded toward the handgun resting on the floor near the bed. "I didn't see any dogs. Or anyone, for that fact. I was fine."

"But you didn't see Eddie or Kevin?" I asked, becoming more and more alarmed. That wasn't like them to disappear without saying anything. Eddie was always adamant about either him or Kevin staying to watch over us.

"No," she said. "But maybe they went scrounging around the neighborhood."

"Yeah, but they've never gone together," I said.

Tracie climbed back into bed. "I think they're fine," she said. "Besides . . . we haven't seen much in the way of people this past week. Maybe they needed to get something that would take both of them to carry. I don't know. But I'm tired." She lay back, her head upon the pillow.

"Yeah, you rest," I said, swinging my legs over the edge of the bed. "I'll see if I can find out where they went to. Can I get you anything?"

"I'm good, thanks," Tracie said, getting comfortable in bed. "Wow . . . I thought I was going to die, there, for a while."

"Not me," I lied. "I knew you were going to pull through."

Suddenly, there was a noise outside. A squealing of tires braking to a halt. Two doors slamming.

A car?

Eddie and Kevin?

57

"What was that?" Tracie asked, propping herself up on her elbows.

"Stay here," I said as I stood and snapped up the pistol from the floor. Barefoot, I hustled up the basement steps, down the hall, and into the living room. I peered out the living room window.

There was a van in the driveway. It was white, with the words *G & N Moving and Storage* printed on the side in blue letters. On the driver's door was a cartoon of a short man, waving, standing next to a truck.

Suddenly, the front door opened. I raised the pistol, aiming at the door, my finger on the trigger—

"Holy shit, Sierra!" Eddie shrieked as he ducked and fell to his knees. Kevin saw the gun and darted quickly to the side. I lowered the barrel as relief poured over me.

"You scared me!" I exclaimed, both glad and mad at

the same time.

"Not as much as you scared us!" Kevin said. "I think I need to check my pants!"

"It's okay, Trace!" I called down the hall. "It's just Kevin and Eddie!" Then I turned back to the guys. "Where did you go? What were you doing?" I asked.

"Earlier this morning, I was out scouting around a few blocks over," Eddie replied. He pointed out the window. "I found this van in a garage. It's got a full tank of gas, but I couldn't find the keys. But it seems Kevy-boy has a little experience in that department."

"I did a lot of tinkering on cars with my uncle," Kevin said. "It's an older van, and they're easy to hot-wire. It's pretty simple, really." He stepped closer and slipped his arm around my waist. "How are you?"

"Fine," I said. "What are we going to do with a van?"

"First, we're going to put it in the garage so nobody sees it," Eddie said. "Then, we're going to stockpile it with food and water and clothes. Guns, too. Then, if and when we're forced out of here, we'll be ready to go."

"And sooner or later, we *will* have to go," Kevin added.

I knew what they meant. Over the past few days, we'd spotted more smoke. More fires were burning, more houses were being torched. We were a month into this thing, this bird flu pandemic, and the survivors were beginning to realize the televisions and DVD players and computers they'd stolen were useless. They couldn't play their PlayStations. Nobody bought jewelry, no matter how valuable it was. Money, no matter how much of it you had, was worthless.

They needed food and water, though, and they knew where they could find it: in the suburbs. Places outside of Ann Arbor and other big cities. They would be looking for quiet neighborhoods that hadn't yet been completely pillaged of their goods.

And that's where *we* were.

58

Eddie rolled up the garage door, and Kevin hastily turned the van around and backed it inside to hide it away. Then the garage door came down, and Eddie and Kevin came back into the house.

"How's Tracie?" Eddie asked.

"Better," I said. "She really seems better."

"Really?" Kevin said in surprise. It was a relief for all of us. If Tracie had been infected by H5N1, it would be a death sentence for her—and us.

"Yeah," I said. "When I woke up, she was standing. Said her fever broke. She'd drank some water, ate some Triscuits. She even went outside to pee."

"She probably picked up something from the dog," Eddie said. "Hopefully not rabies."

I shook my head. "She looks a lot better, but we've got to watch her. If what she has is rabies, her chances aren't going to be any better than with the bird flu."

"Speaking of which," Eddie said to me, "we saw a lot of dogs. If you go outside, take a gun and be careful."

"You don't have to tell me twice," I said.

59

Tracie continued to improve over the next few days, to our great relief. Gradually, color returned to her face, and her leg healed well. She'd have a few scars on the shin and calf of her left leg, but that was the least of her concerns . . . and ours. We were so worried that she had become infected . . . and we knew what the result of that would be. Our best guess was that some infection had been passed on through the dog bite. Eddie had been bitten by a schnauzer a couple of years ago. The dog had been vaccinated against rabies, but Eddie picked up some bug that made him sick for a couple of days. He became really sick, but he recovered fine.

But, while Tracie was getting better, things around us were getting worse. We saw more fires and a lot more smoke. Closer, too. Gunfire had died down in the past few weeks, but now we were hearing distant shots a few times each hour.

And they sounded closer and closer each day.

Eddie and Kevin took turns at night, doing their own scrounging. I don't call it 'looting', because that's not what it was. It was survival. They came back with all sorts of things: nonperishable food, bottled water, clothing, soap, some knives. They also found more guns. Two handguns, and a rifle with a scope. The rifle was a 30-30 Winchester semiautomatic.

"Whoever had this," Eddie said, showing us the firearm, "was starting his own militia. It took me two trips to bring home all of the ammo he'd stored up. We were lucky to find the stash before anyone else."

Sadly, the man we'd given the water to several weeks before had died. Kevin said he'd found his decomposing body, and that of his daughter, in a home several blocks away. Kevin said they were so bloated he couldn't tell for sure how they'd died . . . but he was fairly certain it was the result of the bird flu.

It was, as best we could tell, the middle of June, give or take a few days. The days and nights were warm. It rained several times, and whenever it did, we went outside and showered. Modesty remained, however: if it rained during the day, Tracie and I would go into the back yard and soak up the shower. After toweling off and putting clothes on in the kitchen, Eddie and Kevin would come up from downstairs and take their turn.

My relationship with Kevin had gotten better, too. We'd been talking a lot more, and he was sharing things with me that I never knew about. His father left when he was only four or five, leaving he and his mother alone. He was really resentful. His uncle had stepped in, taking him to ball games, fishing, doing all the 'Dad' things that Kevin's father wasn't there for. He said his uncle was the only father he ever knew. He only saw his dad a couple of times a year, and he said they usually argued a lot. And the death of his mom had ripped him up. Up until now, none of us had spoken too much about losing our parents. We were too busy just trying to get by. Kevin can be kind of quiet, and doesn't share a lot of his deep feelings. The more he opened up, the more I came to respect him. Sure, he was fun. Smart, and handsome. But his openness told me that he trusted me, that he cared. I found myself caring for him more than I'd known.

And I began wondering if there was something going on between Eddie and Tracie. I'd seen them talking alone a couple of times, like they were sharing a secret. Eddie had a smile and a glow in his eyes I hadn't seen before. Tracie did, too.

One afternoon, after we'd showered in the rain and dressed, we went downstairs to get Eddie and Kevin.

"Your turn," I said as we walked down the steps. Eddie and Kevin were already on their way up. Kevin and I kissed, just a quick peck, and I saw Eddie squeeze Tracie's hand. I waited until the guys were upstairs, and then I spoke.

"All right," I said as I plopped onto the bed and shot Tracie a knowing smirk. "Spill."

Tracie looked at me. "What?" she asked, but her grin betrayed her.

"You know what I'm talking about," I said. "What's going on between you and my brother?" I picked up a brush and began running it through my damp hair.

"Oh, you know," Tracie said.

"No, I don't," I replied, still smiling. "Why don't you fill me in?"

Tracie blushed, and she didn't say anything. She began to towel-dry her hair, which had grown past her shoulders.

"Are you guys . . . I mean . . . is there something there? Between you and Eddie?"

"I . . . I don't . . . well, there *might* be," Tracie admitted sheepishly. "Are . . . are you mad?"

"Trace, why on earth would I be mad? Are you kidding?" I stood up and walked to her. "Eddie's a great guy. And you're a great girl. He's changed when he's around you. I've seen it. He's . . . *happier*. He's happier than I've seen him in a long time."

"Really?" Tracie replied with surprise.

"Really," I said, and I gave her a hug, then backed away. "And that's A-okay in my book."

Tracie spoke. "He's really been—"

And that's when a gunshot shattered an upstairs window.

67

The explosion thundered through the house. I grabbed the shotgun that was leaning against the wall, and Tracie and I bolted up the stairs and ran down the hall.

Kevin and Eddie were in the living room. Kevin was rain-soaked, frantically fumbling with his clothing. Eddie had a towel wrapped around his waist. He was carrying one of the handguns.

There was another gun blast from outside. Eddie motioned for us to stay back as he crept to the shattered living room window. Glass was everywhere, and he had to be careful where he stepped with his bare feet. He fired off several rapid shots out the window, then ducked down.

Kevin had finished getting his clothes on. He snapped up a pistol that was on the table, taking up a position on the opposite side of the window. Rain dripped from the roof outside. Eddie shot a glance toward us.

"Stay back!" he hissed. *"Stay in the hall!"*

"Do you need this?" I asked, holding up the shotgun.

"It's only one guy!" Eddie said. Then he peeked around the window. "Now he's running away!"

Eddie took aim with the handgun, fired through the rain. Fired again.

"Gone," Eddie said in disgust.

"You wanted to *kill* him?" I asked.

"Sierra, he *saw* us. And he shot first! That's the first person we've seen in a long time. If he's with a gang or something, he's going to go back and tell them. If they know we're hiding here, they'll know we also have food and water and supplies. He might be back, and he probably won't be alone."

Somewhere in the distance, thunder growled. The rain fell harder.

"Guys," Eddie said as he carefully stepped away from the window. He was still soaked, and his wet hair dripped water as he walked to the kitchen and picked up his clothing that was heaped by the door. "We have to make a decision," he continued. "We have to decide if we're going to get out of here and take our chances . . . or if we're going to stay and fight. We all know it's only a matter of time before someone finds out we're here. They could come tomorrow, they could come next week."

Eddie was wrong.

Oh, he was right about one thing: the man came back, and he didn't come back alone.

But they hadn't waited a day or a week.

They came back . . . that very same afternoon.

61

We were sitting around the kitchen table after eating a meal of corn flakes, water, and potato chips. Eddie had the atlas spread out on the table, discussing possible routes out of Saline.

"Whatever we do, we've got to dodge the cities," he was saying. "That's where we'd probably run into our biggest problems. The streets will be filled with junk cars and trucks. Not to mention there will probably be gangs of looters. We wouldn't have a chance."

"But, where are we going to go?" Kevin asked. "We don't know what we're getting ourselves into. We don't know what's going on the next block over, let alone other places in Michigan."

"Don't you think we'd be safer if we headed north?" Tracie asked. "There are a lot less people, and more forest land."

"Tracie's right," I said, glancing down at the map. "If we can skirt Ann Arbor and make our way north, we'd probably be safer."

"I'm sure other people have had the same idea," Eddie said.

"Yeah," I agreed. "But not everyone is out to loot and steal and kill," I reminded him. "There have to be people like us, people who want to live, people that won't hurt anyone else. People who want to survive. There might even be a place where lots of people have banded together."

"This whole thing is reminding me more and more of that old Mad Max movie with Mel Gibson," Kevin said. "You know . . . where a bunch of people had gathered in the desert to save a huge supply of gasoline? Remember all of the nutcases who tried to overrun them?"

I smiled. I'd seen the movie. It was good. Funny, too, in some places.

But it wasn't all that funny now.

"How far do you think we can go in the van?" I asked.

"It's got a full tank, so we could probably go three hundred miles or so," Eddie replied. "That could take us almost anywhere in northern Michigan, if that's where we wanted to go. Depending, of course, on what we run into. If we have to drive a hundred miles an hour, our gas isn't going to last that long."

I looked at the map. Saline was south of Ann Arbor, which was on the outskirts of Detroit. If we headed north, there were several cities we'd have to stay away from: Jackson, Lansing, Flint. If we could make it north of Lansing, toward the center of the state, we would be able to follow rural roads, winding our way up . . . depending on how far we wanted to travel.

I placed my finger on the map. "Suppose," I began, "suppose we head over here." I glanced up at Eddie, but he wasn't paying attention. Instead, his gaze was in the direction of the living room window. He looked alarmed.

"Wait a minute!" Kevin suddenly exclaimed. "I know where we could go! My uncle's got a—"

"Guys," Eddie said interrupting. "I think we've got company."

62

Kevin, Tracie, and I turned our heads. Far down the street, we could see movement.

People.

We didn't wait to see how many there were. It was just one of those things we *knew*. We knew who they were and what they wanted. This wasn't a group of neighbors paying a friendly visit. None of them would be bringing cheesecake or brownies. The people walking up the street were parasites. Wolves.

"Pack up!" Eddie ordered. "Let's get what we need and get into the van! It's time to go!"

Eddie stood, snapped up the atlas, and the four of us ran down to the basement. The van was already loaded with most of our necessary supplies, but there were several items downstairs that we needed: shoes, a couple of extra bottles of water, the shotgun, the rifle, and the handguns.

"Hurry!" I said as we hastily scraped things together. We filled a big, red Coleman cooler with our bottles of water. Of course, it wouldn't do anything to keep them cold, but it held quite a few bottles and was easy to carry.

By the time we made it back up the stairs, the group was only a few houses away. They were walking quickly, carrying clubs and guns. Both men and women, and they looked ragged. Their clothing was in tatters, their hair disheveled. They looked like they'd been living in a garbage dump. Maybe they had. I'd read a book a couple of years ago about the witch hunts they had back in the 1800s, and that vision instantly came to mind. Bloodthirsty, sneering faces. Eyes wild, crazed. Almost demonic. They were all looking at our house, and it was obvious they weren't just passing through.

There were seven of them. Two of the men had guns.

"Kevin . . . get the rifle!" Eddie hissed. "Tracie! Sierra! Get in the van!"

The Winchester was leaning near the breezeway that led to the garage. Kevin picked it up and tossed it to Eddie, who snapped it out of the air. He shouldered it immediately, aimed—

Jesus, Eddie, I thought. *What are you—*

—pulled the trigger.

Instantly, one of the men carrying a gun fell, and the group quickly scattered in different directions.

Tracie and I had run through the kitchen. Kevin was by the door, and he pushed us into the breezeway. In seconds, we were in the van. Kevin fumbled with some loose wires, and the van's engine chugged. It turned over, but it didn't start.

Outside, we could hear gunshots and shouting.

"Hurry it up!" Eddie shouted from the passenger seat.

"I'm trying!" Kevin shouted back.

Eddie turned. There were no seats in the back of the van, which was packed with our supplies. The cooler was pressed against the back of the passenger seat. The van engine churned and chugged.

"Lay flat, both of you!" Eddie snapped at Tracie and me. "Stay as low to the floor as you can!"

The van suddenly roared to life, snarling like a lion.

"Go! Go! Go!" Eddie shrieked.

Kevin dropped the van into gear and hit the gas. We lurched forward, slamming into the fiberglass garage door, which shattered in an explosion of scrapes and scratches. It fell away, crunching beneath the tires.

Then we were in daylight, and the van's wheels squealed as we rocketed down the driveway. Since the van had no side windows, I couldn't see what was going on around us. Our only line of vision was the windshield in front, or the two square windows in the back.

I heard gunfire, and a bullet punctured the van a few feet above my head.

Eddie rolled down his window and poked the handgun through, firing off several rounds. Another bullet struck the van from behind, burying into the console between Eddie and Kevin. A few feet to the left or right, and one of them would have been hit.

"Faster!" Eddie demanded.

"This isn't a Ferrari!" Kevin snapped. "We've got a

ton of gear in here, man! I'm going as fast as I can!"

I heard another flurry of gunshots, but they were farther away now. Eddie returned fire, but he was aiming behind us. We were putting distance between us and the looters. Soon, we had left them behind.

I lay on the floor of the van, on my belly, holding Tracie's hand. She looked at me. Grinned meekly.

We both knew.

We knew that something had ended, that something was over. It was a feeling of accomplishment, I guess. But it was more. We knew we couldn't stay in that house anymore, that it would have been pointless to stay and fight. More marauders would have arrived. We'd have been overrun soon enough.

No, we couldn't stay. And I was thankful that Eddie and Kevin had the forethought to think about hiding the van and filling it with supplies. I remembered the television interview with the man who was a survivalist.

From here on out, he'd said, *you can't count on the government. You can't count on law enforcement. The only people who are going to survive are going to be the ones who are ready. The ones who are prepared.*

The van slowed.

"Jesus," Eddie said. "This looks like a war zone."

I crawled to my knees, then helped Tracie sit up. We stared out the windshield, dazed.

What once had been homes were now piles of rubble. Charred foundations grew like mold around piles of burned lumber. There were a few homes that hadn't been torched, but their windows were broken, and dirty curtains fluttered in the breeze. Some buildings were nothing but blackened cinder blocks. Bloated, decayed corpses lay scattered in yards, driveways, along sidewalks. Some had been eaten by animals. We passed a car where the near skeletal remains of a man lay hanging from the drivers' side window. What remained of his gray flesh was hanging from his bones like dripping jelly, slowly falling off, piece by piece. There was a small pile of decaying tissue on the ground beneath the door, so rotting and decomposed that even the dogs wouldn't touch it.

It really is true, I thought. *It's the end of the world. It's the end of civilization as we know it. Like that announcer said on the radio: we're on our own.*

"Head west," Eddie said. "Let's get onto 12 and take it to Austin Road, up Schneider, and take East Pleasant Lake Road over to 52. That'll take us north, and we can bypass Jackson and Ann Arbor."

Tracie crawled forward and sat on a cooler.

"You guys all right?" Kevin asked as he glanced at us in the rearview mirror.

"Fine," I said.

"Yeah, me too," Tracie said. She reached out and took Eddie's hand.

I looked around in despair. Seeing the level of devastation, of complete destruction was unbelievable. Obviously, we'd *known* what was going on around us. But seeing it, being within the ruins, a vessel speeding through chaos . . . it was just something I wasn't prepared for.

And yet, there was another emotion I was feeling.

Hope.

Oh, it was only a glimmer, just a seed. But it was there. I had Kevin. Eddie. Tracie. We'd survived almost two months on our own, while billions of people around the world hadn't. We'd foraged for food, we were healthy—considering our limited nutritional menu to choose from. We'd escaped a gang of looters. We had a van, we had a plan. Oh, we had no idea where, exactly, we were headed . . . but we were on our way.

PART TWO:
FLIGHT

63

The ride to highway 52 was uneventful, thankfully. We saw no other live humans. Lots of dogs, however, and most looked ravenous. Some of them, drooling at the mouth, snarling and growling, were obviously rabid. A crazed German shepherd tried to attack the van.

There were cars strewn everywhere. Some were burned. However, along the rural route we'd taken, most were simply parked haphazardly on the shoulder of the road. There was a big silver Dodge Ram truck abandoned in the middle of an intersection. There was a window sticker at the bottom right corner of the rear cab window. It was a caricature of a deer, surrounded by bold letters that read: *DITCH THE BITCH - LET'S GO HUNTIN'*. All I could do was shake my head.

We saw a number of bodies, too. I couldn't look at them. All were bloated and gray. Some had been gnawed by dogs or other animals, and their clothing as well as their flesh had been shredded.

"Check that out," Kevin said, pointing at a charred mass on a side street.

"That's a helicopter," Eddie said.

"It *was,"* Kevin replied. "I wonder if that's the one we saw."

The chopper was on its side, blackened, with a broken blade pointing straight into the air. It was mangled and crunched, like an old, decaying tortoise shell. I wondered how it had crashed, and if, perhaps, someone on the ground had been responsible. Maybe people shot at it. Sad.

"Where are we headed?" Tracie asked.

"North," Eddie replied. "We'll stay on 52 up through Chelsea. Then we can follow some back roads and keep heading north, without having to go into any bigger cities."

"Here's an idea," Kevin said. "I don't know why I didn't think about this before. Actually, I was just about to bring it up when those guys came."

"What's your idea?" Eddie asked as the van hit a bump, jolting us around.

"We head to my uncle's lodge at Otter Lake," he replied. "He's got a private lake surrounded by about five hundred acres. It's in Cheboygan County. There's no one around for miles. In fact, he and my aunt might even be there. The lodge is huge. I mean, it's *big.*"

"Hey," Tracie said, "I'm all for that."

"How do we get there?" Eddie asked.

"We just keep heading the way we're heading," he said. "We go north. Cheboygan County is right at the tip of the lower peninsula. The lodge is really cool. It's built all of logs, with a huge deck. And it's way back in the woods. You have to go down a gravel road about a mile, and then take a two-track the rest of the way in. My guess is, knowing my uncle, he's probably there with my aunt, if they were able to escape the flu."

Eddie had already flopped open the atlas. Kevin leaned over, glancing from the highway to the map, back to the highway. Eddie placed his finger on the map. "Here's Cheboygan County," he said.

"My uncle's lodge is about six miles south of the city," he said. "It'll be perfect."

"Do you think he's going to mind us showing up on his doorstep?" I asked.

Eddie looked at me. Smirked. "It's the end of the world," he said. "He'd probably be happy to see a familiar face."

"What about gas?" Tracie asked.

"I think we have enough to make it there," Kevin answered. "If not, maybe we'll be able to syphon some from the vehicles on the side of the road." He reached behind his seat and pulled out a coiled hose. "I got my Detroit credit card right here."

"I say we do it," Eddie replied. "We should stay away from the main roads, though. It will take us longer, but we should stay as far away from any cities as possible."

I knew what he meant. We had no idea what we might run into, no idea how many people had survived—or what they were doing to survive—but we had a pretty good idea. People would do whatever they needed to do to get by.

Survival of the fittest, I thought. *The law of the jungle.*

"I've gotta pee pretty soon," I said, and Tracie

nodded as well. *Me, too,* her eyes said.

We pulled over to the side of the road, slid the panel door open, and got out. It felt good to stretch our legs. The rain had moved on, and the sun was beginning to peek through huge gray and white clouds.

While Kevin and Eddie had hiked a short distance into the woods on the drivers' side of the van, I teased Tracie.

"Tracie's got a boyfriend, Tracie's got a boyfriend," I sang sweetly.

She blushed. "Maybe," she said.

"Oh, come on, Trace. I'm only kidding. I think it's great. You've been holding his hand for the last half-hour. And I think he really likes you."

"Has he said anything?" Tracie asked.

"He's my brother," I said, rolling my eyes. "He doesn't have to."

64

Necessities completed, we were on the road again. Still, we saw no signs of any other people. *Live* people, that is. I imagined if anyone saw our white van, they would probably think we were dangerous and would stay out of sight. The roads we took were clear, for the most part, except for the fact that Kevin had to slow occasionally to go around an abandoned vehicle, or—worse yet—a dead body. Ugh.

We snacked on granola bars and water. While we had a lot of canned food, cereal, and the like, we decided to save it until we were someplace where we might be able to start a fire. We'd brought pots and pans, of course, and just the *thought* of a hot meal was enough to make my mouth water. Until then, we'd settle for eating whatever was handy.

"How far are we from Chelsea?" I asked.

Eddie looked down at his map. "We just passed Jerusalem Road," he said, "so we don't have too far. We'll go under I-94, and Chelsea is only a few miles from there."

I-94 is a major east-west thoroughfare through Michigan. If you begin in Detroit, the freeway takes you through Ann Arbor, Jackson, and Kalamazoo, before it begins gradually winding south, exiting Michigan into Indiana. Most days it's flooded with traffic, including lots of large semi-trucks. Of course, that was before the bird flu wiped out everyone. Now, I was sure we'd find the freeway empty.

Wrong.

65

"There's the overpass, way up ahead," Kevin said. "We're not far, now."

As we drew near, we saw more of what we'd seen on the outskirts of Saline: burned and overturned cars scattered about. A few bodies wasting away on the side of the highway. Kevin wasn't paying attention, and he ran over someone's leg that protruded onto the highway. It made a dull, squishy thud, and Tracie and I winced.

"Sorry about that," Kevin said, glancing up into the rearview mirror. "I don't think he felt it, though."

Eddie opened the map on his lap. "We can go through the town, or we can bypass it by using some side streets," he said. "Whatever you guys think is safer."

"So far, we haven't seen much in the way of human life," Kevin said.

Which got me to wondering: *Just how many people are*

there left alive in the world? Thousands? Did the bird flu really wipe out nearly everyone in the world? It was impossible to know.

"Can you hand me a bottle of water, Sierra?" Kevin asked as we passed the on-ramp to I-94. The overpass was coming up.

I moved from the cooler and knelt next to it, opening up the lid. "Anyone else?" I asked.

"I've still got some," Tracie said.

"None for me," Eddie replied.

I handed the bottle of water to Kevin, but a movement on the overpass ahead made me pause.

"Look!" I exclaimed, pointing. "There are people on the bridge! On I-94!"

Kevin eased off the gas. There were four or five people leaning over, looking at us as we approached. One of them was waving at us.

"They don't look all that hostile," Kevin said.

"Yeah, well, don't stop," Eddie warned. He picked up the pistol that he'd placed between his legs.

Suddenly, another form appeared on the bridge. The man was holding something—but not for long. All too late we realized what was happening.

The man had been holding a cinder block.

The operative word: *had.*

Now, the heavy, cement rectangle was hurdling through the air, falling rapidly, on a collision-course with our van.

66

Kevin cranked the wheel so hard that I thought the van was going to roll over. Tracie and I were thrown into the side wall, and I smacked my head hard. Tires squealed. Then, Kevin spun the wheel in the other direction, and Tracie and I were thrown to the opposite side of the van. There was an enormous thud from beneath the van that shook the whole vehicle. It felt like we'd hit . . . well . . . like we'd hit a cinder block. Then, there was the sound of dragging metal as the van passed beneath the overpass. Clearly, the cement brick had done some damage. Apparently—and lucky for us—it hit the pavement too soon, but Kevin couldn't avoid running over it. I'm sure its intended target had been the windshield or the front of the van.

Kevin let off the gas.

"Keep going, keep going!" Eddie ordered as he looked into the side view mirror. "Don't stop now!"

"I'm not going to!" Kevin said. "But we're dragging something!"

"As long as the van moves, we'll be all right!" Eddie exclaimed. "We'll check it out when we get farther down the road!"

I glanced through the rear windows. On the overpass, the group of people had gathered on the north side, watching as we drove farther and farther away. They'd tried to stop us . . . and they'd nearly succeeded.

"Friendly bunch of people," I said to Tracie.

"Yeah," she said, as she, too, glanced at the small group on the overpass. "A real welcoming committee."

The metal screeching was terrible. When I was in fifth grade, there was a kid named Jeremy Roberts who would always scratch his fingernails on the blackboard. Everyone in class cringed, and he drove us all nuts. The more we reacted, the more he did it. That's what the screeching sounded like, only a lot louder.

After we traveled a few miles, Kevin found a spot where we could see clearly in every direction, so we knew there wasn't anyone around. He limped the van to the shoulder of the road. The awful metal screeching ceased as the van came to a stop. Even at a simple idle, the van was unbearably loud.

Eddie slid out, and so did Kevin. Eddie pulled the panel door open, and Tracie and I got out. Kevin was already laying on the ground inspecting the undercarriage.

"It's the exhaust pipe and the muffler," he said. "We were lucky. That cement block could have ripped the underside of the van to shreds." He stood quickly and searched the contents of the van. He pulled out two towels and handed one to Eddie.

"Use this," he said, "so you don't burn your hand. Help me pull the exhaust pipe the rest of the way off. The van will be really loud, but at least it'll run."

Eddie fell to his knees, rolled onto his back, and slid under the van, and they worked at yanking the exhaust pipe from the catalytic convertor.

Tracie suddenly spoke, and her voice was cautious and tense. "Hey guys, maybe we weren't so lucky, after all! Someone's coming!"

I spun. In the distance, on the highway behind us, through shimmering heat waves, a car was approaching . . . and *fast.*

67

"Get back in the van!" Eddie shouted from beneath the vehicle. His voice was muffled. "Kevin! Pull harder! Get this thing off! Hurry!"

Tracie and I dove into the van. There was a loud clunking sound beneath us.

"Got it!" Eddie exclaimed.

"Leave it! Leave it!" Kevin said. "Come on!"

They got up in a thrash of gravel. Eddie slid the panel door closed, then climbed back into the passenger seat. Kevin floored the gas pedal and the van rocketed forward, sending Tracie and me crashing into the pile of supplies behind us.

"Hang on!" Kevin said as the van picked up speed.

"Now he tells us," Tracie said as our boxed supplies tumbled around us, spilling onto the floor.

Eddie looked in the rearview mirror.

"Is it them?" I asked. "The ones from the overpass?"

Eddie shook his head. "I can't tell," he replied. "Probably." He gripped the pistol in one hand.

"Trace, get that other handgun!" Kevin ordered. "It's under one of the bags right behind you!"

Tracie turned around and found the pistol, a .38 revolver. Kevin reached back, and Tracie placed the weapon in his hand.

I turned around and looked out the back windows of the van. The car was really coming fast.

"If he doesn't slow down, he's going to hit us!" I said.

"Maybe that's what he wants to do," Eddie said.

The vehicle chasing us was big. A Cadillac or a Lincoln of some sort. Suddenly, a long gun barrel poked out from the passenger window.

"He's got a gun!" I shouted. "He's got a gun!"

Eddie turned and looked out the back of the van, then he rolled down his window—just as the back windows shattered. Tracie and I screamed and fell to the floor as tiny pellets of glass snowstormed within the van, making tinny splintering sounds as they ricocheted off metal.

Eddie turned once again. Now that the back windows were gone, it gave him a clear shot at the car behind us.

"Stay down!" he ordered, firing several times. The gunshots within the van were unbelievably loud. As I lay on the floor, I cupped my hands over my ears, but it didn't help much.

Behind us, I heard the squealing of tires.

"I think you got one of 'em!" Kevin exclaimed.

"Yeah, well, they're not done yet," Eddie replied. He

fired off several more rounds. "You guys stay down," he ordered us again. Which was silly . . . because the last thing I was going to do was stand up and get shot.

"Hang on!" Kevin said. "He's going to try and pass!"

The van rolled to the left, then shot back to the right. Eddie fired off another shot.

"You got a tire!" Kevin cheered, pounding on the steering wheel with his palm. "You hit his right front tire!"

Eddie shot once more, and then there was only the loud roar of the van for nearly a full minute.

"Did we get away?" Tracie asked. She was laying on the floor of the van on her belly, next to me.

"Maybe," Eddie said. "They aren't going to be able to chase us with a blown tire."

I got to my knees and looked out the back windows of the van. The car behind us was leaning to the right, slowing, pulling over to the shoulder.

"That was a close one," Kevin said, wiping the sweat from his brow with the back of his hand. "Let's hope we don't have to go through that again."

"Nice shooting, cowboy," Tracie said to Eddie as she got to her knees.

"All in a days' work," Eddie said as he watched the car behind us pull to the side. We had already put a lot of distance between us and our attackers. Their car had pulled to the shoulder, and it was barely moving.

This is madness, I thought. *This can't go on. It just can't.*

Well, maybe it could.

68

We thought about circling around Chelsea, taking side streets, instead of going straight through town. We wanted to avoid another encounter like we'd just had, and if we went downtown, there might very well be people around. The last thing we needed was another cinder block to come crashing down on us. Without the muffler and exhaust pipe, the van was really loud, and was certain to attract attention, if anyone was nearby. It sounded more like a race car or a Harley-Davidson motorcycle than a street vehicle.

"The only problem," Eddie said loudly as the van cruised along, "is this map. It's not detailed enough to show any of the side streets or routes around town. I don't want to make any wrong turns and wind up getting lost, driving around and wasting gas."

"Well, we'd better make up our minds pretty quick," Kevin said. "We're going to be in town soon, whether we like it or not."

"How big is Chelsea?" Tracie asked.

"Not very big," I replied. I'd been to Chelsea several times for some high school basketball and football games.

"If we went fast, we could be through the downtown area in only a few minutes," Eddie said. "And once we're out of town, we'd be into lots of forest and farm land."

"I say we just head straight through town," Kevin suggested. "Let's just stay on the main drag, and watch out for any trouble. If anyone comes after us, we'll deal with it then."

Eddie placed the atlas on the floor and picked up the handgun. He pointed to the shotgun on the floor behind Kevin's seat and looked at me.

"How are you with a scattergun?" he asked with a grin.

I shook my head. "I've never shot a gun before in my life," I replied. "You know that."

"Yeah, well, if someone comes up behind us, don't be afraid to learn," he said.

I glanced at Tracie for a little comfort. She smiled, but it was a nervous smile.

Kevin sped up, and the van grew louder. "Okay," he said, nearly shouting over the thundering engine, "we go through. Everybody hang on."

69

As we neared the downtown district, we saw more of what we'd seen in Saline: burned houses and cars, cars on their sides. Some of the vehicles were in the middle of the street, and Kevin had to slow the van to go around them. A few dead bodies, some of them partially eaten by animals, were on the sidewalks. The dead body of a man was seated on the cement, leaning back against a lamppost. There wasn't much left of him except tattered clothing and bones caked with what remained of his decaying flesh.

Downtown, most of the buildings had burned, and their skeletal shells were scorched. Some of them had crumbled, scattering bricks on the street and sidewalks.

"It sure doesn't look like there's anyone around," I said.

"It looks like this place has been deserted for years," Tracie said.

"If there is anyone around, they'd hear us coming for miles," Eddie said.

We traveled on, cautiously making our way downtown, looking for any signs of life, or for anything threatening. The failed ambush on the I-94 overpass was a reminder of just how desperate people had become. I was sure there were more gangs around . . . and I didn't want to run into them.

But I also knew that not *everyone* who had survived was living like barbarians. There had to be some people, somewhere, who were banding together to make the best of their situation. The trouble was finding them. If they were keeping low, and we were keeping low, how would we ever know where they were? Perhaps there were people like that in this very city, watching our van pass, thinking that we, too, were animals on the loose. Maybe they were staying out of sight, waiting for the loud van to pass, hoping it didn't stop, hoping they weren't spotted.

I knew how that felt.

We went over some railroad tracks, followed by a small stream. To the left of us was Veteran's Park. Oddly, it was the only thing that didn't look like it had been damaged. The grass had grown long, but, all in all, the place looked normal.

"I think we're going to make it," Kevin said. We had passed through the downtown district, and now there were houses—or, what was left of them—lining the street on both sides. Many had been burned. Most of the windows had been broken out. Cars were parked in driveways, some with their doors hanging open. In one yard, ragged laundry still hung on a line, swaying gently in the breeze. One house had a message painted sloppily on the side of it: *Please Help Us*. The white paint had dripped and dried, and the letters had already begun to crack and fade.

And up ahead . . . movement.

I pointed. "What's . . . what's *that?*" I asked.

Kevin slowed.

"It's a guy on a bicycle," Eddie said. "He's riding a damned bike."

20

"Go slower," Eddie said.

Kevin eased off the gas, and the van slowed. The engine quieted a little.

"It's just an old guy on a bike," Tracie said. She and I had crept forward, leaning on the back seats of the van, peering out the windshield. Rain had started to fall again, and the street was shiny and slick. The man on the bike was several blocks ahead of us.

His head suddenly snapped around, and he saw our approaching van. Startled, he suddenly turned onto a side street and he began to pedal away quickly.

"Catch up to him!" Eddie said. "Maybe he knows something!"

Kevin pressed down on the gas pedal, and the van sped up. "He's probably afraid of us," he said.

"Just pull up to the road and stop!" Eddie said.

"Maybe we can convince him that we're not going to hurt him!"

When we reached the street where the man had turned, Kevin slowed to a near stop.

"There he is, down there!" Eddie exclaimed. "Catch up to him!"

Kevin turned the van and sped up, splashing through several shallow puddles that had formed in the street. It was raining harder now, and Kevin turned on the windshield wipers.

It didn't take long to reach the man on the bike. Terrified, he steered over the curb and onto a lawn. The bike wobbled and the man tumbled into the wet grass, spilling the contents of a basket that was affixed to the handlebars.

Eddie leapt out of the van. He took the pistol with him, but he stuffed it into the right front pocket of his jeans.

"Stay here," he said. "I'll try and talk to him."

Eddie hustled in front of the van, raised his hands in the air in a nonthreatening fashion, and walked toward the man who was frantically getting to his feet.

"We aren't going to hurt you," Eddie pleaded. "Please . . . I just want to talk. I'm not going to hurt you."

"Stay away from me!" the man squawked as he faced Eddie. I could see him clearly now. He was unshaven, and his hair was dirty and long. His clothing was filthy. He looked like a street bum.

Eddie stopped walking. He was about twenty feet from the man, who stood over the fallen bike. Several food items—a can of tuna, a box of crackers, and a bag of potato chips—were scattered on the ground.

"We aren't going to hurt you," Eddie repeated. "We

aren't going to take your food."

The man glanced at us in the van, then back to Eddie. He seemed to relax a little.

"What do you want?" he growled.

"Are . . . are there more like you?" Eddie said. "Are there any more survivors?"

"Sure there are," the man spat. "A few. Fiends."

"But, what about you?" Eddie asked. "Do you live alone? Are you with anyone?"

The man shook his head. "I live by myself. Stay out of sight when I can. Only go huntin' for food when I have to."

"How come you don't drive a car?" Eddie said. "There are lots of cars around."

"Too much attention," the man said. "Cars will bring them coming."

"Who is 'them'?" Eddie asked.

"You know," the man said. "Them. Those gangs. Steal all your food. Kill ya, even. Criminals."

"Are there more like you, living alone?" Eddie asked.

The man thought about it. "I suppose," he said. "I see some people, once in a while. I stay away, though. I don't want no trouble. And I want to go now."

The man stood his bike up and began gathering the spilled items.

"Do you . . . do you need anything?" Eddie asked.

The man turned, looked at the van. Looked at Eddie. "You's got some water?" he asked.

I got off the cooler, opened it up, and pulled out two bottles of water. Then I handed them to Kevin, who held them up for Eddie to see. Eddie came to the van, took the bottles of water, and walked toward the man.

"That's close enough," the man warned. "Don't come any closer."

"Hey, that's cool," Eddie said. He tossed a bottle to the man, who snapped it out of the air. Then he tossed the other bottle. The man caught it as well, and placed both of them in his basket.

"Thank you," he said, and began pushing his bike toward the house.

"Good luck," Eddie called out.

The man stopped and turned. "Luck?" he said. "Luck? You need a lot more than luck to get by, these days." Then, he continued pushing his bike until he vanished alongside the house.

Eddie came back to the van, got inside. "Let's get out of here," he said.

Kevin spun the van around, then hit the brakes.

"Shit," he breathed.

Ahead of us, in the gray drizzle, was a gang of about twenty people. They were standing in the road, carrying guns, knives, clubs.

"I think we've overstayed our welcome," Eddie whispered.

71

They walked toward us slowly, cooly, like arrogant cowboys strolling through a prairie town. Their guns and batons and bats swung easily at their sides, and I had no doubt they knew how to use them.

And there were both men and women, mostly younger: maybe our age on up through their thirties. They were a bit ragged, but looked nowhere near the disheveled appearance of the man on the bicycle.

One man in the middle of the group—tall, with long, black hair, wearing a dirty black leather trench coat, blue jeans, and black boots—was most obviously their leader. He carried a shotgun at his side. He didn't walk . . . he swaggered. His movements were confident and cocksure.

Kevin stopped the van.

"Turn around," Eddie said. "Let's get out of here."

Kevin glanced in the side view mirror. "Not so fast," he said. "We've got 'em comin' up behind us, too."

I turned and looked through the shattered rear windows and saw the dark shapes of at least a dozen people coming toward us from behind.

The group fanned out, over the sidewalks and into yards, their eyes focused on us. As they drew nearer, their strides became quicker, more purposeful.

Kevin spoke quietly, and his lips barely moved. "Trace. Sierra. Get down."

We heard him, but we didn't obey. Maybe we couldn't. Maybe we were too scared, maybe we felt we'd be safer if we knew what was going on around us. I don't know. But Tracie and I didn't move an inch.

So this is what it's come to, I thought. *The law of the jungle. Survival of the fittest. People are now hunting in packs, like wild dogs. Without basic law enforcement, people are doing pretty much whatever they wanted.*

In what seemed only a matter of seconds, we were surrounded. The mob kept their distance, except for the tall man in the black trench coat. Using his shotgun like a cane, he strolled forward, toward us, until he was only several feet in front of us. Eddie held the pistol in his lap. Kevin had grabbed his, and he let it hang at his side, concealed from the surrounding hoard.

The man in the trench coat raised the shotgun . . . and pointed it at the windshield of the van.

72

The gun remained trained at our windshield, and I realized then that if the man fired, we would be as good as dead. The pellets from the shot shell, combined with the shards of flying glass, might not kill all of us at once . . . but I was willing to bet if that's what the man intended to do, he wouldn't hesitate.

"Get out," the man ordered. "Slow."

"Sierra and Tracie," Eddie whispered, *"you two stay here."*

The driver's side and the passenger side doors opened simultaneously. Eddie and Kevin slowly slipped out. Both carried their weapons.

The man in front of the van lowered his shotgun, but others in the group trained their guns on Eddie and Kevin. I looked behind us, and saw a couple of people with their guns aimed at Tracie and me.

"You people are a little ways from home, I imagine," the man sneered.

"Not far," Eddie said. "We don't want any trouble."

The man glared at him. A grin spread on his face, widening, more, until he started laughing.

"Trouble?!?!" he exclaimed. "Trouble?!?! We're all in trouble. Every one of us. It's just a matter of what degree of trouble we're in. Us? Well, we ain't doin' too bad. Now, *you—*"

He raised the shotgun and pointed it at Eddie's head.

"—you people are in a little more trouble than we are."

"What do you want?" Kevin said.

The man quickly swung the gun barrel, and now it was pointed at Kevin, who flinched and began to raise his pistol. He stopped when several others in the group took steps forward, their guns aimed at him.

"I wouldn't think about doing that, if I were you," the man snarled. "Now . . . what *we* want doesn't really matter right now. It's what *you* want. Why are you here?"

"We're just passing through," Eddie replied. "Like I said, we don't want any trouble."

"Suppose'n we don't let you through?" the man said. He'd lowered his shotgun, but the others around the van still had their guns aimed at us.

Kevin and Eddie didn't respond.

The man cocked his head and looked at us. Nodded toward the van. "Who ya got in there?" he asked.

"My sister and her friend," Eddie replied.

"How old are they?" the man asked.

"None of your business," Eddie snapped.

The man in the trench coat laughed, then he looked directly at Eddie. "I could *make* it my business," he said.

Nothing was said for a few very tense seconds. Then the man spoke again.

"Get 'em out," he ordered.

Suddenly, the sliding side door opened. Tracie jumped and grabbed my hand. We crawled back.

At the door stood a woman in her twenties. She looked like she had once been attractive, with high cheekbones and a strong chin. Her skin was sun-weathered and dry, however, and her blonde hair was stringy and windblown. She wore black denim pants and a white T-shirt that was damp with rain, and her dark nipples were clearly visible through the wet fabric.

"You heard me," the man said, speaking to Tracie and me. "I said *out.*"

Slowly, Tracie and I climbed out of the van and into the drizzle, which had now slowed to a fine mist. We walked up behind Eddie and stopped.

The man motioned for Kevin to join us. "You two put your guns down on the ground. Now."

Eddie and Kevin, without any other choice, did as they were ordered. It would have been senseless to try and fight, anyway. There were too many of them. If Kevin and Eddie had tried to shoot their way out of this, we'd all wind up dead.

But we might wind up dead, anyway, I thought. *These people don't look like they're here to throw us a Welcome-to-Chelsea party.*

The guns lay on rain-glistened pavement in front of Eddie and Kevin. A kid who couldn't have been more than ten years old scurried up like a rat, snatched both guns, and scampered off.

"Whaddya got in the van?" the man asked.

"Our supplies," Eddie said. "Look. I told you. We don't want any trouble. We just want to be on our way."

"Oh, we might just let you be on your way," the man said. "But there is a price to be paid." He looked at Tracie and me, and I cringed. His eyes were cold and menacing. Wolf-like.

"You might say," he said, looking at Tracie and me, "you might say that we'll make ourselves a little trade."

73

A dagger of fear splintered down my spine. My skin crawled. Tracie was holding my hand, and now she squeezed it so tightly that it hurt. Somewhere, a crow cawed.

"Get over on the sidewalk," the man ordered us with a sweep of his shotgun. We backed over the curb, across a thin strip of long, un-mowed, wet grass, and onto the walk.

"We're taking everything in your van," the man said. "Then you can be on your way."

The hopeful optimism we'd felt only an hour or so ago was gone. Instead, that familiar despair settled in once again. True, they could have just killed us on the spot. They didn't need us, but they wanted our supplies. But if they let us go with the van, well, that was one thing to be happy about.

And, although the man looked at Tracie and me like we were freshly-cut meat, he didn't threaten anything more.

While we stood on the sidewalk, several people went to our van. They began pulling out our hard-earned supplies . . . supplies Kevin and Eddie had hunted for over the past few weeks. We could only watch as they took our cooler filled with bottled water, our boxes of canned food, our clothing—everything. They piled it up alongside the van. A girl pulled out the shotgun, rifle, and ammo that was on the floor, but the man wearing the trench coat stopped him.

"Leave them," he ordered. "We have enough weapons. They're going to need those, anyway." He turned and looked at us. "Bonus, huh?" he snickered.

When they had stripped our van of our supplies, he looked at us. His face beheld a question, and he looked genuinely confused.

"Tell me," he said. "Just where do you think you're going to go?"

Eddie shook his head. "North," he replied. "Somewhere safe."

The man snorted, and placed his gun over his shoulder. "Kid, don't fool yourself. No matter what you do, no matter where you go . . . you'll never be safe again." He nodded toward the van. "Go. Get out of here. And if we see you again—you might not be so lucky."

The four of us climbed back into the van. I slid the side door closed. Kevin fumbled with the exposed ignition wires. The engine spluttered, turned over a few times, then roared to life.

The man gestured to a few people who were still standing in the street, in front of the van. "Let 'em pass," he ordered. The mob in the street thinned. Kevin dropped the van into gear, and we slowly pulled away.

74

"Turn here," Eddie said. "On Werkner."

Kevin slowed, and made a right turn onto a gravel road. Tires crunched, but the sound was drowned out by the muffler-less van.

We'd been traveling for about twenty minutes, following the main highway north out of Chelsea. Eddie and Kevin had discussed the situation we'd found ourselves in, cursing the fact that we now had no food, water, fresh clothing—nothing. No soap, no toilet paper. We had the shotgun, rifle, handgun, and lots of ammunition, which was good. Other than that: nothing. All our weeks of preparation and work had been for nothing.

"I guess it could have been worse," Kevin said. "If we didn't have any supplies at all, they might have done something a little more drastic."

I shuddered. When he put it that way, perhaps we

weren't in as dire straits as we thought we were. We had guns, ammo, our van . . . and our lives. That wasn't all bad, considering the shape of the world. When you compared it to that, we were rich.

Eddie was holding the atlas in his lap. "This road should allow us to connect with a bunch of other roads that will still take us north, without going through any cities."

Tracie hadn't said a word in a long time. She was seated cross-legged on the floor of the van, behind Eddie. Her eyes were glossy, and I reached over and placed my hand on her leg. "You okay?" I asked quietly.

She nodded. Sniffled. "Yeah."

"Things are going to get better," I said.

"Of course they will," she said, looking away. She stared straight ahead, and a single tear tumbled, streaking her cheek. "How can things get any worse?"

75

The van bumped along the gravel road. Wildlife began to appear more frequently. We saw several deer, a couple of raccoons, a porcupine, and a half-dozen rabbits—one of which almost fell victim to the van. We saw an occasional dog, usually mangy and wild-eyed. We didn't see any that looked like they'd be friendly.

We followed the back roads, turning left or right, depending on Eddie's orders. Occasionally, we passed large farms and homes, and I wondered if there were people inside, watching, wondering who was passing by in the van. Wondering if trouble was coming.

"How's our gas?" Eddie asked.

"Just under three quarters of a tank," Kevin replied. "This thing doesn't get very good gas mileage, but the tank is big. And we're not going very fast, so we're not burning up a lot of fuel."

"See?" Eddie said, turning to look at Tracie and me. "More good news."

"How long do you think it'll take us to get to the lodge?" Tracie asked.

"Probably late tonight," Kevin replied. "Taking these back roads is going to make the trip a lot longer."

I managed to smile, and so did Tracie. She reached up and touched Eddie's arm. He lowered his hand, and took hers in it. That seemed like a good idea, and Kevin must've been thinking the same thing, because his right arm dropped, and I took his hand.

And we traveled on.

76

The skies cleared, and the sun came out. We'd been bouncing around back roads, through forests and farmland for most of the afternoon. There weren't many abandoned cars, and we hadn't seen any dead bodies in over an hour.

"Hey, hey," Kevin said, leaning forward in his seat. "What's that up ahead?"

We peered out the windshield.

"Looks like a store," Tracie said.

"Some sort of little convenience store, way out here," Eddie said.

It was. The store was small and rural-looking, not at all like the big mega-convenience marts that dotted the freeways of Michigan. It was nestled beneath a cluster of maples and oaks, completely engulfed in shade. Despite its run-down appearance, it looked homey, friendly. I could almost see small children riding their bikes to this place, going inside, and coming out with ice cream or candy. On a normal summer evening, maybe a couple of old men would be seated at a bench, talking, swapping fishing stories.

But that would be a *normal* summer day. This little country store would never be seeing days like those again.

Kevin slowed the vehicle and pulled into the gravel parking lot. We looked all around for signs of danger: people, dogs, whatever. We didn't see anything.

Kevin disconnected the ignition wires and the motor died. The ensuing silence was welcome: I hadn't realized how loud the van was without the muffler. Now, as we exited the vehicle to the sounds of birds and day crickets, it was a nice, peaceful change.

"Feels good to stretch out," Tracie said, raising her arms in the sky and arching her back.

Eddie stepped into the back of the van and retrieved the shotgun. He rested it on his shoulder as he scrambled back out, joining Kevin at the front of the van.

We stood in the sunlight, staring at the dilapidated store. The front windows were smashed. Two gas pumps had been knocked over, and their metal shells were dented, crumpled and rusting like giant tin cans. There was a flashing arrow sign (unlit, of course) with plastic letters that read: *OLD BEER - WINE- I UOR.*

"Old beer," Kevin quipped. "Sounds yummy."

The front door had been pane glass, but it had been shattered. The only thing left was the sturdy metal frame.

"It's probably pretty picked over," Eddie said. "But we might as well see what we can find."

The four of us walked to what was left of the front door. Eddie pulled it open cautiously, holding the shotgun to his shoulder with one arm. His eyes scanned the room quickly as he took a step inside. While it was doubtful we would find anyone around, we'd learned precautions had to be taken—always.

A sign on the wall behind a smashed counter read: *Sorry, no public restrooms.* Next to that sign was a picture of a small girl, wide-eyed, holding a Starbucks coffee cup. The caption beneath, in capital letters, read *UNATTENDED CHILDREN WILL BE GIVEN AN ESPRESSO AND A FREE PUPPY.*

"All clear," Eddie said as he took another step inside. Kevin was next, followed by me, then Tracie.

The place was a wreck, but we'd grown accustomed to such scenes. Actually, we would have been surprised to find anything in proper order.

However, as we looked around the room, our hope grew. There were lots of things the looters had left. Sure, they'd probably taken the most necessary items: food and water. But there were other things scattered about that would prove useful: sealed rolls of paper towels, toilet paper, tampons, a pocket knife, and numerous items such as toothpaste, toothbrushes, deodorant, soap, shampoo, and bottles of multivitamins. Little things became big things really quick in our brave new world. There were even a few T-shirts we'd be able to wear. They were all the same color: red, with a screen-printed picture of a small log cabin surrounded by trees. Beneath the cabin, printed in letters made to look like logs, was *Island Lake General Store, Island Lake, MI.* We'd look like quadruplets in some campy 70s movie, for sure.

"Cool beans!" Kevin exclaimed. "Let's get this stuff

into the van."

"Yeah," I said. "We might starve, but at least we'll have clean teeth. And we won't smell bad."

Eddie had gone into a back room. "We're not going to starve," he called out. "There's some canned food back here." He appeared in the doorway holding a can of Hormel chili. The can was dented, but it was intact.

"With our luck, we won't be able to find a can opener," Tracie said as she picked up a couple of rolls of paper towels.

I smiled, and Tracie saw me. She grinned back. "I told you things would get better," I said.

Tracie just kept grinning, picked up a small can of Right Guard, and carried her items to the van.

77

We finished packing all the supplies we'd found at the store. Actually, there had been far more things than we'd originally thought. In addition to the toiletry and hygiene items, we'd found nearly a dozen cans of chili, along with some canned vegetables. And a can opener. There was also a single bottle of water Tracie had uncovered beneath a tipped shelf. We shared it sparingly. Kevin found some large pieces of clear plastic wrap and a roll of duct tape, and he and Eddie had covered the exposed back windows of the van that had been shot out. As we'd traveled, exhaust was rising and backing up into the van, and it reeked. Hopefully, the plastic would provide a good seal.

"Just think," Eddie said as he'd carried the chili into the van. "When we get to the lodge we can build a fire and have our first hot meal in almost two months."

That alone made my spirits soar. Hope was

returning, in the form of a fire and a dented can of Hormel chili. Like I said: it's the little things.

For a change, I was sitting in the passenger seat. Eddie and Tracie sat behind me on the floor. The van was about half-full with things we'd pilfered from the store. We'd even found some blankets, still folded and wrapped in plastic, with price tags on them. They'd come in handy, for sure. Evidently, whoever had originally looted the store was much more concerned with food and water . . . which was fortunate for us.

"How about this," Kevin said as he glanced at me. "How about we travel for a little while, then find a place to spend the night? It's going to get dark soon. Even though we have a map, we don't know these back roads very well. I don't want to take a chance of getting lost."

Kevin had a good point. While we really wanted to get to Otter Lake as soon as possible, it wouldn't be smart to take unfamiliar back roads after dark. Many of the roads were unmarked, and we didn't want to take a wrong turn and wind up driving around, wasting gas.

"Fine with me," Tracie said. I nodded, and Eddie unfolded a local map he'd found beneath the counter of the general store. It was a county map, and it was very detailed, showing lakes, rivers, back roads, two-tracks and the like—things the larger atlas didn't show.

"We're right here," he said, placing his finger on the map. "If we continue following Island Lake Road, it'll take us up to Island Lake. It looks like it's a big recreation area. There might be a camping area there . . . or, better yet, cabins."

"Just like summer camp," I said. "We can all wear

our matching shirts."

"Yeah," Kevin said. "We'll break out the marshmallows and weenies and sing 'Kumbaya' into the wee hours of the night."

I laughed, leaned over, and gave him a kiss on the cheek. Once again, things were looking up for us— at least for the time being.

78

Our drive to Island Lake was smooth. There were a few trees down, and Kevin had to slow the van and go around them. We encountered a few abandoned cars and trucks, but we saw no one. I began to wonder if people had left to find someplace safer, or if they had all died.

"I'm glad we're out of the city," Tracie said.

"Me, too," I replied.

"Left, here," Eddie said, looking up from the map. Kevin eased off the gas and the van slowed, turning onto a gravel road. A sign that was nearly falling over read *Island Lake Pt. Rd.*

Gravel crunched beneath the wheels. We were now headed south, but, if Eddie's map was correct, this road only went about a mile before it dead-ended.

To the right of us, Island Lake appeared. The sun was setting, and honey-lemon rays glistened on the gently rippling water. A flock of ducks, perhaps seven or eight, flew low above the lake. It was odd that most birds in America hadn't been infected with the bird flu, but like the guy on the radio had said: the mutated H5N1 virus that passed from human to human had no effect on birds, or any other animals. It was a deadly strain all its own.

"You're right, Sierra," Eddie said. "This is going to be like camp."

"Keep going?" Kevin asked.

Eddie glanced down at the map. "Yeah," he replied. "This road should end at a picnic or camping area. It's not clear on the map. But keep your eye out for cabins."

We didn't see any cabins, but Eddie was right: the road ended abruptly at a small, rustic camping area, complete with fire pits. Quite obviously, no one had been there in a long time. Weeds had taken over, giving the area a bleak, desolate look.

Kevin stopped the van. The sun was dipping behind the trees on the other side of the lake, and the western sky burned orange and rust. It would be dark soon.

Eddie picked up the shotgun. "You guys stay here," he said. "I'll go check things out."

He slid the van door back, and a fresh, woodsy smell washed over us. It was a clean smell, awash with gummy pine and cedar, and the airy-fresh aroma of wild flowers. Much better than the stale air we had to breathe in post-flu Saline. I hadn't realized how polluted the air in our city had become. The constant fires, the smell of noxious fumes had become incessant. And driving the van with the broken windows had filled the vehicle with grimy, thick exhaust. Thankfully, the plastic sheeting over the back windows had done the trick.

Now, with the windows down and the side door open, we were breathing fresh, clear air. I wanted to take huge gulps, savoring the wonderful, woodsy sweetness.

"We don't have any tents, but we can sleep in the van if we have to," Kevin said. "It'll be cramped, but at least we'll be out of the weather."

"And away from dogs," Tracie said.

Eddie circled all the way around the van, carrying the shotgun. He found a trail and followed it, looking cautiously to the left and right. He continued warily, until we could no longer see him through the knotted limbs.

"I can't wait to have a hot meal, even if it's only chili," I said. "We haven't had a hot meal since we ate macaroni and cheese at our house."

"Yeah," Tracie agreed. "Chili and french-cut green beans are going to be a gourmet dish."

"There's nobody around," Kevin said. "Come on." He opened the van door and slipped outside. "Let's stretch out a little."

I opened the door and got out. Tracie scrambled from the side of the van, and the three of us walked down to the lake. Above, an osprey soared, searching for its final meal of the day. Crickets chimed in unison, and unseen frogs bleated from their hiding places along the shore. To the south, a small island was visible. Island Lake wasn't very big, but it sure was a beautiful, peaceful place.

I sat in the sand, kicked off my sneakers, and pulled my socks off. Then I stood and waded into the water. It was surprisingly warm, and I began to plan a bath. To shower in a warm rain was one thing, but to be totally immersed, soaking in water would be a joy beyond comprehension.

Kevin and Tracie stood at the water's edge, admiring the beauty of our new surroundings.

"Sure is a pretty place," Kevin said.

Tracie turned her head. "There's certainly nobody around, that's for—"

Tracie's voice was abruptly halted by the sharp report of a gun blast.

79

"Tracie! Sierra!" Kevin barked. *"Back to the van!"*

I sprang from the shallows, snapped up my shoes, and ran barefoot back to the vehicle. Kevin had leapt through the side door and began rummaging around for the Winchester 30-30. Tracie dove into the vehicle, and I threw open the passenger door and leapt inside.

"Stay here!" Kevin ordered after he'd found the rifle. *"Lock the doors!"*

Which wouldn't do much good with the back windows of the van shot out, but I think Kevin had forgotten about that.

He leapt from the van and slid the door shut. I hit the automatic lock button on the passenger door, and there was a loud *ka-clack* as the doors were secured.

Kevin took off running, following Eddie's path, carrying the rifle like an infantryman. Just before he was out of sight, he stopped. Then he lowered the rifle and walked forward, vanishing in the trees.

"What do you think is going on?" Tracie asked nervously.

"I don't know," I replied. "But not much would surprise me."

But, in the end, I had to admit . . . I was surprised by what had happened.

30

Eddie and Kevin soon appeared, side by side, on the trail. Both were carrying their guns over their shoulders.

Eddie, however, was carrying something else in his other hand.

Tracie leaned forward in the van, crawling up near the console. "What on earth is *that?"* she asked.

I didn't answer. Instead, we both remained silent, watching the pair approach until we suddenly, simultaneously realized what Eddie was carrying.

"It's a rabbit," Tracie and I said in unison.

"He shot a *rabbit?"* Tracie asked.

"My brother the mighty hunter," I replied.

"He shot a rabbit?" Tracie repeated. "What for?"

I shrugged. "To eat, probably," I replied. "He and Dad go—used to go—hunting rabbits all the time. In the fall, of course. During rabbit season."

"He eats . . . *rabbits?"* she asked incredulously. It was apparent this was some new and vile idea—in Tracie's mind, at least. "Have . . . have *you* eaten them before?"

"Yeah," I replied with a shrug. "They're pretty good, but you've got to cook them right. Their meat is really tough unless you cook them for a long time."

"You eat *rabbits?"* Tracie again said.

"Come on, Trace," I said. "It's a rabbit. They're good eating." I unlocked the van doors and got out. Kevin and Eddie heard the door close behind me and looked up. I walked toward them.

Eddie held up the rabbit. "Guess what's for dinner?" he asked, displaying a proud grin. "This oughtta add some chunk to our chili."

31

Although there weren't any camping cabins, Eddie had found a small ranger station that was just out of sight of the parked van. The building was rustic, built of wood and painted dark green. It had a tiny office with a counter, but there was an attached living area that had a couch, a kitchen area, and, off to the side through a short hallway, a small bedroom with a dresser and a double bed. Although there wasn't much in the amenity department, the place hadn't been ransacked, and would make a nice, comfortable place to spend the night. Apparently, no one was occupying the station when the pandemic hit. There were no food supplies whatsoever, but no sign of damage or forced entry. Even the windows were unbroken . . . a sure sign looters had overlooked this place . . . or hadn't arrived, yet.

"It's probably just far enough out of the way that nobody found it," Kevin said. "Most looters would have picked easier targets."

And in the bedroom, above the small dresser, was a mirror. Sure, we had one in the van, but this mirror was bigger, and for the first time since we'd set out earlier in the day, I was able to get a look at myself.

Oh, God, I thought. *I look like some of the looters we've seen on the street.* My hair was messy. It was getting longer, as I hadn't cut it since before my birthday. Now it hung over my shoulders to my chest. My green T-shirt wasn't dirty, but it was far too big to fit properly. There was a faint grease stain on my forehead, and I had no idea how it got there. I wiped it away with my palm. It would be good to finally clean up with warm water.

One thing we discovered behind the ranger station, to our great delight, was an outhouse—complete with a cement floor and a porcelain flush toilet. On the outside wall, someone had ingeniously rigged up a fifty-gallon drum several feet off the ground with a pipe on the bottom that led to the toilet's holding tank. When we found it, the drum was filled with rain water. Eddie went into the small bathroom and flushed the toilet, and it worked perfectly.

The little things.

32

Eddie cleaned and prepared the rabbit, while Kevin, Tracie, and I unloaded supplies from the van and hauled them to the ranger station. It was getting dark quickly.

"Sierra," Kevin said, "you and Tracie build a fire in the fire pit over there. I'll go scrounge up some more wood before it gets too dark to see."

There was a pile of tinder stacked near a tree—thin, dried branches, all about two feet long—and Tracie and I grabbed handfuls of it and placed it into the fire pit, which was only several yards from the cabin.

"So, how's it going with you and Eddie?" I asked.

Tracie shrugged. "Hey, you know as much as I do," she said. "The four of us have been together twenty-four hours a day. I feel like I'm living in a sitcom."

"I know what you mean," I said. "Maybe you'll have a chance to be alone with him while we're here."

"I hope so," Tracie said.

I lit the pile of tinder with one of the wooden matches I found in the small kitchen. The flames quickly grew, licking and twisting. Tendrils of smoke curled and rose. Kevin had found a large pile of chopped wood at another campsite, and he hauled over several arm loads and stacked them near the ranger station. When the pile of thin sticks in the fire pit was completely engulfed in flames, he placed three logs on. We stood in the flickering light, bathing in the warmth of the fire. Once again, this was something we hadn't experienced in quite a while. Not just a fire, but heat, in general, other than the sun. Although the evening was warm—hot, actually, as we were all sweating—we couldn't tear ourselves away from the magic of the fire.

The wood-framed screen door whisked open and smacked closed, and Eddie joined us by the fire, holding the skinned, headless rabbit. It was pink and red, with white strands of tendons and ligaments exposed. I'd seen skinned game before, but Tracie looked away. I thought she was going to throw up, but she didn't.

"Hey, Sierra, go get the grill," Eddie said. "It's leaning against the wall in the kitchen."

I went into the kitchen, which was now dimly lit by a single, flickering candle we'd found in the dresser drawer. Eddie had opened three cans of chili and two cans of green beans, leaving the contents in the cans on the counter. The large grill, which looked more like a grate, was leaning against the wall. It was banged up and a little bent, but it would work fine. I picked it up, carried it outside, and handed it to Eddie. He dropped it over the fire pit. Then he placed the skinned rabbit on the grill, off to the side, away from the flames so it wouldn't burn.

"We'll let him cook a little while," he said. "The chili and the beans will cook fast, so we'll just wait a while on those."

"Great," Tracie said. "I'm going to go for a swim and get cleaned up." Tracie looked at me, and I could see the firelight reflecting in her glassy, dark eyes. "You wanna?"

"You bet," I replied, and we walked into the small ranger station. I picked up the candle and walked into the small bedroom. Then I placed the candle on the dresser and unzipped my jeans.

"And where will *you* be sleeping tonight," I asked as I pulled my shirt over my head.

Tracie was slipping out of her clothing.

"Don't get any ideas," she said. "It's not that way."

"It's not that way for Kevin and me, either," I said. "But I like being next to him. I feel safe. Warm."

We didn't have any towels, but the blankets we'd taken from the general store would work just fine. After we'd stripped, we each wrapped a blanket around ourselves. Tracie pulled out a bottle of shampoo from a box where they'd been stored. Then I picked up the candle, and we walked outside.

Eddie and Kevin had found a couple of large logs. They'd dragged them close to the fire and were now sitting down. Eddie was poking the slow-roasting rabbit with a stick.

Tracie and I walked the short distance to the water's edge. The sand was still warm from basking in the sun all day. I set the candle down, then we dropped the blankets onto the ground and stepped into the water.

"Ooh, it's kinda warm," Tracie said. "It feels great."

"This is gonna be awesome," I replied. I wanted to dive in, to leap into the water and be suddenly, wholly immersed. But, I was a little nervous. I'd never been swimming at night before, and I was wary. If I dove in and hit a submerged stump or log, I could really be hurt. Last year, a kid at school had done that. He'd broken his neck and died.

We waded slowly into deeper water. An almost full moon and a clear sky provided enough light to see, and the silvery-reflection danced upon the dark waters. Tracie carried the bottle of shampoo we'd taken from the general store.

When the water was up over my breasts, I slipped beneath the surface, totally submerged. It was beyond fantastic, even better than I'd imagined. I wanted to hold my breath forever, to let the fresh water wash against my skin for all of eternity. Beneath the waves, the bird flu pandemic was gone. The looters were gone, the vandalism, the senseless rioting and killing. Beneath the surface was like a new world.

After a few seconds, I stood up, breaking the surface. The water was up to my neck, and my wet hair clung to my face. Tracie popped up next to me.

"Oh, God!" she cried. "This is awesome! I never thought water could ever feel so good!"

She popped the lid of the shampoo bottle, poured a small amount into her palm, and handed the bottle to me. After squeezing out a small dab, I closed the lid and tossed the bottle to shore.

As I scrubbed the lathering shampoo into my hair, I looked at Eddie and Kevin in the distance, seated by the fire not far from the small ranger station. Kevin laughed, and it echoed across the lake. Eddie got up and adjusted the rabbit on the grill, then he sat back down again.

There was a question I had been dying to ask Tracie for a long time. Even from before this whole bird flu thing. I almost asked her a couple of weeks ago, but I didn't think it was quite the right time.

"Trace, have you ever . . . ."

I paused, wanting to choose my words carefully. It would be really tacky to come right out and say something like: *Tracie, have you ever had sex before?* I mean, I'm sure some people might put it that way. But not me. And I certainly wouldn't put it that way to *Tracie.*

"Have I ever what?" she asked. "Hold on . . . rinse time." The silhouette of her head vanished beneath the inky surface, only to reappear a moment later.

"Now," she said as she pulled wet hair from her face. "Have I ever what?"

"You know," I said, feeling a bit sheepish, and maybe a little silly.

"Have I ever . . . ." her voice trailed off, and I knew she knew what I meant.

"Yeah," I said. "You know."

"First, I have two questions for you. One: have you? And two: why do you want to know?"

"Okay," I replied. "That's fair. No. No, I haven't. And why do I want to know? I . . . I don't know. I was . . . I was just curious, I guess."

"You're curious because of what you've heard about me and David."

Caught. She was right. I *had* heard. But I'd never

asked about it. She'd only gone out with David once, just a couple of weeks before the bird flu hit.

"Here's the truth," she said. "No, I haven't. Ever. Not with David, despite what you heard."

"But—"

"I know what you *heard,* Sierra. Here's what happened. David and I went out. Once. He wanted to—you know—run the bases, if that's the right term for it. I didn't. Nothing happened."

"But that's—"

"Let me finish. Because I *didn't,* he made up some story for his pals, saying I *did."*

"No!"

"Yes," Tracie said.

"Hold that for a sec," I said, and it was my turn to slink beneath the surface and rinse the shampoo from my hair. I stood back up, opened my eyes, and pulled the hair out of my face. "Okay," I said. "Did you say anything to him about it?"

"Sort of," she said. "He was in the lunch line with his friends. They were all looking at me. I could feel it. By then, I'd heard what he'd said, but I hadn't had a chance to talk to him. I called him at home once, but he wasn't there, and he never returned my call."

"So, whadja do?" I asked. We began wading back to shore.

"I walked right up to him in the lunch line, gave him a kiss on the cheek, and told him—loudly, so everyone could hear—that he was great. But then I went on to say that it was too bad that a particular part of his anatomy didn't measure up. I mean, those weren't my *exact* words. I was much more blunt about it, if you know what I mean."

I gasped, and thought I was going to choke. "You *didn't!*" I exclaimed.

"I *did!*" Tracie said. "He turned nine shades of red. Left the lunch line, in fact. Haven't heard or spoken to him since."

We reached the shore, found our blankets, and patted ourselves dry in the faint glow of the candle.

"But, then, people still think you and he—"

"Sierra, people are going to think what they want to think, whether it's the truth or not. You can't change it. People believe what they want to believe. Your friends—the ones you know and trust—will know better."

"I didn't mean to pry," I said. "I was just curious, that's all."

"I know, and you weren't prying," Tracie said. "Come on. I'm hungry, but I still don't think I have the stomach for a dead rabbit."

33

We changed into the same jeans we had on before our swim, but we both put on the red T-shirts we'd taken from the Island Lake General Store. Then we joined Eddie and Kevin at the fire.

"You're going to feel like a million bucks," I told Eddie. "The lake is really warm. How's dinner coming?"

"Good," Eddie said. "The rabbit will be ready in about half an hour."

While Tracie wasn't all that thrilled at the prospect of eating rabbit meat for dinner, we convinced her she wouldn't be able to tell what kind of meat it was.

"It'll be a little tough," Eddie said. "But mixed in with the chili, you'll never know. It'll taste just like chicken."

"I've heard *that* before," Tracie said, rolling her eyes.

Kevin and Eddie left to take a dip and wash in the lake, and Tracie and I prepared the chili and beans. It was pretty simple, really: all we did was pour the chili and the beans into separate pots and place them on the grill. Meals don't get much simpler than that, unless you're ordering at a drive-thru window.

The fire had burned down into a pile of orange embers, and it wouldn't be long before the food was ready. My mouth watered every time I got a whiff of the chili. And the rabbit didn't smell too bad, either. Dad and Eddie used to cook rabbits at our house, along with other animals they'd shot. Dad was a great chef, and every wild game dinner he prepared was delicious. Mom was a bit squeamish when it came to handling the dead animals—especially rabbits, because they looked like they could have been cats after they were skinned—but she didn't have a problem eating them after they were all dressed out and cooked.

Tracie, for her part, had a hard time looking at the well-browned rabbit that slowly cooked at the edge of the grill. Oddly, she seemed drawn to it, curious-like, but then hastily looked away, repulsed by the sight of the freshly-killed animal.

"Do you ever think about your parents?" she asked, snatching the topic from God-knows-where.

"All the time," I said.

"I think about Mom," Tracie said. "Jesus, Sierra. Why does everything have to be so final? What happened to 'Mommy can fix anything?' No matter what, I always knew my mom could make things better. No matter what. Used to be that problems seemed to just go away. Now, they just keep coming at us. We're alone. We're completely alone."

"I'm here," I said. "So's Eddie. And Kevin. You're not completely alone."

"I know, I know," Tracie said. "It just feels like it, though. Us against the world."

Kevin and Eddie emerged from the shadows of the lake with blankets wrapped around them, their faces and hair shiny and wet. They went into the ranger station to change.

"We're doing better already," I said. "It's safer here, out of the city. We have food, water, and a toilet that works! I never thought we'd see another one of those. I've been on worse camping trips. And in the morning, we'll head to Kevin's uncle's lodge at Otter Lake. I'll bet things will be a lot better up north."

I stirred the chili in the pot, and Tracie stirred the green beans.

Suddenly, we heard a rifle shot. It was far away, but there was no mistaking it. We'd heard enough of those in the past two months.

Perhaps we weren't as alone as we'd thought.

34

Kevin and Eddie came out of the ranger station a moment later, both wearing their red Island Lake General Store T-shirts.

"We heard a gunshot," I said.

"We heard," Kevin replied, glancing up into the night sky. "Sounded like it was a long ways away, though."

"Chili and beans are ready," Tracie said.

Eddie sat on the log and poked the cooked rabbit with a stick. "Easter bunny's done," he said, and Tracie winced and looked away. Eddie laughed. "Just kidding," he said.

"I think I'll use the facilities," Tracie said, getting to her feet.

While she was gone, Eddie used the pocket knife he'd found at the store to cut small pieces of meat from the rabbit. He dropped them into the chili, stirred, then cut more meat. When the entire rabbit was stripped of its flesh, he pushed the tattered carcass off the grill.

"Bowls," I said, and I got up and went into the ranger station. In a kitchen cabinet I found a half dozen plates, but no bowls. They would have to do. Most were well-used and beat up, but they'd work fine. There were also knives, forks, and spoons in a drawer. I snapped up a few and took them down to the lake to rinse them off. When I returned to the fire, Tracie had returned and was sitting on the log next to Eddie and Kevin.

I laughed out loud, and they looked at me.

"What?" Kevin asked. "What's so funny?"

"With our shirts on, we look like a bunch of camp counselors," I said, still chuckling. "We look like we're gathered for the evening meal."

I passed plates out, along with silverware. I forgot to grab napkins, but it was too late. I was too hungry, and so were Kevin, Eddie, and Tracie. We started eating as soon as Eddie began dishing out the chili, which was actually pretty chunky with the rabbit meat mixed in. It was thick, and the fact that we didn't have bowls wasn't going to be a problem at all. In fact, there was so much meat in the chili that we used forks instead of spoons.

And the chili/rabbit concoction was tremendous! Perhaps it was partly because it had been so long since I'd had a hot meal, but at the time, it didn't matter. The chili was spicy, chunky, hot, and good. The rabbit meat was a bit chewy, but it really was quite tasty. Even Tracie, who was a bit hesitant at first, began gulping down her meal.

"Hey, hey, save room for green beans," Kevin said.

"Screw the beans," Eddie said. "This chili's great!"

We served ourselves 2nd and 3rd portions. Even after the chili/rabbit was gone, we were still hungry enough to divide up the green beans. We washed everything down with lake water, which, to my surprise, tasted good. I'd always heard you shouldn't drink water from lakes and streams, since you didn't know what was in it. We could've boiled the water to purify it, but we hadn't thought about it, and now, none of us wanted to take the time to boil it and wait for it to cool down.

Besides . . . we had no other choice. The looters in Chelsea had taken all of our bottled water. As my mom used to say: beggars can't be choosy.

The fire had burned to a red, glowing carpet of ashes and chunks of burned wood. The four of us, still seated around the fire, hadn't said anything for a few minutes. I think we were so stuffed from a satisfying, hot meal that we all took a little bit of time to let the experience sink in. I felt more full than I had in a long time, and it felt good. I'd noticed in the mirror earlier that my cheeks had sunken a little bit, and I assumed it was because I'd lost a couple of pounds. We all had, as a matter of fact. Eddie, who was never really 'chunky' had once had a little roll to his belly. I noticed in the past few weeks that his stomach muscles now showed, and there was no trace of fat on him anywhere. Kevin, too, looked leaner and more muscular. Tracie, for her part, looked pretty much the same, but she's always been thin, anyway.

"I'm calling it a night," I said, and I stood up.

"I'm kind of tired, too," Kevin said. He stood, slipped his arm around me, and I did the same. We walked into the ranger station and into the dark bedroom. There, we lay on the bed, his arm around me, my nose nestled against the side of his chest, my hand resting on his stomach.

I giggled.

"What?" he asked sleepily.

"Our camp shirts," I replied. "We look silly."

Kevin giggled. "Yeah, we do," he said. He shifted and kissed my forehead.

And then we were asleep.

35

In the morning, I was awakened by warm sunshine streaming through a window, caressing my face. Kevin was gone. The air in the room was fresh and clear, and I couldn't help but smile when I looked down and saw the silly red T-shirt I was still wearing.

Camp counselors, I thought.

The past few months in Saline suddenly seemed a thousand years ago. We'd only begun our journey the day before, but it seemed like a week had passed. So much was happening, moment by moment, that it was hard to look back and put things in chronological order. But, while we might not know what would happen from day to day, we were surviving. We'd made it this far, out of the city. We were safer here.

I swung my legs to the side of the bed, stood, stretched, and yawned. Then I walked into the small living room.

Eddie and Tracie were sleeping on the fold-out couch. They, too, still wore their red T-shirts. I smiled and shook my head. I guess I'd never imagined Eddie and Tracie getting together, but, now that I thought about it, they *did* make a good pair.

The wooden screen door whisked open, startling me. Kevin appeared, and his face was a mixture of concern and confusion.

"What?" I asked. "What is it?"

He nodded, motioning me outside. I followed, and I closed the screen door slowly, silently, so as not to wake Eddie and Tracie.

"What?" I whispered. *"What's wrong?"*

Kevin pointed down to the ground. *"Those aren't ours,"* he said.

I didn't know what he meant—at first. Then, I knelt down and saw exactly what he was talking about.

There. In the soft earth.

Footprints.

36

Ten minutes later, after Eddie and Tracie had awoken, we were standing outside. Kevin explained how he'd spotted the footprints on his way to the outhouse.

"Well, *somebody* was here last night, that's obvious," Eddie said. "Question is: who?"

"And why?" I added.

We stood in the morning sun, staring down at the footprints. We'd followed them all around the ranger station, where they stopped beneath the bedroom window. Then, they wound around to our van, down to the lake, and back up to the campfire before vanishing down the trail. We checked the van, but nothing was missing. Nor had they entered the ranger station, as Eddie had latched the screen door, locking it, when he and Tracie had come in from the fire.

"Whoever they were, they must not have needed

anything very badly," Kevin said. "Nothing *we* have, anyway."

We looked around the woods, peering suspiciously into the thick limbs and branches. I wondered if, perhaps, someone was watching us right now. I wondered how they'd known we were here, and if they had been watching us last night, around the campfire. Perhaps they were near the lake when Tracie and I went swimming. Maybe someone was huddled in the brush, not far from where we were, watching us at that very moment.

If so, what did they want? They didn't take anything last night. Were they just curious, checking to see who was staying in the ranger station? We hadn't a clue. Maybe they were just like us, trying to survive in a world gone mad. Wondering who the new kids were at the ranger station. I didn't like the fact that someone had spied on us, in the dark. That really bothered me. Sure, no harm seemed to be done, but I just had a weird feeling. In the girls' high school locker room, there were windows that were beveled and wavy, and you couldn't see in or out. However, a small rock had broken out a tiny hole, and while I was showering with some other girls last year, we noticed an eyeball peering in at us through the hole. It was some dumb freshman boy, who was caught and suspended. But the feeling of being watched, of being spied upon, was like having dirt all over your skin that you couldn't scrub off.

"Anybody hungry?" Kevin asked.

"I'm still full from last night," Tracie said, rubbing her belly. "I don't think I'll need to eat for a week."

"Let's just get on the road and get to the lodge," I suggested. "The sooner we get there, the better. Whoever was here last night . . . well, maybe they'll be back. Maybe they'll be back with others."

Kevin nodded. "Let's pack up. We can take some of the supplies from the station, just in case."

I glanced down at the footprints, happy to be leaving.

And soon.

37

We spent the morning rearranging the inside of the van, storing our supplies so we'd have as much room as possible. We decided to take the mattress from the bedroom, so we'd have somewhere soft to sit or lay down. The mattress fit perfectly in the back of the vehicle. At the very least, two of us could lay down and stretch out, as opposed to having to sit on the floor while we traveled. We stored our other supplies in boxes, organizing what little food we had, along with other items we'd taken from the ranger station. Of course, we hoped we wouldn't have to use them, that we'd be at the lodge on Otter Lake in a few hours. But the past few months had taught us to be prepared for anything. The plates might come in handy, along with the utensils, cups, and other kitchen items we'd found.

Seeing that we hadn't gotten sick from drinking the lake water, we filled several mayonnaise jars we'd found at the ranger station. Hopefully, we might find some bottled water somewhere, but we couldn't count on it. There hadn't been any at the Island Lake General Store, but we thought there were probably some other stores like that one. Maybe—*maybe*—we'd come across one, and be able to salvage more necessary items.

Within an hour, we were ready to leave.

"I'm going to miss that flush toilet," I said to Tracie as we left the ranger station for the last time. "I hope Kevin's uncle has something like that at the lodge."

"Don't count on it," Tracie said.

Kevin and Eddie were at the lake, washing their hands. Tracie and I began walking toward the van.

"So, how's it going with my brother?" I asked her. "How late did you guys sit around the fire?"

"Quite a while," Tracie replied. "We just talked, mostly."

"Mostly?"

Tracie grinned. "Mostly. Yeah. We talked about this whole flu thing. Talked about your parents. My mom. He's really strong, but he's still really hurting over losing your mom and dad."

"I've talked to him about it a little," I said. "He gets pretty emotional, and he doesn't like to say much about it."

"He did last night," Tracie said. "And he talked about you. He talked about you a *lot.*"

"Me? About what?"

"He really does love you, Sierra. He really cares about you, and he says he never tells you that. He feels like he has to take care of you, now that things are the way they are."

"I'm pretty good at taking care of myself," I said.

"I know that, and so does he. He knows you can take care of yourself. He knows Kevin won't let anything happen to you. But you're his sister. He loves you. He *needs* to take care of you. Of us. Get it? He feels responsible, like he owes it to you. Not only for *you,* but for your mom and dad. Now that your parents are gone, you don't really have anyone to look after you."

"None of us do," I said.

Tracie stopped as we reached the van. She turned and looked at me. "We have each other," she said. "Kevin and Eddie are smart. We're going to be all right, I think. We just all have to take care of each other."

33

Tracie and I loaded the last few items into the van. Eddie and Kevin returned, gave the ranger station and the immediate grounds a quick once-over, and climbed into the vehicle. Tracie and I sat in the back, on the mattress, while Kevin took up his position at the wheel. He fumbled with the ignition wires for a minute, and the engine roared to life.

"We need to trade this one in on a quieter model," I said loudly. The broken tailpipe and missing muffler made the engine sound even louder than ever.

"It'll get us where we need to go," Kevin said.

"At least the plastic on the back windows will keep the fumes out," Tracie said. "There were a couple times, yesterday, when I thought I was going to puke."

Eddie unfolded the map he'd picked up from the general store and began plotting a course.

"This is a great map," he said. "We can follow back

roads for a long ways and skirt all of the larger cities."

The day was hot. Kevin and Eddie had their windows rolled down. Last year at this time, I would have been laying outside in the sun. Or going for a walk in the park. Or riding my bike to the beach. It would have been a perfect day to do those things.

Of course, when your first precedence is survival—simply staying alive—you have to prioritize. I dreamed of getting to the lodge at Otter Lake where, hopefully, it was safe enough to do things like that. Where we could sit back and soak up the sun, swim, go for walks in the woods. Things like that.

The little things.

We drove along back roads, winding and weaving. We saw several dogs, a few abandoned cars—nothing we weren't used to. Houses we passed were cold and lifeless. Some of them had burned.

After driving about half an hour, however, Kevin suddenly gasped.

"Oh, shit!" he said. "Shit!"

"What?" Eddie said.

Kevin shook his head. "I can't freakin' believe it!"

"What?" Eddie repeated with more insistence. "What's up?"

Kevin slammed the steering wheel with his hand. "Our 'visitor' from last night? The one who didn't take anything?"

"Yeah?" Eddie said.

"Well, he took something, all right. We're almost out of gas!"

39

We were able to travel about twenty miles on the remaining tank of gas, stopping along the way when we saw a vehicle parked along the road or in someone's driveway. All of their tanks had been syphoned dry.

"Looks like there were a lot of people with the same idea we had," Kevin said, after he'd checked for gas in a blue Chevrolet Blazer. "Everybody wants the gas."

We were cautious when we checked vehicles in front of houses, wary that there might be people inside. We even went to several houses to see if there was anything that would be useful, but most homes had been pretty much stripped of anything that wasn't bolted down. Several homes stank of death, and we stayed away, knowing what we'd find inside.

Soon, the engine began to sputter and cough. The van had finally run out of gas.

"Damn!" Kevin cursed as the van slowed. He pulled it over to the shoulder.

"Is there anything around here?" I asked Eddie. "Anything on the map?"

Eddie shook his head. "A few lakes. No towns or anything."

Tracie unscrewed the lid of a mayonnaise jar, took a drink of water, and handed it to me. I drank, and passed the jar to Kevin.

"I can't believe that every single car for miles has been drained of gas," Eddie said as he scoured the map. "It's only been two months! How could all the gas be gone?"

"Easy," Kevin said. "There were a lot of people with the same idea we had: get out of the city. If those people were driving, like we are, they'd have to get gas from somewhere. It's a lot easier to syphon gas from a car's tank than it would be to try and get it from the underground tanks at a gas station."

"We could always walk," Tracie said.

"Yeah, and get there in the spring," I said.

"Well, we can't stay *here,*" she replied.

"Yes, we can," Kevin said, turning. "We can stay right here. Or, rather, *you guys* can stay here." He looked at Eddie. "I'll hike on up ahead and see if I can find another vehicle. If I do, I'll drive it back here."

"And if you don't?" I asked.

"I will," Kevin said. "I will."

90

By nightfall, Kevin still hadn't returned.

91

"Where do you think he could be?" I asked Eddie. He was sitting in the driver's seat, and I was in the passenger seat. The clock on the dashboard displayed five minutes after midnight. Tracie had fallen asleep on the mattress behind us. The windows were open, and warm night air breezed through the van. We were serenaded by thousands of crickets.

"I don't know," Eddie replied, shaking his head. "But he said he wasn't coming back without a car."

"But what if something happened to him?" I asked. "What if—"

"Kevin is smart, Sierra. You know that. He can handle himself. And he's got the rifle, too. He's fine. I promise."

We sat in silence, staring at the black ribbon of highway, dimly lit by the near-full moon.

"How's it going with you and Tracie?" I asked quietly.

"Us? Fine. Good, I guess. She's really great. How about you and Kevin?" he deflected.

"Fine," I said. "He seems quieter these days."

"Kev's a pretty deep thinker," Eddie said. "There's a lot on his shoulders. There's a lot on all of our shoulders."

"I think about mom and dad a lot," I said.

"Me, too."

"I miss them."

"Me, too."

"It was bad enough to lose them," I said. Then I looked at him. He turned to look at me. I shook my head. "I'd never make it without you," I said. "Kev and Trace, too. I wouldn't have made it this far. Certainly not on my own."

Even in the darkness, I could see that Eddie's eyes were wet with tears. My own tears spilled onto my cheeks. He leaned forward, and we hugged and held each other for a long time.

92

An hour later, Kevin still hadn't come back.

"Get some sleep," Eddie said. "You need it. I'll stay up for a while."

Eddie was right. I was worried about Kevin, but I really was tired. Besides . . . there was nothing I could do.

"Go on," Eddie urged. "Lay down and get some sleep. If—when—Kevin comes back, I'll wake you up."

I spun slowly in the chair and lowered to my knees, crawling to the back of the van. There was a jar of water next to a box, and I picked it up, unscrewed the lid, and drank.

"You want some?" I asked Eddie.

"Yeah," he said, reaching his arm back. I handed him the jar, and he took a long drink. Then he handed it back to me, and I screwed the lid back on and set the jar back down next to the box.

Tracie was still sleeping soundly on the mattress,

making soft, airy whistles as she breathed. I snuggled up next to her, and soon, I was sleeping, too.

Not for long.

93

Two things woke me up. The sound of a distant, roaring engine, and the sound of crunching gravel close by.

"Sierra! Tracie! Wake up!" Eddie shouted as the side door slid open. The dome light came on, providing a thin, yellow glow. *"Get up! Get up!"*

"Wha . . . what's going on?" I asked groggily, trying to focus and wake. Tracie, too, had awoken with a start, and she was on her hands and knees. Then Eddie had grabbed our arms and was pulling us from the van.

Far off down the road, two headlights were approaching—fast. We could hear the engine roar, growing louder.

"Into the woods!" Eddie ordered.

"What?!?!" I exclaimed.

"Into the woods! Into the woods! We don't know if that's Kevin or not! I'll stay here . . . you two hide in the woods! Just duck down, and stay out of sight!"

He pushed us away, and Tracie and I stumbled down a short embankment. Weeds whipped at my pants and scraped my bare arms. Shadows began to grow as the headlights drew nearer, and Tracie and I frantically stumbled on, still not fully awake, seeking the safety of the shadows in the forest.

The oncoming vehicle began to slow. It was big, it seemed, bigger than our van. I could see Eddie's silhouette on our side, next to the passenger door, out of view of the approaching vehicle, shouldering the shotgun, ready . . . .

Suddenly—a familiar voice, as the headlights slowed to a stop at the van. The vehicle was a motor home. Not a huge one, but at least twice the size of our van. Then, a familiar voice—

"Hey you guys! Eddie! Tracie! Sierra!"

It was Kevin!

Tracie and I sprang from the bushes, ran back up the embankment, and to the driver's side window. There was a light on inside the motor home, and I could make out Kevin behind the wheel.

"We've got to go!" Kevin shouted frantically. "Now! Leave the van!"

"But, we've got—"

"Leave it! Leave it!" Kevin ordered. "I'll explain when you get in!"

We ran around to the other side where the door was. I yanked it open and dashed inside. Tracie followed, and she closed the door. Eddie leapt into the passenger seat, aiming the shotgun at the floor. He dropped the atlas and the folding map at his feet.

"Hang on a sec!" he said. "I've got to get the shotgun shells and the bullets for the Winchester!"

He vanished for a moment, then returned with an armload of small boxes. He dumped them on the floor of the motor home, leapt into the passenger seat, and closed the door. I sat down on a cushioned chair next to a small dining table. Tracie took a seat on the couch.

The motor home suddenly surged forward as Kevin hit the gas.

"What's going on?" Eddie asked excitedly.

"Well, I got this thing," Kevin said as the vehicle picked up more speed. "But they're after us."

"Who's 'they'?" I asked.

"I don't know," Kevin said. "A gang, looters, who knows. I might have lost them, though."

I turned around. At the back of the motor home was a small bedroom. The door was open, allowing a view through the rear windows.

A pair of headlights suddenly appeared in the distance.

94

"I found this thing in a pole barn about four miles from here," Kevin explained as the dotted-yellow line came at us like machine gun fire. "The pole barn had been broken into and looted, but no one bothered to check out a back room that had been locked. I kicked the door in . . . and this was on the other side . . . keys and all, with a full tank of gas! There's even some cans of food in the cabinets, a gas stove, water—this thing's got it all!"

We went around a turn and the headlights far behind us vanished . . . but we knew the car was still after us.

"Hang on, hang on!" Kevin said, and he hit the brakes so hard that the tires squealed. Tracie and I were sent sailing to the front of the vehicle, and we had to brace ourselves to keep from slamming into the console and the back of Eddie's seat. Things clattered and clanged within the closed cupboards, but it didn't sound like anything was broken.

"Sorry, sorry," Kevin said as he turned the vehicle so hard I thought we were going to roll over. "Time to lose these guys once and for all!"

We were now on a thin two-track that must've had potholes as deep as wash tubs. The motor home bounced and jostled, throwing us back and forth. Tracie and I held on to one another for support, but it didn't do much good. I grabbed part of a cabinet, and Tracie supported herself by grabbing the back of Eddie's seat.

"I don't know where those guys came from," Kevin said. "But I was driving along, and all of a sudden there were headlights coming at me. They spun around and pulled up along side. It was dark, but I could see they had a gun sticking out of the passenger window. They shot once, and missed."

Suddenly, Kevin halted the vehicle and killed the lights. Keys jangled in the darkness, and the motor died.

"How did you get away from them?" Tracie asked.

"I stuck the rifle out the window and fired," Kevin said. "I didn't even aim, but I got a lucky shot and hit their windshield. I don't know if I hit anyone, but the car stopped. I floored it, and I thought I'd lost them . . . but apparently not. Maybe now, we will, though. We're off the road far enough that they won't see us unless they come down this trail. Let's hope they just keep going."

It was dark inside the motor home, but I could make out the faint silhouette of Kevin in the driver's seat, and Eddie in the passenger seat. Tracie was next to me, nearly invisible in the darkness. Beyond the motor home, however, the light of the moon reflected on the thick foliage.

Behind us, the highway began to glow. Trees began to turn a murky gray as the headlights approached.

We waited.

95

Headlights illuminated the trees on the opposite side of the road. A car suddenly sped by, very fast—and kept right on going. A surge of relief flowed through all of us.

"That was luck," Kevin said.

"No, that was brains, man," Eddie replied. "It's great to have you on the team. Way to go." They high-fived.

"Yeah," I said, leaning forward and giving Kevin a hug. "It's great to have you back."

"What's great," Kevin said, after pulling me into his lap, "is we've got this thing with a full tank of gas. Everything works, as far as I can tell. There's even a shower on board . . . and a bathroom that works. Fresh water, too! No more lake water from a mayonnaise jar. Towels, some blankets. And soap."

"This thing is better than the ranger station," I said.

"Yeah," Tracie said. "More room, too."

Kevin continued. "We can stay here for the night and go back to our van to get our stuff."

"Do we really need it?" Tracie asked. "I mean . . . if we're going to be at your uncle's lodge soon?"

Kevin nodded. "Nothing's for certain, Trace. We don't know for sure what we're going to find up there. Might as well save everything we can. And besides: whoever was chasing us probably has no idea our van is loaded with supplies. We'll hang here until morning, get our gear out of the van, then keep heading north."

If only things were that simple.

96

At the very back of the motor home was a bedroom. Granted, it was small, but the bed was comfortable. Kevin and I slept there, while Tracie slept on the couch in the living area, if you could call it that. Eddie reclined the passenger seat and slept, cradling the shotgun in his arms. It had been a long day for all of us, and we didn't have any trouble sleeping.

In the morning I awoke first, but I didn't move for a long time. It was just beginning to get light outside. I lay in bed, listening to Kevin snoring softly next to me. I was so glad he made it back safely. And yes, I must admit, proud. He'd made a fantastic discovery—a motor home—and he'd brought it back . . . just like he said he would. For us, it was like a mansion on wheels.

After a while, I got up. Kevin stirred and rolled to his side, but he didn't wake. Softly, I tiptoed toward the front of the motor home, stopping at the sink. I turned the water on . . . and it worked! I quickly shut it off, not wanting to waste a single drop. I don't know why I was so surprised. I guess when you're not used to having running water for a couple of months, you get used to getting water in other ways. A faucet seemed fantastically futuristic, a miracle invention.

I searched the cupboard, found a plastic cup, and filled it beneath the faucet. I sniffed the water before I sipped—just in case. It had been sitting in the tank for two months, at least, and probably longer. It didn't smell bad, so I drank. It was awesome. Smooth, cool. Clean.

I placed the empty cup in the sink and walked to the front of the motor home. I didn't know how old the vehicle was, but, judging by its clean appearance, I figured it couldn't be too old. The odometer read just over twenty-thousand miles.

Eddie was snoozing in the passenger seat, still cradling the shotgun. I sat in the driver's seat and picked up the atlas, opening it to the state of Michigan. I had a rough idea where we were, and I found the general area on the map. Then I looked north, to where we were headed. Cheboygan county. I'd never been there before, and I wondered what it was like.

I glanced down to the southern part of the state, where we were, and traced a route north with my finger. We'd been on the road for two days, yet it seemed longer. And normally, the trip would only take about four hours—at the most. *Normally,* that is. Taking back roads, winding in and around farms, forests, and fields was going to take longer. Were we being too cautious? Would it be better to take the freeway and race north as fast as we could? Or would we encounter more gangs like the one who threw the cinder block from the I-94 overpass?

It was impossible to know. All I did know, however, was I'd be glad when we were finally at the lodge up north. We didn't know what we'd find, to be sure . . . but it was bound to be safer. Anywhere remote, away from hoards of desperate looters, was fine with me.

I put the map on the floor, looked into the forest, and waited for Kevin, Tracie, and Eddie to wake up.

97

Eddie had awakened first. Then Kevin woke, and when he stumbled to the front of the motor home, Tracie stirred. I laughed. Not only did we all look very groggy with our bleary eyes and messy hair, but we were all still wearing the same, silly red shirts. Revenge of the Nerdy Camp Counselors.

"Quiet night?" Kevin asked Eddie.

Eddie nodded and yawned. "Nothing. But I fell asleep pretty quick."

I swapped places with Kevin and he started the motor home, backed up, turned onto the highway, and headed toward our van. The sun was shining, the sky was a crisp, baby blue, and the trees lining the road were thick and green. It was a new day, and it was filled with colorful promise.

By some miracle, our vehicle on the side of the

highway had remained untouched. With our luck the way it had been, I was sure it would have been discovered and looted of our supplies and gear. We were thrilled to find it exactly as we'd left it.

After loading most of the items into the motor home, we discussed which route to take.

"According to this," Eddie said, tapping the unfolded map, "we're still in the Pinckney State Recreation Area, near Unadilla. If we head directly north, cutting in and around these back roads, we'll be able to stay away from Lansing to the west, and Flint to the east."

"What about the freeways?" I asked.

"This far south, I think we should stay away from them," Eddie said. "But once we make it farther north—past Bay City—maybe then we could pick up I-75, or US-27. But until we reach less populated areas, we should stay on back roads, away from the major highways."

"But there could be people anywhere," Tracie said. "Kevin found that out last night."

"True," Eddie said. "We just have to think like looters. They're going to want to stay together. They'll want to stay where their chances of surviving are the best. These are people who probably don't know how to fend for themselves, other than stealing from someone else."

"Well, we were stealing, in a way," Tracie said.

"We're not taking from someone else," Eddie said. "We're not hurting anyone to get the things we need. There are mobs out there that will do anything to get what they want. We're just doing what we can to get by."

"Yeah," Kevin said light-heartedly. "It's the end of the world. Who gives a rat's ass about laws anymore?"

Kevin turned the vehicle around and headed in the opposite direction, with Eddie once again navigating from the passenger seat. Tracie and I opened a couple of cans of chili and used the propane stove to warm the contents.

"Gee, a real, working stove," Tracie said, watching the blue circle of flame. "I feel spoiled."

"And deservedly so," I replied.

"What's on the menu for breakfast?" Kevin said as he managed a quick glance at us.

"Ham, eggs, bacon, and wheat toast," I answered. "But we're disguising it to look like chili."

"I'll bet it tastes like chili, too," Eddie said.

"But we've got clean water," I said. "No more mayonnaise jars with lake water. No matter how clean it was, we were lucky we didn't get sick."

"Yeah," Eddie snickered. "After all . . . fish have to piss somewhere."

Trace grimaced, and I laughed.

We ate while we traveled, with Eddie telling Kevin when and where to turn. We made it north, past Unadilla, up around Fowlerville, around Antrim Center and Bancroft. The towns weren't very big, but neither was Chelsea—and we'd already learned our lesson there. The roads we'd taken were paved, mostly, traveling through more rural areas, forests, and fields. We continued seeing burned cars and looted houses. Lots of wildlife, too. Deer, rabbits, squirrels, and several dogs, some with collars, some without. They looked mangy and dirty, but most of them didn't look like they were starving. We saw an occasional dead body here and there, on the shoulder of the road, hanging out of a car, or laying in someone's driveway. But two months of scenes like this had made our skins pretty thick. Seeing a dead body, no matter what condition it was in, just wasn't a big deal anymore.

A live body? Now, *that* was a big deal—and that's why it was such a shock when Kevin rounded a corner to find a man and a woman, standing in a yard, staring at the motor home as we passed in front of their house.

93

They stood in the yard, nonthreatening, watching us. I think they were as surprised to see us as we were to see them. Kevin instinctively took his foot off the gas and pressed the brake. Tracie and I got up from the couch and peered out the window.

The man and woman were walking away, hurrying back to their house. When the motor home stopped, Kevin began backing up.

"Do you think this is a good idea?" Tracie asked.

"Did you see them, Trace?" Kevin replied. "They're in their fifties. They don't look like the killing, looting type. They look like Mom and Dad, only a few years older."

Kevin slowly backed up until he was past the driveway. Then he pulled forward and nudged the motor home toward a graying, old farmhouse.

"There they are, in the living room," I said, pointing.

"They're watching us."

"They're probably wondering the same thing we are," Eddie said. "You can't trust anyone, anymore."

"They'll trust me," I said, moving toward the door.

"Sierra, wait—"

"They'll trust me," I repeated. "A girl is going to seem less threatening than a guy. Besides . . . look at you. Your hair's a mess, your shirt is untucked and wrinkled. You look like you've been tossed around a mosh pit."

"A mosh pit," Eddie echoed. "Well, you don't look much better."

I ignored him and opened the door, stepping into the early afternoon sun. As I walked across the un-mowed lawn, I made sure the people in the house saw that I was empty handed, and I made eye contact through the window. I could see them speaking to one another. Finally, I stopped on the lawn, several feet in front of the porch.

The front door opened, and the man stood behind the screen. He was wearing dark slacks and a white shirt. His hair was short and trim, and he was clean-shaven.

"What do you want?" he said. He spoke a bit harshly.

"If you're thinking we are going to try to take anything from you, that's not the case," I said. "I'm Sierra. My brother, Eddie, is in the motor home, along with my friends, Kevin and Tracie. We're headed north. We don't want to hurt you. Or anybody, for that matter."

The woman joined the man at the door. Her hair was graying, shoulder length, and she wore a blue denim dress. Good Housekeeping Poster Parents.

"Then, why are you here?" the man said, his voice softening a little.

"What do you know?" I asked. "About what's going on? We haven't spoken to anyone in two months. The only thing we know is what we heard on the radio stations, before they all went dead. We decided to head north, to a lodge Kevin's uncle owns. You know . . . to get away from the city and the gangs. We . . . we're just trying to survive."

The man stared at me, then he looked at his wife. Then he looked back at me, nodded toward the motor home, and spoke.

"Anybody sick in there?" he asked.

I shook my head. "No," I replied. "We haven't been around anybody in a long time."

He looked at the woman again, then me.

"Tell your friend to drive the motor home behind the house. Then come to the back door."

99

Their names were Jerry and Sarah Morgan. Like us, they were just trying to survive . . . and keep out of sight of others who might not be so friendly.

"There's no law, no order anywhere," Jerry said. We were seated in their living room. Sarah had made iced tea—without the ice, of course—and we sat around sipping and talking.

"The first few weeks of the pandemic were bad enough," Sarah said. "We thought they'd get it under control."

"We thought the same thing," I replied. "But it only got worse."

"When it was clear that we were on our own," Jerry continued, "we knew we were going to have to protect ourselves. Gangs of people were coming house-to-house, stealing and looting. Killing. They killed our neighbors, just to the west of us. Shot the whole family, stole their food. Took whatever they wanted. They came to our house, but we've got guns, and we used them. We've had several attacks like that. Mostly, though, we haven't seen any gangs in a few weeks. There are others like us, too. Not many, I'm afraid. Everybody lays low. Don't go out much in the daytime. We try to make the place look as deserted as possible, so no one knows we're here. You folks kinda surprised us when you went by. Your motor home is quiet. Didn't hardly hear ya comin' 'til you had already passed."

"But what are you doing for food?" Eddie asked.

"We've got a storm cellar stocked with canned goods," Sarah replied. "Mostly, things I've canned myself. We have a good supply, but we try to conserve what we can. Jerry shoots a rabbit now and then, and we're growing some vegetables."

"I got a deer a few weeks ago, and make jerky out of most of the meat," Jerry interjected.

Sarah nodded. "We're getting along better than most, I think. More tea?"

We all nodded. Even at room temperature, the tea was refreshing.

"You're heading north?" Jerry asked.

We nodded, and Kevin spoke. "My uncle has a large log home up in Cheboygan County," he replied. "It's way back in the woods on a small lake. And there's a good chance my aunt and uncle are there, safe. We were thinking that if we could get there, we could do what you guys are doing. Maybe there are others like us, and we could sort of get together."

Jerry shook his head. "There are others, sure," he

said. "But no one wants to get together just yet. Not around here, anyway."

"Why?" Tracie asked.

"Gangs are getting bigger. More powerful. When they find a group of people, they fight them. Take their stuff. They know that if there are a lot of people in one place, well, they'll need a lot of supplies to survive. Food, water. Gas. Gangs are even starting to fight each other. It's insane. There's nobody to stop them. Mostly, though, they stay near the cities. I don't know much more than that. There are a few people doing what we're doing. The Arlingtons, about a mile to the south. We had two-way radios for a while, but the batteries are dead. I hike over once in a while, and Fred Arlington sometimes comes here. Company's nice. Mostly, though, I'm afraid to leave Sarah and the house alone. You're smart, though, to head north. I hear it's easier up there."

"Have you folks eaten?" Sarah asked.

My eyes darted to Eddie, then to Tracie and Kevin. They were doing the same. We were all looking at each other, not wanting to impose. But we *were* hungry. We'd only had chili that morning, and it certainly didn't fill us up. But the Morgans needed food, too. We didn't want to take what they had.

"No, we're fine," Kevin said.

Sarah, knowing we were only being polite, got to her feet. "Really," she said. "I'll put a couple of things together. It won't be much, but it'll fill the holes, as my mother used to say." She whisked off to the kitchen.

"You think heading north is a good idea?" Eddie asked.

Jerry nodded. "Talked with Fred last week. He hears that more and more people are heading to the country. Me and Sarah, we're thinking of doing the same thing, after winter. If things don't get better, if the gangs don't go away, we'll head north come spring. We have enough food, and we have a well out back, with a hand pump. But if it gets too dangerous, we'll try to make our way north."

Sarah returned with plates of peaches. "From last year," she said. "Grown right here."

My mouth was watering even before she handed me the plate. It had been a long time since I'd had fruit, let alone peaches.

"If I were you," Jerry said, "I wouldn't be driving that thing around during the daylight hours. Someone will see you for sure. That thing you got there, that's a traveling gold mine for looters."

"You think we should drive at night?" Eddie asked.

Jerry nodded. "Yep. Lights off. With the moon the way it's been, you'd be able to see okay without the headlights. In fact, tonight will be a full moon. Lots of light to see by. Sure, it might be risky. But it'll be a lot less riskier than driving that thing around during the day. If it's not cloudy, the moon will give you enough light to see."

"Then we can take I-75 or US-27," Kevin said thoughtfully.

"Yep," Jerry said. "You barrel along the expressway as fast as you can safely go. If you run into any gangs along the highway—and you probably will—they'll never see you comin'. By the time they do, you'll be past 'em. That is, if they see you at all."

That made sense. Driving at night without lights

might not be the safest thing to do, but, like Jerry said, it might allow us to slip by gangs unnoticed.

"Yeah," Eddie said. He seemed excited by Jerry's idea. "And if we're able to jump on one of the expressways, we could make it to Cheboygan in only a few hours, as opposed to creeping along back roads for a couple of days."

Eddie and Kevin talked excitedly while we ate the peaches, tossing around different ideas, thinking about pitfalls we'd encounter if we drove at night. Tracie and I listened, not saying anything. Finally, Eddie looked at me.

"What do you think?" he asked. Then he glanced at Tracie, wordlessly posing the same question.

"Sounds like a plan," I replied.

"Yeah," Tracie said. "And we've got a traveling bathroom and a shower. I'd fight to the death just for those two things."

Tracie had no idea she just might get her wish—that very night.

100

We left at two o'clock in the morning.

Earlier, Sarah had prepared a meal consisting of venison jerky (salty, but it was very good), corn, and green beans that we'd brought in from the motor home. They also filled some jars with fresh water from the well, and we hooked a hose to the motor home and topped off all of the water ports. We were all able to take showers that evening. The water wasn't very warm, but it didn't matter.

But leaving Jerry and Sarah had been hard. We'd spent the day with them, talking about what had happened to the world . . . and what might happen. They both seemed very gentle, wise, and optimistic. They treated us like family, and I enjoyed our conversations. Kevin even drew them a map to the lodge on Otter Lake and gave it to them, saying if they ever *did* make it north, that was where we would be. "You're welcome anytime," he said. "Any time at all."

Now, we traveled the back roads in darkness. The moon provided a stale, ashen glow, enough to see the highway clearly. Eddie found a pen light in the glove compartment, and he plotted our course on the map.

"We'll take East Grand River Road over to US-27," he said. "We've only got to make a couple of jaunts here and there. If all goes well, we'll be at Otter Lake before the sun comes up."

And all *did* go well. We made it to US-27 without any difficulty. Soon, we were barreling north at over eighty miles an hour. The full moon and a clear sky gave us plenty of light to navigate. We had several tense moments, however, especially when Kevin had to swerve to miss abandoned vehicles. One of them was in the middle of the freeway, but we saw its dark shadow early enough to slow and go around it.

Most importantly, the plan was working. If there were any gangs laying in wait, we didn't see them, and they didn't see us. We nosed up through Mt. Pleasant, Clare, Houghton and Higgins Lakes, and Grayling. The motor home ran smoothly and quietly.

"We should be there in about an hour," Eddie said. "We've made great time."

"Speaking of time," I said, "what time is it?"

Kevin clicked on the dashboard lights, then shut them off. "Four-thirty," he replied. "I think we'll make it to the lodge right around sunrise, maybe a little after."

And that's when the front of the motor home exploded.

101

There was no warning.

I had been seated in a chair a few feet behind the passenger seat, behind Eddie. Tracie was sleeping on the couch.

Suddenly, there was an ear-shattering crash, a violent clamor of metal, fiberglass, steel, and glass. The concussion sent shockwaves through the entire vehicle. There were more sounds of destruction: a loud hissing, metal dragging, tires squealing. I was flung forward by the initial collision, and forward again as Kevin stomped on the brake. Tracie was flung over the couch and into the back of the chair I had been seated in. Kevin and Eddie had been wearing their seatbelts, and both air bags deployed with a loud, huffing *pop!* Kevin was struggling with the bag as he tried to steer and stop the skidding vehicle, which was leering to the right, then the left.

"What the hell happened?!?! What the hell happened?!?!" Eddie shrieked.

"We hit something!" Kevin replied, pulling the deflating air bag away from his face. It was murky-dark in the motor home, and the dimness only added to the confusion and chaos.

"No shit!" Eddie snapped, struggling to pull the deflating air bag away from his lap.

The vehicle finally skidded to a halt. The engine was running, but there was a loud ticking sound, and a sharp hiss of steam. The air had an acidic, burning smell . . . rubber and electricity.

"We hit something," Kevin repeated. "I'm not sure what, but I have a pretty good idea." He unbuckled his seat belt, opened the door, and slipped outside. The dome light came on, and Eddie turned around.

"You guys all right?" he asked.

"I'm fine," I said, turning to help Tracie to her feet.

"Yeah, me too," Tracie said groggily. "What happened?"

"We hit something," I answered.

"Where are we?" she asked.

"South of Gaylord, on I-75."

Eddie pushed the deflated air bag out of his way and slid off the seat and onto the pavement. Kevin reappeared on the driver's side and fumbled for a flashlight that was clamped to the console.

"If it's not one thing, it's another," I said.

"What did we hit?" Tracie asked.

"I don't know," I replied, opening up the side door. Cool night air washed in. Crickets chimed, interspersed with the loud ticking of the motor and the steamy hissing noise, which was fading.

Eddie and Kevin were in front of the motor home, inspecting the damage. The hood was up, badly dented and kinked. The flashlight beam swept over what was left of the grill and the jumbled mess of shadows swarming the engine.

"Right there," Kevin said. "That's what it was, all right. A damned deer."

There were splotches of blood and tufts of light brown fur intermixed with broken metal and fiberglass. The right front of the motor home was a garbled muddle of jutting, sharp shrapnel.

"Will it still drive?" Eddie asked.

Kevin shook his head as he swept the beam back and forth across the front of the motor home. "I don't know," he said. "Probably. But it looks like the radiator core is damaged, and the radiator hose is broken. We won't be able to travel very far if the engine overheats. We're going to have to pour some water into the radiator and see how bad it leaks. Maybe it can be fixed. We're actually lucky it's not worse. I think the best thing to do is to find the nearest exit and see if we can hide out in the woods somewhere. Whatever happens, we're not going very far for a while."

Tracie appeared by my side. "What's up?" she asked. "What'd we hit?"

"A deer," I replied. "Kevin says it'll still drive, but not for long. We're going to find a place to hide, figure out if it can be fixed, and make plans from there."

"Let's move," Kevin said. "The sooner we get off the freeway and find a place to hide, the better."

The four of us climbed back into the wounded

motor home. Kevin and Eddie had to push the deflated air bags out of their way, but their husks were still attached to the dash. Kevin shifted into gear, and the motor home lurched forward with creaks, groans, scrapes, and that insanely loud *tick-tick-tick-tick* from the engine.

"We could go back and find the deer," Eddie said, trying to make light of our situation. "You know . . . fresh venison steak."

"I think I'll stick with chili and green beans," Tracie said.

102

Kevin inched the motor home along, unwilling to press the vehicle any faster than thirty miles an hour. Thankfully, we found an exit only a mile down the road. There was a dark, abandoned convenience store on the right, its hulking, monolithic shadow glowing faintly in the moonlight. There were no other buildings, no other structures. A few cars littered the parking lot, and a *United Van Lines* semi-truck was on its side in the ditch.

Kevin flicked on the headlights, but only the driver's side lamp worked. Still, it provided enough light to illuminate the road ahead of us. He steered right, following the ribbon of blacktop as it passed the dark convenience store and snaked between two walls of thick forest. Stars twinkled in the early morning sky. It would be daylight in an hour or so.

"Over there," Eddie said, pointing. He'd spotted a

small trail on the left of the road. It was overgrown and thin, but Kevin turned the motor home, anyway. Branches and brush scraped the sides and the bottom of the vehicle as it bounced its way into the forest. The insane scraping dredged up more 5th grade memories of Jeremy Roberts, scratching his fingernails on the blackboard.

After we'd driven a hundred feet or so, Kevin stopped. He turned off the lights, killed the engine, and the loud ticking died. There were a few lingering pops and clicks, and a hissing sound that faded quickly.

"We're about two miles from Gaylord," Kevin said. "Let's lay low here. I think we'll be safe. There's nothing else around, as far as I can tell. We all need some sleep. Then, we'll figure out what to do."

"Sleep sounds good," I said.

Eddie rolled the passenger window down and reclined his seat. "I'll stay here," he said. "I think if anyone comes, I'll hear them, even if I'm asleep."

Kevin remained in the driver's seat, and he, too, rolled the window down. Tracie was already asleep again on the couch. I poured a cup of water from the sink, drank it down, then strode to the back of the motor home and climbed into bed.

Sleep came easily.

103

I awoke to the pleasant sounds of morning: birds chirping and a gentle breeze murmuring through the trees. The air was fresh, clean, and cool, with a bitter hint of chemical: a reminder of the damage to the front of our motor home. Kevin, Eddie, and Tracie were awake, talking softly up front. I lay in bed for a moment, stretched, then swung my legs out of bed.

"Hey, sleepyhead's awake," Eddie called out.

I stood and walked to the front of the motor home. Sunlight brightened the interior. Through the windshield, the deserted trail stretched on, tunneling through thick limbs and branches.

"Breakfast is on the table," Tracie said, nodding at a bowl of dry corn flakes and a small plate of peaches. Sarah Morgan had insisted we take a couple jars from their cellar stash. We all had protested, not wanting to take food that, no doubt, they would need, but both Sarah and Jerry insisted. Now, I was kind of glad, because the peaches on the table looked enticing.

"What about you guys?" I asked.

"We ate," Eddie said.

I picked up the plate of peaches, found a spoon, and hungrily scooped them into my mouth. I ate slowly, savoring the thick, syrupy sweetness.

It was just after nine. Although I still felt tired, the short sleep had refreshed me a little. But I couldn't wait to climb into a bed and sleep for half a day, straight.

"What's the plan?" I asked as another sliced peach slid off my spoon and into my mouth.

Kevin looked at me. "How do you feel about taking a hike?" he asked.

"What do you mean?"

"We're thinking Eddie can stay here and make some repairs to the front. He can pull out the radiator, which is going to take some time. Tracie can stay with him. You and me . . . we can hike into Gaylord, maybe find an auto parts store. We need to get some stuff to repair the radiator, along with some antifreeze. I'll be taking the Winchester with us, so I'll probably need some help carrying everything back."

I finished the last of the peaches, placed the empty plate on the table, and picked up the bowl of dry corn flakes.

"Fine with me," I said with a shrug. "How far do we have to go?"

"About two miles," Eddie said, looking at the atlas, which was open on his lap. "We have no idea where we'll find an auto parts store—"

"—or if we'll be able to find what we're looking for,"

Kevin interrupted, and Eddie continued.

"—but we don't have too many other options. I already hiked back to the store at the off-ramp. None of the abandoned cars or trucks are driveable. Being that we're only a half hour or so from the lodge, I thought we might be better off to just find another vehicle, but no luck. This motor home is still our best bet, considering the amount of water it holds. Not to mention all the supplies we have. If we can fix it, that would be great."

"Do we have a map?" I asked. "I mean . . . do we know how to get to the city?"

Eddie shook his head. "No map," he replied. "But we do have this."

He opened up the glove box and pawed around, until he found what he was looking for: a compass. It was one of those little globe deals with a suction cup to stick to the dashboard. Simple, but it would work. "Just head straight north, through the woods," he said. "You can start by following this two-track. It shouldn't take you much more than half an hour to reach the city limits."

"And Gaylord's not a very big city," Kevin said. "It should be safe."

"Let's just hope," I said. "Let's just hope."

104

True to Eddie's words, it hadn't taken much more than half an hour to reach the outskirts of Gaylord. We'd followed the two-track for about a mile before it turned and went east. From there, we followed the compass, hiking directly north. We didn't have too much difficulty—except for a thick swamp with tightly-knitted alders. Moving through the tangle was difficult, as we had to push wiry branches away just to move, but it was quicker than going around. The swamp ended at a small embankment clustered with trees, and, at the top of the hill, the forest stopped abruptly.

Kevin and I stood at the edge of the forest, where the trees gave way to an expansive field. In the distance, a single, massive maple tree stood in the middle, full and round and thick with dark green leaves. On the other side of the field, a half mile away, we could see the fringe of the city: buildings (some of them charred and blackened), homes (mostly burned), and dozens of cars and trucks, some of them on their sides, some of them upside down. Gaylord wasn't very big—there were certainly no high-rises or tall office buildings—but the circumference of the city was wide and sprawling.

We saw nothing else, no signs of life, except for a few birds. Not even any dogs.

"The only problem now," Kevin said with a gesture of the rifle, "is going across the field. If anyone's around, they'll be able to see us, plain as day. The only other choice we have is to follow the tree line east, and hope we can get to the city without being exposed for so long."

"We could run," I suggested. "We could make it across the field in only a few minutes."

Kevin thought about it. "We could," he said. "It's up to you. We won't be able to run on our way back, though, with all of the stuff we'll need to carry—if we're able to find the stuff at all."

"We'll find it," I said, squeezing his hand. "We will. Let's go."

"Head for that small outbuilding, this side of that gas station," Kevin said, using the rifle to point. "We'll take a break there, and stay out of sight for a few minutes. Check things out." We set out across the field, running, but not at breakneck speed. The grass was tall, and we had to watch where we were stepping. The last thing we needed was to trip and fall, twist or break an ankle. As we ran, Kevin swung the rifle at his side, and he glanced in all directions ahead of him, on constant lookout for people.

When we reached the small building (it was more of a shed, really, with a caved-in roof and a kicked-in door) we dropped to the ground, huffing and puffing. I sat against the outside wall, leaning back. Several old bottles and rusted cans were scattered on the ground, within long, stringy grass. Kevin crawled around to the side to get a better look at what once had been a small but thriving city.

I looked up and saw over a dozen turkey vultures pin-wheeling beneath an unblemished, blue sky. Their massive wings rode currents of air, tilting and drifting, lifting and soaring in wide, arcing circles. I marveled at their ease of movement, their precision of flight. Up close, I thought they were perhaps the ugliest birds on the face of the planet, with bald, fleshy heads and a down-curved beak. In flight, however, their movements were definitive and graceful, a majestic display of mastery.

Kings of the new world, I thought. *Their job has always been scrounging and foraging for food. With so many dead people, it must be like a buffet for them.*

Kevin knelt at the edge of the dilapidated, graying shed, cautiously peering around the corner.

"Anything?" I asked, still panting heavily from the sprint across the field.

"No," he replied. "Looks pretty dead."

I crawled to him on my hands and knees and peeked over his shoulder. The scene was all-too familiar: blackened shells of houses and cars, vacant buildings. Grass was overgrown, and everything looked mangy and littered. A few billboards still stood, their colors faded and dull.

"Over there," Kevin said, pointing. In the distance was a blue building with a *NAPA* sign. "That's what we need, right there," he said. "Let's just hope it's not too picked over."

"Why would looters steal radiator repair supplies or antifreeze?" I asked.

"I don't understand why anyone would loot in the first place," Kevin replied. "People don't have to have a reason, Sierra. They just have to have the opportunity. But I'm going to bet you're right. People aren't going to steal automotive supplies when they're busy searching for food."

We waited for several minutes, watching for any signs of human life. After seeing nothing, Kevin decided it was safe to proceed.

"We'll go from building to building," he said, pointing to the gas station. "When we get there, follow me closely. We'll stay against the wall, and go around the other side. Then we'll have to cross the road to get to the *NAPA* store. Keep your eye out for anyone. Ready?"

I nodded, and we got to our feet. We walked this time, but quickly, and made it to the back of the gas station a moment later. Then we crept around the side, where I grimaced at the sight of a human corpse. It was seated, sort of, propped against the red brick building. From what I could tell, it had been a girl—probably my age or younger—and her remains were withered and gray, nearly mummified. Part of her leg was missing, most likely gnawed by a hungry animal. Her mouth was open wide in a grotesque, silent scream. Her tongue was shriveled and dried, and her teeth were stained a tobacco brown-yellow. Several shiny, black beetles were eating away at the dried tissue of what once were her gums. Kevin stepped over her, not giving the rotting remains a second glance. I hopped around the corpse, wincing.

Across the street, the windows of the auto parts store

were shattered. Nothing new: there wasn't a single window, anywhere, in any building, that was intact. Even the plastic *NAPA* billboard was sheered in half, and simply read *PA*.

At the front of the gas station, we stopped. There were two islands with four gas pumps each. The *Mobil* logos were still visible, but most of the pumps were smashed and dented. Their hoses lay on the ground like limp, black snakes. A van was parked at one of the islands, and the body of a dead man was slumped over the steering wheel. A hole was clearly visible in the side of his skull. This man hadn't died of the bird flu . . . he'd been murdered in cold blood.

And up and down the street in both directions: more of the same. A few cars and trucks strewn here and there, buildings reduced to rubble. Those that *were* still standing were charred. Some were marked with strange, spray-painted scribbles that looked like gang insignia—which I thought odd, being that we were this far north. Gang activity, for the most part, was usually confined to the larger cities in the southeastern part of the state. Regardless, it didn't mean anything to us, and we didn't give the markings a second thought.

We should have.

105

Kevin nodded to me and we darted across the parking lot, behind the van with the dead man at the wheel. We slowed, and Kevin shot wary glances in both directions of the four-lane road. Not seeing anything in the distance, we sprinted across the street. The door of the auto parts store had been shattered, so we didn't stop until we were inside the building.

If there was any good news, it was this: the building hadn't been torched. Most of the buildings around the *NAPA* store had been burned, but somehow, the auto parts store had survived.

Another bit of good news: the inside of the store had been ransacked, but there were still all sorts of products that hadn't been stolen. Shelves had been pulled down, their contents knocked to the floor. It was nearly impossible to walk with so much junk at our feet. But, I was actually relieved to see so many items remaining, despite the disarray.

"Well, it doesn't look like much has been taken," Kevin said. "We might find what we need, but we're going to have to hunt for it."

I walked to the front counter, stepping over upended shelves and pushing things to the side with my feet: cans of paint, hoses, cables, several cans of WD-40, and a few catalogs. Behind the counter was a large poster, one of those laminated ones required by the state, detailing all of the rights a Michigan worker had. All employees were entitled to the minimum hourly wage, as required by state law, according to the poster. There was also a toll-free number to call, if you felt you've been discriminated against. There were acres and acres of fine print. The whole poster seemed oddly irrelevant, considering.

There was a calendar on the wall, opened to the month of May. The picture above the calendar displayed a very skimpily-dressed, large-breasted woman, splayed over the hood of a red corvette. Her arms were squeezed close, causing her breasts to nearly fall out of the tiny yellow bikini top she was wearing. I wondered if they were real.

Beneath the photograph was the actual calendar. *Danny - dentist - 9:30am* was scribbled in on May 2nd. For a moment, I wondered who he was. One of the owner's children? An employee? What had he been doing when the bird flu pandemic hit? I wondered if Danny made his dentist appointment, or if, by then, it had already been too late.

Probably.

"Hey, here we go," Kevin said from the other side of the room. "Here's a hose we need. Help me look for some quick set epoxy or some type of glue. Muffler cement will work, too, if you come across a tube of that. That would probably be best."

"What about antifreeze?" I asked.

"That, too," he said. "But if we don't find it, we'll be able to get by with water. We've only got about forty miles to go."

I searched through the rubble of what was left of the auto shop. I found filters, lubes, tools. Oil pans, hoses, plastic funnels. I found lots of things I hadn't a clue what they were . . . but they didn't appear like anything we were looking for.

Then, beneath a broken shelf, I found two, one-gallon containers. They were green, and on the label was a picture of a kid holding a puppy. It was *Sierra* brand antifreeze, and, according to the label, it was less toxic and safer than other brands of antifreeze.

"Hey," I said, holding up my find.

Kevin turned. "Whadja find?" he asked.

"My antifreeze," I said with a smile. "See? It says 'Sierra' right on the front."

"Good going," Kevin said. "How many?"

I looked down. "Two, it looks like," I said, shuffling some debris with my feet. "I don't see any more."

"That will probably be plenty," Kevin said. "All we've got to find now is some kind of sealer."

I looked around. On a far wall were more of the strange markings we'd seen on a building down the street. It was the same design:

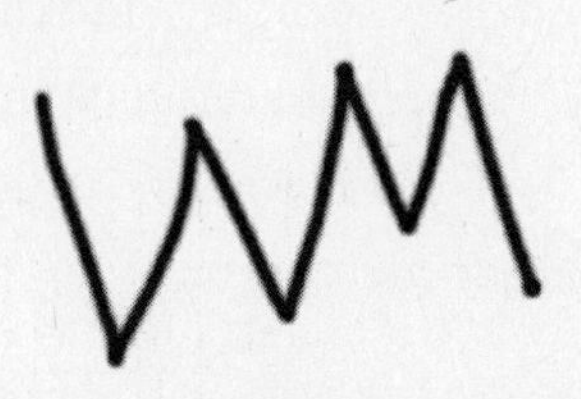

It seemed simple, not at all like some of the complex gang symbols I'd seen in and around Detroit. But it meant something. Someone had taken the time to paint it on a building down the street, and on the wall inside the *NAPA* store.

I looked outside.

There was another marking, the same design, on the side of a black Chevy Blazer. The letters were spray-painted white, and had dripped before drying. But it was unmistakable. What it meant, however, I hadn't a clue.

"Got it!" Kevin said excitedly as he reached down and snapped up a tube of something. "C-16 Muffler Cement! This stuff'll work great!"

I was relieved to hear he'd found it. Yet, I had a bad feeling, and I didn't know why. I just felt . . . *tense.* I felt like I wanted to get away. I felt like we were being watched. I'd felt this way the day previous, when we'd discovered the footprints around the ranger station and our van. It was the same feeling I had when I'd found out that kid had watched me and a few other girls in the gym showers last year.

"Let's go," I said, picking up the containers of antifreeze.

Kevin strode through the rubble and met me near the front door. He was about to step outside.

"Wait," I cautioned.

He stopped. "What?"

"I . . . I don't know," I replied.

We stood in the doorway, looking around at the ruins. A few turkey vultures soared high in the sky. The sun baked the pavement, and heat waves rose in the distance like a fluttering, transparent membrane.

"What do you think?" Kevin asked.

I turned and looked at the odd writing on the wall, then I glanced at the calendar with the large-breasted model and the scribbled appointment for May 2nd. Then I looked back to the street.

"I don't think Danny made it to the dentist," I replied quietly.

106

We crossed the street. I carried the two gallons of antifreeze, one in each hand, while Kevin carried the hose and the muffler cement in one hand and the Winchester in the other. The day was hot, and we were both sweating. It would be nice to have a pair of sunglasses, but that little luxury would have to wait.

I looked down the street . . . and stopped.

"Kevin," I said quietly.

"What?" he said, and he stopped, turned, and looked at me. He saw me staring, and followed my gaze.

Several hundred yards away, four people stood in the middle of the street. Four men, I think. I couldn't tell for sure because they were a long way away.

We stood there in the middle of the street, watching them watching us. We didn't move, they didn't move. But I was sure they'd spotted us.

"Let's go," Kevin said, and we started off again. When we reached the convenience store I turned and looked back.

The men were gone.

Kevin and I slunk along the side of the building, past the rotting corpse of the girl. A few more beetles were gnawing around her teeth, and there was some sort of grub or worm in her eye socket. I looked away.

Then we were at the back of the building, rushing to the shed. When we reached the graying old building, I looked behind us, and all around. The four people we'd spotted just moments before were nowhere to be seen. Perhaps they'd spotted us and had been afraid.

A shadow zipped past on the ground, and my heart skipped a beat. It was fast-moving, but as it passed by, I realized instantly what it was, and glanced up. Above, the turkey vultures were still prowling the skies, on the lookout for a fresh kill. I read somewhere that turkey vultures don't kill animals, but, rather, eat the leftovers of other killed animals. What's left is picked at by crows and other scavenger animals.

The Kings of the New World, I thought again.

"Let's head across the field," Kevin said. We were both really sweating now, and my T-shirt was hot and clammy against my skin. My jeans felt loose and grimy, slimy, and I couldn't wait to take a shower in the motor home. Or a dip in Otter Lake, which Kevin said was clean and cool.

I followed Kevin, and we hustled into the field. Our previous path was still visible, as evidenced by the pushed-down appearance of the tall grass and weeds. We followed the shadowy line through the field, and I watched the shadows of the vultures circle around and around with no clear or definitive pattern to their flight.

I heard something—a droning sound—and turned. Then I stopped.

"Kevin!" I called out, and now he, too, stopped. Then he heard what I heard, and turned his head.

To the east, two trucks were racing through the field, kicking up orange-brown debris in their wake.

They were headed right for us.

107

Realizing we weren't going to outrun them, we held our ground. Kevin stuffed the tube of muffler cement into his back pocket and dropped the hose. Then he gripped the rifle with both hands, aiming the barrel into the air, not pointing it at the trucks, but holding it ready.

The trucks continued coming. One was a green Dodge truck, and the other was a red Ford. I could see the dark silhouettes of two people in each vehicle, rocking back and forth to the unsteady rhythm of the bouncing vehicles.

As the trucks drew near they slowed, until, about fifty feet away, they stopped altogether. The shadows remained within the trucks for a moment.

Then, doors opened. Four figures—men—slipped out, each one carrying a rifle or shotgun. They weren't aiming them at us, but they didn't look like they were here to give us a ride across the field, either.

Then they started walking toward us. Kevin made a motion with the Winchester, and they stopped. All four of them shouldered their guns, aiming directly at us.

"Who are you?" one of the men asked.

We didn't reply.

"Maybe you didn't hear me," the man said. "Who are you?"

"I'm Kevin, and this is Sierra," Kevin said.

"Not what I'm looking for," the man said. "Who are you with?"

Kevin paused before answering, considering the question. "We're . . . we're not with anyone," he said. "We're alone."

"Nobody's alone anymore," another man said. "Who are you with? 'Cause you ain't WM. I ain't never seen ya's before."

WM? I thought. *That was the insignia on the side of the building. And in the auto parts store. And on the black Chevy Blazer.*

The men began to walk toward us, and Kevin shouldered the Winchester. The men halted, but one of them laughed.

"In case you can't do math," he snorted, "you're outnumbered. Oh, you might get one of us, but if you fire that thing, I guarantee both of you are gonna be vulture food."

"What do you want?" Kevin asked, keeping the rifle to his shoulder.

"We're the ones askin' the questions," the man said. "And you're on our property. So you'll answer, and you'd better be quick."

"I told you," Kevin said, "we aren't with *anyone.*

We're alone."

"What were you doing in that store back there?" one of the men asked.

"Just getting some supplies," Kevin said.

"Not without our say-so," the man replied. "In other words, you're *stealing.*"

They began walking toward us, slowly, guns still shouldered.

"Boy, you can drop that rifle anytime, now," the man drawled.

Kevin kept the Winchester at his shoulder. There was a faint click as he took the safety off.

"All right," the man said. "We'll do it your way."

Slowly, the man turned toward me. He was only about twenty feet away, and I could look right down the barrel of the gun.

"You got 'til I count ta three," the man continued, "then your girlfriend's gonna have nothing but pulp from her tits on up. One . . ."

I could hear Kevin breathing, could see his back spreading and deflating with every breath.

" . . . two . . ."

Kevin's finger tensed around the trigger.

" . . . three . . ."

108

"Okay, okay," Kevin said, lowering the rifle slowly.

"Drop it," the man ordered. Kevin let the Winchester fall into the grass.

The four men moved quickly toward us, but they kept their guns ready.

"Let's go," the man said. "Into the back of the truck. Chuck . . . get the duct tape."

They herded Kevin and me to the back of the Dodge. One of the men pulled out a roll of silver-gray duct tape. He bound Kevin's wrists, then mine. Then, he lowered the tailgate, and we were lifted and pushed roughly into the bed of the truck.

"You can try and run away," one of the men said, "but I think even *you* can tell you won't get far."

I looked at Kevin. He looked angry, defeated. His face was shiny with sweat.

The truck began to move. Soon, we were bouncing across the field. I worked at the duct tape on my wrists, but it was useless. And there wasn't anything in the back of the truck that had a sharp edge.

Where are they taking us? I wondered. *What's WM? Some sort of gang?*

The truck rocked and bumped, and we jostled onto the road. Traveling was smoother now, less bumpy, but it wasn't much of a comfort.

And in the sky above, turkey vultures rode hot currents of air, circling like shadowy demons, searching, watching, and waiting.

109

Not being familiar with the city, I had no idea where we were going. But we traveled over I-75, made several turns, and drove through what once must have been an industrial park or industry center. Wide open fields with manufacturing facilities, storage buildings, and loading docks. Only now, the huge buildings had mostly been reduced to rubble. Semi-trailers, long and boxy, were mostly burned or tipped over. And the sun, high in the afternoon sky, seemed to be melting what was left of the destruction, only adding to the devastation. We passed a small airfield where a twin-engine plane was in two pieces on the runway, its silver fuselage upturned like a bloated whale. There appeared to be several dead bodies—what was left of them—on the tarmac, baking in the sun. I couldn't imagine what they smelled like. Perhaps they'd been baking on the pavement for so long that they had no smell at all.

Then we approached what looked like a larger, main road—four lanes wide, with a turn lane in the middle—and turned left onto it. We jarred to the side of the truck bed. Apparently, our captors didn't care whether we were being tossed about.

"Look at that, Sierra," Kevin said quietly.

To the south—our left—a barricade had been constructed, completely from cars and trucks. Some were on their side, some were upside down. Some were burned. There were even a few semi-trailers. Razor wire had been hung over and on most of the vehicles, which, we could now see, appeared to be arranged in a circle, like some sort of reverse moat of sharp steel and metal. Most obviously the barricade was intended as the outer wall of some sort of compound. Behind the massive wall of twisted metal was what appeared to be a large strip mall.

The truck slowed, and we turned into a big Wal-Mart parking lot. Then we drove to the barricade where there was a thin opening. A man and a woman stood at the entrance, each carrying guns. Both looked ragged, and they stepped away as our truck rolled through, followed by the red Ford. They leered at us as we rode past, and I remembered seeing that very same look before. It was on television, on the *Discovery* channel. It was a pack of hyenas, in Africa. There were seven or eight of them, waiting in the bush as a cheetah devoured a freshly-killed gazelle. When the cheetah was finished the hyenas pounced, ravaging what was left of the gazelle.

The truck slowed, and we stopped near the entrance of the store.

The two men in our truck got out and ordered us out

of the bed. It was cumbersome, trying to move with my wrists bound the way they were, but I managed. When I was at the back of the bed, one of the men grabbed my arm and yanked me down. Kevin nearly fell, but the other man grabbed him.

"This way," the man said, guiding us toward the shattered doors. We were hustled along past the yellow cement posts, through what would have been automatic doors, and into the dark building. To our right, an older man with a filthy blue Wal-Mart smock stood. He was wearing cracked glasses, and his hair was a rat's nest. Several days' of stubble grew on his crinkly-skinned face. There were several badges that adorned his smock, and a button that read *How May I Help You?* He had a tic about him, as his shoulder twitched noticeably, uncontrollably.

He looked at Kevin and me and flashed a nearly toothless, sooty grin. "Welcome to Wal-Mart," he growled, his words gravelly and gritty. "Welcome to Wal-Mart . . . ."

110

The inside of the department store was unlike anything we could have possibly imagined. First of all, the building was dark, and with no windows, we couldn't see much beyond the front doors. Nearby, the cash registers had been yanked out, along with the checkout counters. The place had obviously been looted, but not as bad as many of the stores we'd seen up until now. There were racks and racks of women's clothing and shoes. Some shoes were scattered on the floor, which was scuffed and dirty. The air was thick and stale with a heavy, greasy smell.

"This way," the man said, and we followed as he turned down an aisle. Here, it became too difficult to see where we were going, but the man obviously knew his way quite well.

Something scurried past, low, brushing my thigh, and it took a moment to realize it was a child. A boy. I heard him giggle as he ran off.

We were led deep into the store, around full shelves and down cluttered aisles. Clearly, the department store had fared much better than most stores. Certainly better than the stores we'd seen downstate, which had been looted of everything, and, in many cases, set on fire.

Then a faint light appeared ahead of us, a vertical, glowing slit between two doors, and two more glowing lines, both at the bottom and the top of the doors. I could only assume this was the entrance to the stockroom. We followed the man to the doors; he pushed them open.

A single small, battery-powered lantern glowed on a desk. There were a couple of people in the room, but they were away from the light, and I couldn't make out their features, or whether they were men or women. They had been talking in hushed voices, but stopped speaking when we entered.

"Stop," the man that was leading us ordered. We did as he told us, and he walked to a dark corner and bent over. Said something to someone, quietly. Then he walked away.

A man in the corner spoke.

"Everybody out," he said, and there was a shuffle of feet, a scraping of chairs. No other voices. Shadows bobbed.

In a corner, I saw the man as he stood. He came toward us, closer to the light. It was a man about Kevin's height, stockier, older. Mid-twenties, perhaps. He was wearing jeans and a black *Ramones* T-shirt. His hair was blond—almost yellow—and it was cut, but the result was uneven and shabby. He wore a four-inch long braided goatee. His cheeks were road maps of ancient acne scars, pockmarked and ruddy. There was a scar on his forehead, too, like a knife wound. It was still a pink-red, and looked to be quite recent.

His blue eyes reflected white pinpoints from the single camp lantern, and he looked first at Kevin, then me, then back to Kevin. Then up and down.

"Auto parts, huh," the man said, his eyes flickering back and forth between Kevin and me. "You guys K's?"

I looked at Kevin. I was terrified, and I hoped it didn't show. Kevin, for his part, didn't look as scared as he did angry.

"I don't even know what a 'K' is," Kevin replied.

The man looked at him, then looked at me.

"You know," the man said, "I'm pretty good at spottin' a liar. And I don't think you're lyin'. I think you're tellin' me the truth."

Kevin and I said nothing.

"Where ya from?"

"South," Kevin replied.

The man looked at me. "You?"

"South," Kevin answered.

The man glared at Kevin. "I wasn't talking to you, was I?" he snapped. Then he looked back at me. "Where you from?"

"South. Saline. Near Ann Arbor."

The man drew back a little. "Ann Arbor? You're a little ways from home, aren'tcha?"

"There's not much left of home," Kevin said.

"There ain't much left of anything, anymore," the man said. "That's why we're here."

"What *is* this place?" Kevin asked.

"It's a freakin' Wal-Mart," the man replied.

"Whaddya think it is?"

"A compound," Kevin said.

"You're right, there," the man said. "We're safe here, protecting our supplies. We own this place, and all the other stores in the strip mall. Other places in town, too. We own the place where you guys were stealin' stuff."

"All we wanted were a few things to fix our vehicle," Kevin said.

"Yeah, well, you were taking things that didn't belong to you. We fought for that street. We beat the K's, fair and square."

"The K's?" I asked.

"K-Mart," the man replied. "Man, you guys really don't know nuthin', do ya?"

Kevin and I shook our heads.

"The K's got their part of town . . . we have ours. Early on, when everyone was getting sick and going nuts, me and a few friends came here. Took all the guns, kicked everyone out. Got some more people together. Shot anyone who tried to come in. And there were a lot of 'em, too. Oh, we let our friends and family in, if they weren't sick. My uncle, there, you met him. At the front doors. He's not all there, as you probably know." He circled his ear with his index finger. "But he's family, and he wasn't sick. He was one of the first to show up here. Others that came, well, we had to kill a few hundred people. Then we got smart, built that barricade with vehicles and barbed-wire. Some people on the other side of the city did the same thing at K-Mart. After things calmed down, the K's decided they wanted what we got. Tried to overrun us. That's when the fighting started."

"How many people are here?" I asked.

"About sixty," the man replied. "We keep to ourselves, mostly. But we gotta protect what's ours, what we fought for."

"But hasn't anyone gotten sick?" I asked.

The man shook his head, and his braided goatee wiggled. "Not since early on. Oh, we were worried for a few days. But nobody got sick. Haven't seen any infects in a while, matter of fact. Anybody who got the flu is long since dead."

"Look, we just wanted some antifreeze and some stuff to fix a radiator," Kevin said. "We didn't know the store is yours."

"'Course you didn't," the man grinned, and I immediately got a bad feeling. Up until now, I had felt the man wasn't going to hurt us. Now, however, I wasn't so sure.

"That's the trouble, these days," the man said. "Nobody knows nothin'. Everybody just assumes everything belongs to everyone, like the city is just one, big, community cooperative. Well, it ain't that way. Never was. We have to survive. Sooner or later, things are gonna start to run out. In fact, some things are in short supply right now."

He glared at me with a catlike grin. Looked me up and down. "How old are you?"

"Six . . . sixteen," I replied.

"You look older," he prompted. I said nothing. Then he placed his hand against my cheek. He was still staring at me, but he spoke to Kevin.

"This here your girlfriend?" he said as he ran his fingers over my chin, down my neck . . . .

"Yeah," Kevin replied, clearly uncomfortable, his anger simmering. But with his hands wrapped in duct tape, there wasn't much he could do.

"You got yerself a hottie, here," he replied, and his fingers found the collar of my T-shirt. "You love her?"

"Yeah," Kevin breathed.

"Lots?"

"Yes."

"How much?"

"A . . . a lot," Kevin stammered.

The man's finger was beneath the collar of my shirt, running it against my skin. I cringed at the sensation. His finger felt like a dirty worm.

"Sixteen, huh?" he said. Then he walked over to the desk where the light was, picked something up. Turned. Faced us. Faced *me*.

"Come here," he said.

I couldn't have moved if I tried. I was horrified.

In his hand was a long, silver knife.

111

After a few seconds, he spoke again.

"I. Said. Come. Here."

"Don't," Kevin said.

"I wasn't talking to you, lover-boy," the man said, and he slowly walked up to me. He searched my face, looked down at my body.

"Sixteen," he said. "You're cute . . . but you're a little young for me." He grabbed my bound hands, inserted the knife blade between my wrists, and drew it forcefully upward. The duct tape severed.

"I'm gonna let you guys go. You don't seem like you're doin' no harm. You left some shit in the field?"

"Yeah," Kevin said as the man turned and cut the tape around his wrists.

"You get it. You get it, and you move on. Or you try and steal some of the K's stuff. But I promise you: if the K's catch you, you ain't gonna be so lucky. The K's . . . well, you might say they're a bit short in the 'women' department. A hottie like you? You'd be a nice treat for some of them guys. I'd be careful if I was you." He turned toward the door. "Harley!"

After only a few seconds, the door opened. The man who had brought us here, who had led us through the darkened department store, appeared.

"Take 'em back to the field where you found 'em. Let 'em go."

I didn't know if a *thank you* was in order or not, so I said nothing. Kevin kept quiet, too, as the man—Harley—led us back through the dark aisles, around clothing (fresh, new clothing that would feel oh, so wonderful against my skin) and to the front doors. There were people watching us, in the shadows, concealed within the aisles. I could feel them, sense their eyes on us . . . but I couldn't see them.

"Thank your for shoppin' Wal-Mart," the crusty old man said, grinning through his rotting teeth. His eyes were wide, wild, and crazy. "Come see us again."

112

"There it is, up ahead," Kevin said, pointing out the motor home.

Harley had dropped us off in the field, right where we'd left our supplies. Then he drove off. He never said a word to us. I picked up the two containers of antifreeze, and Kevin picked up the Winchester. We found our way back through the forest, but we'd had a little trouble finding the motor home. Finally, we saw pieces of it through the trees. We'd missed the two-track entirely, but, thanks to the compass, we knew in what general direction to travel.

"Eddie! Tracie!" Kevin shouted, alerting them to our presence. We didn't want to accidentally sneak up and scare them.

There was no answer, and no movement.

"Trace?" Kevin called out again. "Eddie?"

We approached the motor home. A few birds

chirped in the trees. There was no wind, and the only other sounds were our feet crunch-crunching in the brush.

"Eddie?" I called out. "Trace?"

No reply.

Fear began to coil around my heart like a viper, twisting and squirming, tightening, slithering. We'd been gone a few hours . . . any number of things could've happened, and I feared the worst.

I tried again: "Trace? Ed—"

Kevin placed his fingers to his lips, urging my silence. Then he nodded toward the side door of the motor home.

"Open it," he whispered, shouldering the Winchester and taking a step back.

Slowly, I stepped forward, reached out, and grabbed the door latch. There was a muted click, and I slowly pulled the door open.

Kevin swayed back and forth, peering into the motor home. Then he took a step inside, and looked toward the back of the vehicle.

He lowered the rifle. Smiled.

"What?" I whispered.

"See for yourself," Kevin said quietly, moving aside. I took a step into the motor home, and turned. From where I stood, I could see Eddie and Tracie in the bedroom. They were laying on the bed, Eddie without his shirt. One hand held the shotgun, also laying on the bed, and the other hand held Tracie's. Tracie was also shirtless, her skin bare except for her bra.

"They're sleeping," Kevin snickered. He walked toward them, quietly, stopping at the foot of the bed. "Hey, guys," he said, startling Eddie, who awoke in a huff. He sat up quickly, disoriented. Tracie, too, woke up, groggy and confused.

"Good thing we're not the WM's," Kevin said. "Or the K's. You'd be in a lot of trouble if we were the K's."

"You're back," Eddie said, getting to his feet. "I guess I fell asleep. Didn't mean to." He rubbed his eyes. "Did you find stuff to fix the radiator?"

"Yeah," Kevin replied.

"What's a WM?" Eddie asked.

"I'll tell you while we fix the radiator," Kevin said. "Come on. This shouldn't take too long. We might be able to head out again, after dark, if we can get this thing working. But we're going to have to watch out. Come on."

113

Tracie and I took turns showering. The water was only lukewarm, but it was more than refreshing. There is nothing in the world like being clean. My whole body seemed to heave a sigh of relief, to breathe a gigantic rush of fresh air.

"It wasn't what you think," Tracie said to me. We were in the bedroom with the door closed, getting dressed. Earlier, she'd washed several T-shirts in the shower and hung them out to dry. They were still a bit damp, but they were *clean.*

"How do you know what I think?" I smirked. We were discussing how she'd come to find herself on the bed with Eddie.

"It was just so hot, you know?" she replied. And it was. It was eighty-four degrees in the motor home. "I was tired, and I laid down to nap. Eddie joined me. He said he wasn't going to fall asleep, but he—"

I laughed. "Trace, enough. I know you better. I know my brother. Relax. You don't have to explain a thing."

I told her all about what had happened, about being taken to the Wal-Mart compound, about how there was another gang they called the K's.

"They didn't hurt you?" Tracie asked.

"No," I replied. "But I think they could have. Easily. He said they'd killed a lot of people, and I believe him. We were lucky. But he told us that if we'd run into the K's, we wouldn't be so lucky. He said they're short of women."

Tracie shuddered. "Let's stay away from them," she said.

The motor home's engine suddenly turned over several times, spluttered, then caught. The engine idled. It was a little noisy, but the loud ticking was gone.

"Yay," Tracie said, without much enthusiasm.

I tucked the T-shirt into my jeans and opened the bedroom door. Up front, Eddie was in the driver's seat. Through the windshield, I could see the open hood, and a dirty pair of knuckles holding it up.

"Okay, okay, shut it off," came Kevin's voice. Eddie turned the key and the engine died.

"How's it going?" I asked.

"Radiator still leaks a little," Eddie replied. "But Kev thinks it'll be okay. At least for where we need it to go. Once we get back on the freeway, Kevin says we'll be at the lodge in less than an hour."

Although I'd never seen the lodge on Otter Lake, Kevin had gone into great detail. I had a clear vision of what I thought it would be like: rustic logs, inside and out. A stone fireplace. Thick, green pines. A crystalline lake, virgin blue.

Acres and acres of wilderness.

A haven.

A new start.

A new home.

Less than an hour away.

That is, of course, if we could get there.

114

We discussed our plan of flight. All options were left on the table, including backtracking and heading north by sweeping way around.

“Problem is,” Eddie said, “is that we'd burn up too much gas. We might not even get there.”

“And there might be gangs in other places,” I added. “If there are gangs in Gaylord, there could be gangs anywhere.”

“The WM's and the K's,” Eddie said, shaking his head. His voice dripped with sarcasm. “Northern Michigan's answer to the Crips and the Bloods.”

It was late evening, and the sun had set, leaving the western sky a dirty orange. Crickets sang. Stars began to twinkle as the sky darkened. We'd eaten another Hormel chili dinner, but it was the last of the cans. We had some green beans, two boxes of dried cereal, and a jar of Sarah

Morgan's peaches left. Nothing more. We had plenty of water, but we'd need to seriously begin to plan where our future meals were going to come from. What the lodge at Otter Lake held in store for us was anybody's guess.

"I say we just blast on through, right up I-75," Kevin said. "Let's stick with our original plan. We can wait until the wee hours of the morning—three or four—and fly through Gaylord. It'll take us two minutes to make it through the city."

Tracie stood and went into the tiny bathroom without a word, closing the door behind her.

"I kinda had that same idea," Eddie said, nodding toward the closed bathroom door. He stood up and stuffed the pistol into the front pocket of his jeans. "I'll rough it, though." He opened the door and stepped out into the early night. "Back in a flash." He closed the door behind him.

In front of the motor home, the trees had blended into the night. Kevin and I sat in shadowy darkness, me on the couch, and he in the driver's seat.

We still hadn't spoken about the events of earlier in the day. Oh, sure, we'd explained what had happened to Eddie and Tracie—but we'd left a couple of parts out. Parts that we hadn't even spoken about on the hike from the field to the motor home.

I got up and walked to the passenger seat. Sat. Looked at Kevin.

"Kevin," I began. "Did . . . did you mean that, today?"

"Mean what?" he replied.

"You know . . . when . . . when we were in Wal-Mart. With that guy. He asked you if you loved me. Did you . . . do you . . . mean it?"

Kevin paused. "Yeah," he replied. "I meant it. I do."

"For how long? How long have you known you loved me?"

He drew a breath. "Since . . . since the rain."

I didn't know what he meant.

"The rain?" I replied. "What rain?"

"Back home. In Saline. The night of that rain shower. You got up in the middle of the night, went upstairs, took your clothes off, and stepped out into the rain. I . . . I didn't see you or anything, it wasn't like that. But I *felt* you. I felt you that night. When I stepped into the rain, it was *you.* The rain was you, and you were the rain. I don't know. It's . . . it's silly, I guess. I'm—"

"No, no, it's not," I interrupted. "But . . . how come you didn't say anything? I mean, up until today? Up until now?"

I could see his silhouette as he looked out the windshield. Beyond, there was nothing to see except for the inky night.

"I was afraid, I guess. I've never said that to anyone. I mean . . . like . . . to a girl." He reached his hand over and placed it on my lap. Turned to face me. "I really do love you, Sierra. And I don't ever want anything—*anything*—to happen to you. No matter what. I'll die first." He leaned toward me, and I did the same. Our faces were only inches away in the darkness.

"No, you won't," I said. "I'll kill you if you die before me."

Our kiss was brief, as the sound of the flushing toilet brought us back to where we were, to our present surroundings that had, somehow, vanished for a moment. Time had seemingly stopped . . . ever so briefly.

The bathroom door opened, and a sodium light washed the interior of the motor home. "Well," Tracie said with a smirk, noticing the intimate closeness of Kevin and I. "Sorry to interrupt."

The side door of the motor home opened. Or, rather, it was *thrown* open, slamming against the side of the vehicle. Two gun barrels suddenly poked in. Two bright flashlight beams, like blazing suns, blinded us. We couldn't see, but we could hear.

"My, my, my," an unfamiliar voice sneered. *"What do we have here?"*

115

As the two men stepped into the motor home, their faces reflected the splayed light from their flashlights. They were dirty—filthy, in fact—and they reeked. Their smell was overpowering, and I had to fight the urge to gag. It was as if just breathing the air was contaminating. One of them wore a pair of white painter pants. He had no shirt, and veins of dried, dirty sweat stained his neck, squiggling down his bare chest. His right nipple was pieced with a silver ring, and his left nipple was shriveled and slightly deformed. Most obviously, it had been pierced at one time, but the jewelry had met its demise somewhere along the way, disfiguring the areola.

And on his shoulder was a crude tattoo: the letter 'K'. The tissue around the tattoo was pink and inflamed. Obviously, it was a recent addition to his skin.

The other man wore blue jeans and a filthy, olive-colored tank top. Sweat stained a 'V' beneath his armpits, and there was a splotch of sweat the size of a softball over his sternum. His brown hair was ratty and nappy, and he had apparently been on the every-other-week shave plan, judging by the quarter-inch of growth on his face and neck. Like the other man, he also had a very crude 'K' tattooed on his shoulder.

One Nipple spoke. "How 'bout that," he said, and his breath was repulsive. Again, I had to fight to keep from gagging. "Skull was right. But he was wrong about one thing. We got ourselves *two* hotties, here, not just *one*. That there's a big bonus."

"Leave us alone," Kevin said, but I could hear the fear in his voice.

And I couldn't blame him.

Tank Top waved the gun at Kevin, aiming at his head. "One more word outta you, and your head's gonna be shreds," he snapped. "Matter of fact . . . stand up."

Kevin paused a moment. Not having any alternative, however, he did as he was ordered.

"Out," One Nipple said. "Get out here."

One Nipple backed out of the motor home, motioning with his flashlight. "Come on, boy, we ain't got all night!"

Kevin looked at me. "I'll be all right," he said.

But I knew he was wrong.

Then he squeezed my hand and stepped into the night.

Tank Top looked at me, then Tracie. "Hoo-wee," he said. "We scored. Well . . . we're *about* to." Then he laughed, and I could see his rotting front teeth. They were yellow, streaked with brown. One of them was all black, and looked partially eaten away, jagged and raw, as if it had been gnawed on by some rodent.

"See, Skull owed us a favor," he said. "He told us there was a hottie in the woods. He didn't say they waz *two* of ya's, though. More the merrier, that's what I always say. Now, you gals oughtta feel lucky. See, me an' Jim here, we gonna treat ya real fine. We gonna give you ladies our own version of the 'blue light special.' 'Course, we ain't got no use for your boyfriend, there, so—"

From outside, not far from the motor home, I heard Kevin pleading. "Please! No! Pl—"

There was a sudden, explosive blast—a gunshot—with a simultaneous burst of light.

"—there," Tank Top said, with a burst of satisfaction. His eyes were wild and crazy. Feral. "Now the party can get started."

116

Tracie was sobbing. I was crying, trying to hold it in, but this was madness! My mind was spinning, and I felt faint. We'd come so far, not only these past few days, but the past two months. Surviving on our own, trying to figure out what to do. Now, however, it was all coming to an end. I knew what was coming next, and I knew what the men were going to do to us.

Tracie and I were going to be killed.

After, of course, they—

Or worse. What if they don't kill us? What if they just keep us and use us as they see fit? What if . . . what if we lived, only to be used as slaves or something?

Tank Top kept the pistol trained on me, and began to fumble with his fly with his free hand, tugging at his filthy pants.

"Ooh, yeah," he said, licking his lips. "This is

gonna—"

And his head suddenly vanished in an explosion of hot, red liquid and tissue.

117

Much later.

It took hours to clean the blood inside the motor home. It had covered everything—the walls, the floor, the seats. Tracie and I were drenched in blood, tissue, strands of hair, and bone fragments.

The gunshot we'd heard outside had been from Eddie. He said he was walking back to the motor home when he heard the two men. He got closer, saw them enter the vehicle, heard them speaking. Stayed out of sight while he checked things out.

And when the one man came out of the motor home with Kevin, Eddie knew what the man was going to do.

Except Eddie was first. One Nipple had walked a dozen yards from the cabin, and made Kevin get to his knees. He'd raised his rifle. In the motor home, Tank Top thought the gunshot he heard was One Nipple shooting

Kevin. In fact, the shot had come from Eddie. He'd shot the man in the back just as One Nipple was raising the rifle to shoot Kevin.

That left Tank Top in the motor home with Tracie and me. Eddie turned to sneak back to the motor home and shoot Tank Top, but Kevin stopped him.

"No," he whispered. *"I'll do it."*

Seconds afterward, with the motor home smelling of gunpowder and raw, human flesh, Kevin dragged the headless body from the vehicle, then stepped inside. He held me tight.

"I told you," he whispered, choking. *"I'll die first."*

I cried for a long, long time. Kevin held me, and he didn't let go. I didn't want him to.

113

About the only thing we knew about what we were up against was this: we didn't really know what we were up against.

After hours of cleaning the motor home (we'd found a bottle of 409 in the cabinet beneath the sink, and we used the entire bottle very quickly) it still reeked of filth and flesh. Only now, there was the odor of chemical mixed in. It was disgusting. There were pieces of bone and flesh everywhere, not to mention the blood, which had splattered all over Tracie and me. We each took showers again, and that helped. But the water didn't wash away the vision of the filthy man, pointing the gun at me, eyes afire.

The windows were down in an effort to freshen the vehicle, but the stench of death was awful. Kevin and Eddie dragged the two dead men a few dozen yards into the woods, and left them there. Kevin said they didn't deserve a decent burial.

And he was right.

The only thing we could figure was that 'Skull' was the leader of the WM's, the guy with the braided goatee. There must have been something going on between he and One Nipple and Tank Top. Maybe they were spies or something. We'd probably never know, and it didn't matter, anyway.

It was nearly three in the morning when we finished cleaning, and the four of us sat on the couch (it hadn't been soaked with blood as badly as the chair) discussing what we were going to do. We were tired, but the adrenaline from the earlier events was still coursing through our bodies. The lights were off, but the trees beyond the motor home were awash in moonlight. Inside our vehicle, we could barely make out one another. I sat next to Kevin, holding his hand.

"We're going to make it," Kevin said. "Let's do what we originally planned. Let's head up I-75, straight through. We'll just have to be ready for anything."

"But now that they know about us," Tracie said, "others might be looking for us."

"That's exactly why we should leave," Kevin said. "The sooner the better. The longer we stay here, the more we risk more people hunting us down. And next time, they might send more than two guys. We were lucky . . . *really* lucky. Let's not press it. We risk getting ambushed on the freeway, but at least we'll have a chance of getting away. Here, we're sitting ducks."

"But all we have are a couple of guns," I said.

"No," Kevin said, squeezing my hand. "Not true. We've got more firepower than that."

"How so?" Eddie asked.

"You and Tracie take one of the guns and the flashlight. Hike back to that burned out convenience store, and bring back as many glass bottles as you can. Not plastic. Glass. Sierra . . . tear up a couple of our T-shirts into strips. If anyone comes after us on I-75, we'll be ready."

119

Kevin turned the motor home onto the on ramp. Despite the damage from the previous night, the engine sounded better. The loud ticking was gone, but there was a high pitched whine that increased with speed.

In one of the boxes we'd used to store cans of food were our secret weapons: Molotov Cocktails. Eddie and Tracie had found a half-dozen glass bottles. Kevin used his syphon hose to draw some gasoline from the motor home's tank, and he filled the bottles. Then, we stuffed the bottles with the strips of a T-shirt that I'd cut up. We'd used the shirts that Tracie and I were wearing when Kevin killed Tank Top. They were bloodied, and not good for anything else. I certainly wasn't going to wear them again.

Our lights were off. The moon was even brighter than it had been the night before. However, there were sporadic clouds that passed by every few minutes, darkening the earth. When this happened, it became quite dark, and difficult to see the highway. No matter. We pressed on, merging onto I-75.

I sat in the passenger seat, while Tracie sat on the couch. Eddie stood near a window on the driver's side, holding onto a cabinet for support. None of us spoke as the giant, dark bug sped along the strip of road that snaked through trees on either side.

Within minutes, however, the trees were gone, and the desolate, decaying city of Gaylord appeared. Mostly what we saw were ghosts: skeletal silhouettes of billboards, buildings, cars and trucks off to the side of the freeway, in the ditch, everywhere. There were no lights, no fires. The area looked haunted and forsaken.

Moments later we were going over a bridge that crossed what appeared to be the main road that wound through town. To the left, I saw the dark shadows of several huge buildings, and, unmistakably, the sprawling Wal-Mart compound where we'd been taken earlier in the day.

Then, almost as quickly as it appeared, the city fell away. There were dozens of burned homes on the right, an entire suburb reduced to rubble. Hills rose up on both sides, rising and falling as we passed. Knots of trees became forest. We saw dark billboards here and there, but there were no more homes. We made it through Gaylord without incident.

"How fast are we going?" Eddie asked.

Kevin leaned closer to the dashboard. "Eighty," he said. "We're moving right along. Otter Lake, here we come."

And that's when we saw the headlights behind us.

120

They didn't appear in the distance, far away. They appeared right behind us, exploding like two suns, illuminating the trees on both sides of the freeway and creating a big shadow of our motor home on the road ahead. Someone, obviously, had been following us with their lights off.

"Shit!" Eddie exclaimed. He quickly slid the window open and poked out the screen with the gun barrel.

"He's coming around!" Kevin shouted. "Get one of those bottles!"

There was a gunshot, and Kevin's side view mirror shattered. Eddie took aim and fired a shot at the vehicle, which was now alongside the motor home.

"Trace!" I shouted as I scrambled for one of the gasoline bombs. "Get the matches!"

Tracie found the matches on the counter as I picked up one of the bottles.

"Careful!" Eddie said. "Don't light it yet! Give it to me!"

I handed the bottle to him.

"Matches!" he screeched.

There was another gunshot, and the sound of metal being punctured.

"They're trying to shoot out our tires!" Kevin said as he gripped the wheel. "Hurry it up, Eddie!"

Eddie struck the match. "Sierra! Get another one ready!"

I snapped up another bottle and held it out.

"Hang on, hang on," Eddie said. He touched the match to the gas-soaked cloth sprouting from the bottle. The fiber immediately ignited, and in one swift motion, Eddie's arm shot out the window, launching the flaming missile into the air. There was a sound of shattering glass, and a tire squeal.

"You got him!" Tracie shrieked as she looked into the passenger side-view mirror.

"Just the grill, just the front of the car!" Kevin shouted. "It's burning, but he's still coming! It's not going to stop him!"

There was a flurry of gunfire now, as several shooters opened fire. I handed Eddie another gasoline-filled bottle.

"Get down!" he ordered. "On the floor!"

Tracie and I fell to our bellies and hugged the floor. Eddie lit another match.

"Wait a sec!" Kevin shouted. "I'm going to slow down and see if we can get him to come up alongside! You'll have a better chance with one of those bombs!"

The match was blown out by the rushing wind.

"Shit!" Eddie said.

Kevin slowed, and the car behind us surged forward.

"Now! Now! Now!" Kevin screamed as gunshots riddled the motor home.

Eddie struck another match. As it flared, he touched it to the torn shirt protruding from the bottle. The cloth bloomed a yellow flower. Eddie drew back . . . and threw the bottle out the window. I heard a dull thudding sound.

"Right on!" Kevin howled. "Right through their passenger window!"

There was a sudden crash, and the motor home lurched to one side as the vehicle hit us. I was thrown against the bottom of the couch, and then I got to my knees and looked through the back bedroom, out the rear window.

Behind us, the car was careening to the left, slowing quickly. The front of it was on fire, and flames were coming out of the window. It spun sideways, then stopped. The vehicle was totally engulfed in fire.

Suddenly, a smaller mass of flames took life, moving on its own, and I suddenly realized what I was seeing.

Someone's on fire, I thought. *Someone's burning.*

The ball of running flame fell to the ground. Another flaming human emerged from the burning car.

Suddenly, there was a dull concussion, solid and full. A bright yellow and red mushroom grew as the vehicle exploded. By now, we were several hundred yards from the inferno. Seconds later, I-75 turned to the west, and the fiery scene behind us vanished.

I heaved a heavy sigh. "Good shot, Eddie," I said.

Tracie stood and went to Eddie. They hugged without words.

"This is your driver speaking," Kevin said, really professional-like. He sounded tired, though. "We've just left the northern town of Gaylord, and we're currently traveling at approximately eighty miles an hour. Please remain seated for the remainder of the flight. Next stop, Otter Lake."

I laughed and went to him, kissed him on the cheek.

"You know," I whispered, "I never told you that I love you."

"You just did," Kevin said quietly.

The motor home rolled on, shrouded beneath a watchful, silvery moon.

121

Kevin eased off the gas, and the motor home slowed. It was still dark, but the eastern sky was lightening, turning a dull, salmon color as we exited the freeway.

"We're not far," Kevin said. "We'll take Old 27 north. To get to Otter Lake, we've got to follow a dirt road—Woodmansee, I think its name is—and then cut down a long two-track. The lodge and the lake are way back in the woods."

I was exhausted, but it was impossible to sleep. I tried, but I kept jolting awake. The stench of death, 409, and gasoline didn't help. Tracie didn't have any problem, however, as she had been fast asleep on the bed in the back for nearly twenty minutes.

We'd encountered no problems after our run-in with the car. We had no idea who they were, but that wasn't important. What was important was we'd stopped them.

"Do we have to go into Cheboygan?" Eddie asked. "I mean . . . if there are gangs in Gaylord, there very well could be gangs in other cities."

"No," Kevin replied, shaking his head. "Otter Lake is a few miles south of the city. If I remember, it's a pretty desolate area."

The motor home slowed as it wound down the exit ramp. Kevin turned right onto Old-27, heading north. Here, several cars and trucks were on the side of the road. I'd had hoped that maybe—*maybe*—we'd find some places untouched by the bird flu. I knew the chances were slim, but earlier, as we'd progressed farther and farther north and still saw numerous upturned vehicles and the remains of burned homes, my hope faded.

Now, my hope had grown. I was hoping Otter Lake would be everything Kevin said it was: a tiny lake in a remote setting. A large, log home with a massive fireplace in the living room, and fireplaces in several bedrooms. Maybe Kevin's uncle and aunt would be there. Maybe his cousins.

Of course, there was already a chance the lodge had been looted—or worse. Or, perhaps, someone *else* had the same idea we had, and they'd already claimed the lodge for themselves.

We'd find out soon enough.

122

"I forgot about this," Kevin said as he stopped the motor home. We'd found Woodmansee Road without a problem, and the two-track—but now we had a dilemma. A padlocked metal gate blocked our passage. Because of the density of the trees, we couldn't drive around. If we were going to take the motor home any farther, we were going to have to get the gate open somehow.

"How far is the cabin from here?" I asked.

"About a mile," Kevin said. "I suppose we could walk there."

"Or, we could try shooting the padlock with the rifle," Eddie said.

"Worth a shot," Kevin said. He picked up the rifle and stood. He handed the firearm to Eddie. "Go for it, dude."

I got up from the couch and went to the back to

wake up Tracie. I didn't want her hearing the gunshot and freaking out.

"Hey, sleepy," I said as I knelt next to the bed. Tracie opened her eyes.

"You're going to hear a gunshot in just a second," I said, "so don't—"

The sharp report of the rifle stifled my final words.

Tracie flinched at the noise. "Where are we?" she asked groggily.

"Near Otter Lake," I replied. "We're almost there. There's a locked gate. Eddie's trying to get it open right now."

"Got it!" Eddie's voice echoed. He appeared at the door a moment later and climbed inside. I went to the front of the motor home. The gate was now pushed open, and the two-track sank into the thick forest, a clear path leading through the woods to the lodge on Otter Lake.

The sun was rising faster now. The air was crisp, cool. Clean and fresh. Birds were singing everywhere. The motor home still reeked of flesh, gas, and 409, but with the windows open, the air was circulating. The two-track proved to be bumpy, and tall grass brushed the undercarriage. A few branches slapped the side of the motor home as we made our way slowly to what we hoped would be our new home.

It's burned, I thought. *I know it is. Looters have already been here. They'll have taken everything worthwhile. Worse yet, they might be living there themselves. Squatting.*

"Not far now," Kevin said.

I got up from the couch and stumbled my way to the front, the bumpy road keeping me off-balance. Then I knelt next to Kevin and squeezed his leg. He took his hand in mine.

"It's going to be okay," he said. It was as if he could sense my apprehension. "We're here. It's going to be all right."

A deer walked across the trail in front of us. It stopped, saw the motor home, then darted off with a high flick of its white tail. I took that as a good sign.

We went around a turn, and the forest thinned. Otter Lake appeared, a flat layer of gloss that reflected the sky and the surrounding trees. It was breathtaking. There was no movement, not a single dimple to mar the surface.

"Wow," Tracie said. "You vacation here?"

"I was here a lot when I was growing up," Kevin replied. "The lake is full of fish. Clean, too. Great swimming."

Then—

The lodge came into view.

It sat back from the lake about fifty feet. The home was huge, with a large deck in the front. Numerous windows and a sliding glass door provided an ample view of the lake. The home was still intact, untouched, as far as we could tell. No broken windows, nothing broken or burned that we could see.

But there was a yellow Jeep Wrangler parked in front of the attached garage.

123

Kevin pulled the motor home up behind the Jeep.

"Is that your uncle's?" I asked, nodding to the vehicle.

"I don't know," he said. "You guys wait here. Eddie . . . come on."

Kevin picked up the shotgun and Eddie grabbed the Winchester. He opened the door, and they stepped outside.

"Leave the door open," Tracie said, waving her hand beneath her nose. "It still stinks in here."

"Be careful," I warned as Kevin and Eddie cautiously approached the lodge.

There was no sign of anyone. No one came to the windows. None that we could see, anyway. There was always a chance someone might have seen us coming and decided to hide. That's what I would have done if I was in the house and a strange vehicle pulled up.

Please, I thought. *No more trouble. No more.* I fantasized about being in a big, fluffy bed, the sheets caressing my clean skin. Undisturbed, endless sleep. Waking up slowly, serenely, relaxed and refreshed. It had been so long. Even the nights we'd spent in the basement didn't bring restful slumber. I was always mentally looking over my shoulder, on alert, watchful. You can't get a good night's sleep if you're constantly watching your back. Even with Kevin and Eddie standing watch, it was difficult to sleep for more than an hour without waking up, tense and stressed.

Slowly, Kevin stepped onto the deck, followed by Eddie. They peered into the windows, looking all around. Kevin tried the sliding glass door, but it was locked. Then, they walked off the deck to the front door. It was locked, too.

They spoke, but we couldn't hear what they were saying. Then they walked over to the yellow Wrangler. Kevin tried the driver's door, and it opened. Checked for keys, but he didn't find any.

Instinctively, I got up and left the motor home. There was no one around, I was sure, and I wanted to be in the morning sun, breathing clean air, knowing there wasn't someone around to threaten us. Tracie wasn't far behind me.

"God, that smell in there is *awful,"* she said as she gulped down the fresh air.

"Nobody home," Kevin called out. He walked down to the dock, picked up a gray rock that was about the size of a softball, and found the key hidden underneath. "That's been there since I was little," Kevin said confidently. "Same key, too."

He strode up to the front door, inserted the key, and turned it. The tumblers clunked, the door opened, and

Tracie and I followed Kevin and Eddie inside.

The door opened into a small foyer. True to Kevin's words, the structure was built of logs, and we were greeted with the familiar, musky aroma of cedar. Not overpoweringly so, not like a perfume, but just enough to stir memories. There were several long-sleeved flannel shirts hanging from a coat rack, and a pair of hiking boots next to a closet door.

The foyer opened into a spacious living room. Directly across from the foyer was a large stone fireplace stacked with several long logs . . . logs twice the length of normal fireplace logs. Mounted to the stone was an old, hand-carved mantle adorned with framed pictures. Above the mantle, a moose head hung, wearing dark sunglasses. A single, white sock dangled from one antler, and a cigarette dangled from its mouth.

In front of the fireplace was a large, plush sofa. It looked old, but it was rounded and poofy, inviting, like a dark, fluffy cloud. To the left, a rustic dining room table with eight chairs that appeared to be hand-made.

"Anybody home?" Kevin called out, already knowing we were the only ones there. I think he was just being certain. When no one answered, he walked across the living room. The house was laid out in wings, with an east wing and west wing. A single door closed off each wing, and he opened one of them and vanished down the hall.

"This place is great," Eddie said, looking around.

"Better than that," I said. "It's safe. So far, anyway."

I walked over to the dining room table, where there was a goofy-looking ceramic black bear the size of a baseball. The bear was dressed in waders and wore a fishing vest and a hat. He carried a fishing pole over his shoulder. Several fish were hanging from a stringer that dangled from the bear's waist. In small letters, a caption read *Gone Fishin'*.

The bear was cute . . . but it was the letter beneath the figurine that captured and held my interest.

Out of the corner of my eye, I saw Kevin return to the living room. "I don't know where everybody went," he said, his voice hollow and cheerless.

I picked up the letter. Stared at it.

"I do," I said quietly. Then I looked across the room at Kevin. "This is for you."

124

May 7th

Dear Kevin:

If there is anyone who is going to make it here, it will be you. You've always been smart and strong-willed. If this whole thing goes down like they're saying, then people (if there are any left) are going to be looking for ways to get out of the city and survive on their own.

I heard about your mom. I'm sorry. This whole bird flu thing is really bad, and I'm not sure what's going to happen. Karen and your cousins were in Farmington. They got sick. Neighbors found them yesterday. I got a call from Ashley at Michigan State in East Lansing. She's hiding out. I'm going to get her. If you're reading this, well . . . we probably aren't going to make it back.

I've been stockpiling supplies for the past few days. Of course, it's been nuts in Cheboygan, but there hasn't been any looting yet. Lots of people sick and dying. I've been wearing a ventilation mask everywhere I go. Seems to be working, so far. Knock wood. Today, it's a lot worse, from what I hear. Phones went out earlier. On the radio, they're telling us not to leave our homes.

The garage is filled with as many long-term supplies as I could get. Canned food, winter clothing, whatever I could manage. No propane in the tank, though. There's a generator in the garage as well, but gas is already in short supply. Keys to the Jeep are in the garage, if you need a vehicle.

I'm planning on picking up Ashley tonight, and driving straight back here. I'm hoping I'll see you soon.

But if, for some reason, our paths don't cross again, I want you to know how proud your dad was of you. I know you and him had some not-so-good moments these past couple of years, but he really loved you and was proud of you. He told me that. He knows that you never forgave him for leaving you and your mom the way he did, but he hoped that, someday, you could find it within you to forgive him. He misses you. I told him you're doing good, that you are growing up stubborn just like him. (He's my brother—I know!)

I hope you make it here safe. Stay strong, nephew.

Love, Your Favorite Uncle

125

Flames licked up from the embers, and orange sparks sailed up into the night sky like frantic bugs. The night was cool, and millions of stars salted the sky. Eddie sat on a log near the fire, cradling Tracie's head in his lap. We'd taken a swim in the lake and got cleaned up, and were wearing fresh clothing. Ill fitting clothing, considering that it belonged to Kevin's aunt and uncle, but it was clean and fresh.

Kevin was inside, still sleeping. After he'd read the letter, he'd wept like I'd never seen anyone weep before. I knew there were some big issues between he and his dad: things that would never be resolved, now. I hoped that his uncle's letter would at least help a little bit. We all hugged each other in the kitchen, we all cried. We cried until we were exhausted. Kevin and I went into a bedroom, where he sobbed until he fell asleep. I bathed in the lake, then slipped silently next to him on the bed. Sleep was easy, and it was good.

Tracie and Eddie each took turns washing up in the lake. Two months together, in extreme conditions, and modesty still remained. They chose a bedroom and slept. A clan of vampires, we were, sleeping during the day. But we'd been up all night, and none of us could keep our eyes open.

I awoke as the sun was going down. Eddie and Tracie had risen shortly before me, built a campfire by the lake, and were sitting on the dock when I went outside. They had a bag of marshmallows waiting by the fire.

"They'll be stale, for sure," Tracie said. "But we deserve marshmallows."

I couldn't have agreed more, but we decided to wait for Kevin to get up before we had our little marshmallow-toasting celebration.

"What now?" Tracie asked as Eddie stroked her cheek. The reflection of the fire danced in her eyes. She was wearing a red sweatshirt, a billion sizes too big for her tiny frame, and it made her look like a giant red blob.

"We'll get by," Eddie said. "We're going to make it."

For the first time in two months, I really believed what I was hearing. Life for us—for the world—was going to be much different. The things we took for granted—computers, running water, microwave pizza, cold milk, DVD movies, the convenience of going to a store and buying anything we needed—that was over. Of course, we'd known that for a while now, but here—in the quiet solitude of Otter Lake, and after what it had taken to get here—well, we knew for sure things would never get back to what we'd considered 'normal' for most of our lives.

But we'd made it. We went through two months of

complete hell . . . and we survived. Working together, we all made it to Otter Lake alive. We had clean clothing. We had food. We even had a bag of stale marshmallows. Cool beans.

We were going to make it.

126

Two years later.

Our son was born in May. We named him Robert Theodore Martinchek, after my Dad's first name and Kevin's dad. One month later, Tracie gave birth to twin girls: Faith and Hope.

A year ago, Kevin and I, and Eddie and Tracie married in our own, personal, dual-wedding ceremonies. We made up our own vows, and we took some quotes from an old bible Kevin's uncle had. Eddie performed the ceremony for Kevin and I, and Kevin presided over Eddie and Tracie's. Tracie and I were each other's maid of honor, as Kevin and Eddie were each other's best man. We celebrated our marriage with a bottle of wine we'd found in the basement. It wasn't all that good—quite nasty, in fact—but it was fun.

And we have a dog. She's a mutt of some sort, a

Labrador and something mixed in, like husky. We found her by the lake not long after we'd first arrived. She was sickly thin, filthy, and near death. Her beige fur was matted and caked with mud, and she had several scars, probably from tangling with another animal. Tracie and I nursed her back to health, and we call her Punky. She's fifty pounds of fuzzy love.

Life has changed, that's for sure. Looking back on that first day we'd arrived here at Otter Lake, we never knew what obstacles we would have to face. We just expected everything, and we tried to stay ready. Some of the stores in Cheboygan still had stocks of food and clothing, batteries—things like that. Plus, we met several other families who were doing what we were: surviving. We get together on occasion, talked about forming our own city. We are the youngest of the survivors, as we began to call ourselves. Others look out for us, and we do what we can to look out for them, to do our part and help others survive.

But there are some rumblings we don't like. A man who lives in Cheboygan secretly travels south, to Gaylord, to spy and try to get information about the gangs. He's discovered that the K's and the WM's have banded together after supplies began to dwindle. We were fearful that, perhaps, they might try to head north, to areas that offered at least *some* conveniences. It's a fear that's always there, but I try not to think about it too much.

And the lodge has served us well. Kevin and Eddie chop wood during the summer, and the fireplaces keep the house toasty-warm all winter. We each have our own wing of the home: Kevin and I in the west end, Eddie and Tracie in the east. There are several more rooms in each wing, but with the addition of our children, they'll be filling up. We all work together, eat together. We read to each other in front of the fireplace. We play music on occasion, as we have batteries to power a small compact disc player. But we know that batteries are a non-recycling resource. Once they're gone, they're gone. We have a large garden in a field a few hundred yards from the lodge which yields corn, tomatoes, radishes, carrots, squash, peas, pumpkins, onions, and more. We even grow strawberries and raspberries. Eddie and Kevin have their hands full keeping the animals out. But they hunt all year round, and we're never in short supply of fresh meat. Tracie has long gotten over her squeamishness of dead animals, and she even helps skin the game. Wonders never cease.

And I never think twice about having a family. I know some might find it silly to bring a baby into a world like this, with so much uncertainty. But I remind myself that, for most of human civilization, people got by with a lot less than what we have. Far less, in most cases. We've learned to do more than just survive. We've learned to thrive. Our lives, our world, are so different, and we've learned never to take for granted the things that really are important: our friendship, our love for each other. Our new lives together. Our hopes. Our dreams.

And we've learned that a big, fat strawberry can be heaven on earth. A largemouth bass filet frying in a pan is a feast fit for a king. Sunshine, blue skies. A warm fire. The song of a bird, and crickets at night.

You know—

The little things.

THE END

ABOUT THE AUTHORS

Johnathan Rand is the author of the bestselling *American Chillers* and *Michigan Chillers* series of books for children and young adults. Other works include the all-new *Freddie Fernortner, Fearless First Grader* series, *The Adventure Club* series, and *Creepy Campfire Chillers.* He resides in northern Michigan with his wife and three dogs: Abby, Lily Munster, and Scooby-Boo.

Visit www.americanchillers.com

Christopher Knight is the author of five regionally bestselling thrillers, including *St. Helena, Ferocity, The Laurentian Channel, Bestseller,* and *Season of the Witch*, along with dozens of short stories, magazine articles, and audiobooks. PANDEMIA is his first collaboration with another author.

Visit www.audiocraftpublishing.com

A special excerpt from

FEROCITY

by Christopher Knight

PROLOGUE

Craig Sheldon left the bar after his shift was over, cursing the heat as he started up his car and backed out of the gravel parking lot. It was just after two a.m., and the boiling heat from the kitchen had kept him perspiring for hours. A swim—a quick dip in the lake—was definitely in order. He rolled down the window of the car and sped up, cursing the heat for the umpteenth time that day.

He took a long, final drag on his cigarette, pulled the Marlboro from his lips, and was about to flick the half-smoked cigarette out the window when he thought twice about it and snubbed the butt out in the ashtray. The forest was drier than Wabash County, Tennessee, a county that had been receiving a lot of rain this year, but if you lived in Wabash County, Tennessee and wanted a nice Chardonnay or a Miller Lite, then brother, you knew what *dry* really was.

No sense in burning down the entire goddamn town this early in the summer, Craig thought. *We'll leave that to the tourists.* He nudged the radio volume up a bit with his thumb and forefinger and hummed along to an old Aerosmith tune, tapping the steering wheel in perfect timing with his right palm as Old US-27 sped beneath him, glowing like a black snake in the headlights. The wind rushing through the open car windows was a welcome, cooling relief, and he pushed away the thoughts of sweat and grease and smoke and fryers.

Life was good despite the heat. And despite the fact that the air conditioner at the bar had broken. *Again.* Oh, it wasn't so bad if you were on the floor waiting tables, but if you were in the kitchen grilling up the burritos and the nachos and the burgers like Craig had been for ten hours . . . well, you better look out. The heat from the fryers and stoves kept the kitchen a balmy, tropical hundred and twenty degrees and it was more than just miserable.

Perhaps the only thing that kept Craig going on this particular night was the fact that Cheryl Townsend was going to be waiting for him at her house, clad only in her birthday suit or maybe some itty-bitty fledgling piece of skimpy clothing she'd ordered from *Victoria's Secret*, or any of the other seven or eight mail order catalogs that Brad found laying around her house. His personal favorites were *Frederick's of Hollywood* catalogs, featuring dozens of beautiful, succulent women in clothing so tiny the models probably had to dress themselves with a pair of tweezers. Craig had ordered something from *Frederick's* once and presented it to Cheryl as a Valentine's gift, racking up innumerable carnal favors . . . making the forty-nine ninety-five plus four dollars shipping and handling a very worthwhile purchase indeed. And, although Cheryl left a bit to be desired in the intellectual department, no one would deny that she had breasts that could stop a charging bull elephant . . . which, in Craig's mind, more than made up for the fact that Cheryl Townsend couldn't tell you where the state capitol was. (Somewhere near Flint, she thought, but she couldn't be sure.) Craig and Cheryl had a very simple, respectful understanding: sex was more of a matter of convenience than a matter of commitment, and that was just fine with both. Neither of the two were interested in any type of long-term relationship with each other, which was a good thing—being that Craig had already screwed Cheryl for his last time.

He just didn't know it yet.

✷✷✷✷

Craig turned off the highway and into the lakeside picnic area, a bit surprised to find that there was no one else around. Usually by this time of the morning (right after the bars closed) there were two or three cars parked in the small circle drive that wound dangerously close to the water. Most were just teenagers nervously swigging that glorious *Under Age* brand beer. Which was just like any other brand of beer, but it tasted oh so much better in its youthful prime. *Under Age* brand beer was specially brewed somewhere between the hazy, small towns of Youth and Stupidity and was pretty easy to come by if you knew where to look or who to talk to.

When you reached the legal drinking age of twenty-one, it took the taste and fun away from *Under Age* brand beer, and most enthusiasts graduated to drinking Coors Light or Budweiser or Miller Genuine Draft or some other *Legal Age* brand beer. And if you were a *Legal Age* brand beer drinker, you probably headed to Mullett Lake at this hour with the same idea as Craig Sheldon: a quick, refreshing swim after a long day at work. A day that was made so much longer by that damned broken air conditioner.

Craig reached into the back seat and grabbed a beach towel that, when spread out, looked suspiciously like an enormous *7–Up* can. It seemed like just about every clothing article bought these days had some kind of American corporate logo on it, and beach towels were not immune. The tactic probably wasn't working as well as thought; upon further inspection the article was usually found to be made in Korea or China or Mexico. Or, in the case of Craig's terrycloth *7-Up* can, *Malaysia* of all places. Most people couldn't *pronounce* Malaysia, let alone find it on a map. No doubt Cheryl Townsend would probably say it as Mal-lay-SIGH-yuh.

He stepped out of the car and slammed the door closed, kicking off his Nike's and strolling across the wet grass that grew almost to the shoreline. A heavy rainstorm had raked through earlier in the evening, bringing brief high winds and a torrential downpour. The storm did nothing to drop the temperatures as everyone had hoped. The rain was warm and had moved on as quickly as it had arrived, leaving a gray, hazy mist to rise from the pavement and rooftops like the sleepy steam from a vegetable fryer. The rain had drifted off to the northeast, and for a few brief moments before dusk the sun had peeked through purple and orange thunder heads that hung passively over the horizon.

An old wood pier jutted out from a small beach area and Craig walked slowly along the dock, listening to the sounds of the night as his bare feet padded the weathered planks. The bright chorus of crickets faded as he made his way farther over the water, anticipating a well-deserved swim after a day of slinging burgers and fish baskets and whatever the hell else was written on the endless wave of tickets that the wait staff pushed through the window. He pulled his T-shirt over his head, rolled it into a ball and carried it loosely as he walked, unbuttoning his jeans and unzipping the fly as he reached the end of the dock.

He stopped, gazing out over the dark waters, slowly turning his head to survey the tiny beads of light on the opposite side of the lake some two miles away. The serene stillness of Mullett Lake whispered to him, licking at his ears with the soothing melodies of a sultry summer night.

To the north, about a half mile from where he had parked his car, the jovial laughter of a late night party drifted across the lake. The flickering orange glow of a campfire reflected on the water and in the faces of those who stood around the roaring blaze, and the revelers were laughing and talking, their voices interspersed with broken fragments of reggae music. A car moved steadily north along Old US-27, the low drone of tires on pavement growing stronger, then fading as it passed. Craig turned to watch the car as its headlights continued by, finally disappearing through the trees.

Beneath him the water lapped at the moorings of the dock, gently slurping at the old wooden pilings. Here at the end of the dock the water was deep: ten feet or so at least with a perfect sandy bottom, which made this particular dock and its beach a rather popular swim site. But tonight the water was *black*. Not just a dark, murky black, but a thick, full black . . . a black that seemed to swallow up the night.

Craig dropped his clothes and the *7–Up* towel on the dock, stretched, took a long, deep breath, and plunged headfirst into the cool, dark water.

The water was refreshing and invigorating despite the fact that it, too, was quite a bit warmer than normal. It filled his pores and washed away the smells of grease and french fries and buffalo wings and shrimp ka-bobs that had become trapped in the oil of his skin.

He continued to swim slowly beneath the surface, bringing his arms above his head and pushing himself along as he swept his cupped hands back to his sides, enjoying every glorious, cleansing second. He felt renewed, refreshed and re-energized, and the prospect of burying his face right between Cheryl Townsend's delicious silver-dollar sized nipples grew more tantalizing by the moment. Amazing what a good shower or a dip in the lake can do for your libido.

He suddenly surfaced and shivered. It wasn't a shiver because he was cold or chilled, but he had suddenly sensed something very *odd*. Not at all a premonition, not a vision, just . . . *a feeling*. Craig wasn't afraid of the water; not even at night when demons and ghoulies and ogres came out, if, of course, there actually *were* such things as demons and ghoulies and ogres. If so, they had been slain long ago when Craig was a teenager, when the thoughts of scary monsters lying in wait beneath his mattress and box springs dwindled and were replaced by real fears: getting caught skipping school or having your dad find your pack of *Zig Zags* in the family station wagon.

And yet, oddly enough, that was what *this* feeling was like.

A slight uneasiness began at the base of his neck and trickled down the sliver of his spine. His head bobbed above the surface and he glanced quickly around, watching the waves fade away and distort the moon in the glossy reflection on the surface before him. Tiny lights dotted the shoreline on the other side of the lake more than a half-mile away, and far to the southeast a vertical row of red lights from a radio tower blinked every few seconds.

Craig cocked his chin downward and stared into the black water before him. He could see nothing except the occasional glitter of a reflecting star dancing on the wavering film.

A splash was heard in the distance and the giggle of a woman was cut short as she plunged below the surface, only to re-emerge laughing and sputtering, hollering something unintelligible to the partygoers that had thrown her in. The night was a carbon copy of last night, the night before that one, and the night before that one. Summertime on Mullett Lake, Michigan, and the living was oh, so easy. Spring came early and the warm weather had brought many vacationers to the lake in advance of the season to get a head start on summer, and the lights from their cabins and homes glowed brightly from the shoreline. Everything was beautiful and perfect, just like it should be on a lake in the scenic north. All the travel brochures guaranteed it; tonight was no exception.

And so in the blink of an eye Craig brushed aside his nervousness and began to swim easily, steadily crawling arm over arm through the refreshing water.

His foot kicked something hard, and he stopped swimming immediately and tread water. Once again the odd sensation of apprehension came over him and he turned to look at the dark shadow of the dock some thirty feet away, half expecting to see his father standing there holding a pack of *Zig Zags* in his hand with a *what in the hell do you call this, boy?* expression of boiling rage on his face. Quite obviously he wasn't there, as the elder Sheldon had died of cancer three years ago. A pack and a half a day for thirty years had proven the Surgeon General correct, after all.

Craig snapped his head back around quickly, searching the shadowy, inky waters for . . . for *anything.* His leg had hit something . . . perhaps a sunken log. But then again, he was certain that it was too deep for him to be able to reach bottom. And in the pitch-black water it was impossible to see beneath the surface. He couldn't even make out the vague form of his hand only a few inches away, let alone the object that he had kicked. His head darted nervously around and he decided to return to the dock. After all, he reminded himself, he just needed to get the stench of the bar off of his skin so when the horizontal bop was in full swing later on, Cheryl wouldn't be getting stale whiffs of everything he'd cooked that day. It was just polite.

He turned and began to swim, forcing the demons and ghoulies and ogres back to his pre-teenage years where they belonged.

With the impact of lightning his body suddenly shot

below the surface, and a searing pain screamed from his thigh. In a flash Craig bolted back to the surface, gripping his leg with one arm, flailing frantically with the other, gasping for air. He reached down and his fingers met squishy flesh, and Craig shuddered in horror as he felt his bone through torn muscle and tendons. His leg had been completely severed just above the kneecap, torn away as easily as one of those *take-a-number* roll-tabs at the Secretary of State's office. His mind was a whirling blur of confusion and intense, fiery pain. He tried to scream but another jolt snapped him quickly under water. Now he was moving. Beneath the surface something seized his whole body and was moving, fast. A hundred razors tore through his flesh and powerful, vice-like jaws bound tightly around his torso. In the blackness he could see nothing, but the pressure building in his ears and the movement of water against his face told him that indeed he was being carried deeper and deeper into the lake.

Craig hadn't had time to get a good breath, and his lungs began to throb. Terror and disbelief spun through his head. He was being violently shaken under water, shaken the way a dog plays with its favorite toy. Back and forth and sideways and back again, each motion causing excruciating agony. Sharp incisors crimped his body and forced the remaining of the air from his chest He gurgled and screamed as he exhaled, but the sound was muffled by the rush of bubbles that escaped and began rising to the surface.

He managed to pull one arm free and he flailed it about in the water, trying to struggle away from whatever it was that had attacked him, tearing his flesh away with every powerful, twisting snap. Craig was a good swimmer, but he'd always thought that drowning would be one of the worst ways one could possibly die. *No!!* his mind screamed. *Not this way!! NOT THIS WAY! I don't want to drown! I DON'T–*

He could no longer bear the burning pain in his chest. His air had completely run out. He opened his mouth and water poured in, rushing down his throat, pushing down his esophagus and deep into his lungs. His stomach tried to expel the onslaught of water by regurgitation, but the results were only compounded by more water surging back down.

One arm was still trapped by his side, but his free arm began to grow limp and he felt himself losing consciousness. The pain began to fade and the dark black around him was giving way to a hazy, calming blue. He began to relax, his body growing slack, his muscles relaxing, his eyes wide and bulging.

Suddenly Craig realized that his fears of drowning were unfounded. There was something much more terrible, much more evil to be afraid of than merely drowning. Something that had been lurking in the depths, waiting for its opportunity to attack and devour its next prey. The demons and ghoulies and ogres of his childhood *had* been real, after all. They had missed their opportunity in his golden youth, and they had come back for him.

And man, were they *pissed.*

Hey Craig-geeee, they whispered from the dark depths. *We gotcha now, Craig-geeee . . . .*

No, Craig thought, as consciousness dwindled away. *I'm not going to die drowning. I'm going to die by being eaten. I'm being eaten alive! I'm—*

One more violent, powerful snap shook his body, whipping his head forward and slamming his chin to his chest. He was being carried within some massive mouth, moving swiftly through the water. Craig's world slipped further away and the darkness was no longer. The hazy blue took over, becoming brighter and warmer as the black faded away. Suddenly, even the blue was gone. It was replaced by—

Nothing. There was no color, no sounds. In his mind he saw his father standing at his bedroom door, holding a pack of *Zig Zags.*

You're in one heapa trouble now, boy, he was saying. *One heapa trouble indeed.*

Indeed.

Then, as simply and gently as if someone had clicked off a light switch, Craig Sheldon quietly gave in and succumbed to the overwhelming rush of calming nausea. Horror and terror were replaced by quiet serenity and calm. Craig's light blinked out like the last flicker of a candle that had struggled to burn to the very bottom of the wick, only to run out of wax and diminish into nothing more than a tiny orange spark that grew dimmer and dimmer, finally extinguishing altogether.

Unseen from the surface or the shore, the enormous creature slipped silently back to the murky depths of Mullett Lake.